The Water's Fine

A Novel

Janice Coy

"For if a man is far from his own home and parents, then even if he is housed in opulence..no thing he finds can be more sweet than what he left behind." The Odyssey

Part I

Chapter 1

I've always loved the ocean.

And she's embraced me in return: soothing me as a baby, holding me lightly as I skimmed on her waves, and granting me the freedom to fly on her currents.

I didn't know that passion would break me. That I would be left adrift grasping for something I had never understood.

I was in diapers the first time I saw the Pacific. I don't remember, but my parents said they'd never seen me so calm and mesmerized before. Apparently, I was a cranky baby. Hard to pacify. I was either eating, pooping or crying. They said I never slept. I know that's an exaggeration because why else would they have another baby if I was such a difficult daughter?

Anyway, family legend has it that the first time I was plopped onto a blanket at La Jolla Shores Beach, I stopped fussing. My eyes drooped. The shushing water lulled me to sleep. My parents stayed longer than they had planned that day. I woke up when they strapped me into my car seat. I screamed the whole way home – twenty- five long miles east on the freeway and surface streets. When telling this tale, my parents would inevitably raise their hands to heaven and thank God there wasn't much traffic on the weekend.

For the past six years, I've traveled the world as a scuba dive master. I've visited exotic locations like Australia, Indonesia, Papua New Guinea and the Caribbean. I've seen creatures many will only see on National Geographic specials. I've led underwater tours for all types and sizes of divers. Of course, all this comes with a price. Not every part of the job is glamourous. Not every guest is easy to please. My patience and humility have grown by leaps and bounds. Cleaning toilets and helping seasick divers is as much a part of the gig as 'yes siring' and 'yes ma'aming.'

The job has its ups and downs (excuse the pun). I imagine it's a lot like being a flight attendant jetting around the world. But like any flight attendant, I've had to work for the rewards. I've put up with some not so nice folks who are paying a lot of money to have the experience of a lifetime. If something goes wrong – the whale shark doesn't show or the promised ghost shrimp vanishes from the ledge at one hundred foot depth or the manta rays swim away too quickly – I can only nod at the complaints and murmur that the ocean doesn't offer any guarantees.

I comment that the ocean covers a majority of the earth's surface, and even creatures as large as whales can be difficult to find. I've learned to offer the last part in a very low voice that most don't hear. But it makes me feel better.

These are my thoughts: if you want a guarantee of seeing underwater creatures – visit Sea World or an aquarium. The lions aren't guaranteed on the Serengeti, the ocean is an even bigger place. I've gotten good at projecting empathy.

I joined the crew of the Calypso two years ago. I was looking for a different experience and, as someone who got a bachelor's degree in Greek Mythology and Art, I enjoyed the coincidence of the boat's name. I knew it didn't refer to Odysseus' boat, but to the goddess who held him captive.

Our 115-foot boat leaves out of Cabo San Lucas, Mexico. The Calypso plies the Socorro Islands off the tip of Baja California and the Sea of Cortez, the seven-hundred-mile stretch of water sheltered from the Pacific Ocean by the Baja California peninsula. During the winter months, divers live on board for a week to spend time under water each day with giant manta rays, dolphins, whale sharks, hammerhead sharks and Great White Sharks near the Socorro Islands

I wouldn't really call the Great White Shark experience a true dive – basically, divers are suited up and lowered in a cage to watch the sharks attack bait that's dropped into the water. I've never gotten into the cage. I don't need that kind of thrill.

In the summer months and early fall, we head north for a week into the Sea of Cortez where there is an incredible variety of wildlife for divers to experience. Some have compared the waters to the waters around the Galapagos Islands because of its diversity. I've seen bat rays, whale sharks, humpback whales, sea lions, blue footed boobies as well as seahorses and smaller fish.

The water isn't as warm as other parts of the world. Some of my fellow dive colleagues don't understand why I've stayed so long on a boat that plies the colder waters. They like to be where they can dive in nothing more than a shortie or even just a vest. But it feels more like home to me. A diver who grew up playing in the waters of the colder Pacific. The sea lion pups remind me of Cooper, our old mutt.

The cold water and the sea lion pups sometimes leave me feeling nostalgic. Some nights, I lay in my top bunk listening to the creak of the boat and think about my parents and my younger brother. These thoughts are new to me. I look at the ceiling and wonder if it's time for me to stop "fooling around" (as my Dad says) and get what he calls a real job.

I'm not sure what I'll do with my college degree. Teach in a land-based school I suppose? My stomach clenches when I consider teaching students about art or Greek mythology in an enclosed classroom space. I imagine looking out the window and wishing I was breathing underwater. I tell myself I'm already teaching when I assist the dive instructor in providing additional certifications to the divers on the Calypso.

These conflicting emotions have prevented me from taking the easy two-hour flight to San Diego. Of course, my parents haven't come for a visit yet either. It's weird how we've drifted apart these past years. I used to think we were so close when we spent all those weekends at the beach while my brother and I were growing up.

Besides leading dives for the guests, the scuba instructor and I are assigned five cabins each that we are expected to keep ship shape during the transition between guests and the week the guests spend on board. Each cabin has an attached bath with a sink, toilet, handheld shower head and drain centered in the middle of the steel floor. The bathroom itself serves as the shower enclosure. Much of my cleaning time is spent wiping down the overspray with towels. We also take turns with the cook keeping the mahogany-paneled and carpeted dining room and the less-formal lounge vacuumed and cleaned. It's not really a big deal, but my dad seems to think I'm wasting my brain.

"We didn't raise you to be a maid, Catalina," he says during our infrequent phone calls.

My parents emigrated from Argentina before my brother and I were born. It was difficult for my dad when I chose not to move back home after college. He grew up in a time when girls lived at home until they married. And now, here I am: twenty-eight, single and living somewhere else. My brother is finishing up his studies in Argentina, so at least there's that to keep my dad happy. My mom blows kisses over the phone and asks when I'm coming home.

It's the beginning of another week, and we're expecting a new dive group to arrive at the dock for the next summer dive trip into the Sea of Cortez. As the Calypso rocks and strains against its moorings, I brace myself on the bunk I'm readying for the next guest. I'm nearly done, tucking and smoothing the blanket on the upper bunk. I sway with the boat, waiting for the motion to still. A steady wind started blowing mid-morning, and combined with the passage of other boats, the water is restless, slapping the sides of the boat like a jilted boyfriend.

"Calm down now my love," I say. "I'll be back with you soon."

The rocking and bumping slow. I finish with the top bunk and step to the floor. I've completed making the beds in the other cabins assigned to me. I need to hurry. The guests will arrive shortly. The capitán wants us all to be on deck to greet them.

I lean into the lower bunk, smoothing the blankets I wrinkled when I stood on them to straighten the top bunk. I fluff the pillows. The boat sways, catching me off-balance so that I knock my head against the wall behind the bed. I groan and rub my forehead, pressing on the sore spot, praying the pressure will keep down any swelling.

I'm not superstitious, but I know others who are. They would say a knock on the head is not a good sign at the start of a new journey. It signals bad luck. Sometimes, their ruminations and warnings remind me of the seers who predicted Odysseus' fate, and I joke and call them Greek names they've never heard.

I'll have to smile and pretend nothing happened when I arrive on deck. My unruly black hair is slicked back into a ponytail, and away from my face. Hopefully, a noticeable bump or bruise won't show up on my tanned forehead. Maybe I'll have time to grab a cap from my cabin.

I carefully back out of the bunk and stand to survey the compact space. Every inch is well-used from the placement of the bed to the drawers underneath the bottom bunk. The space is situated below the main deck, the small porthole is speckled with saltwater. Nothing I can do about that. Still, I pull a cloth from my pocket and do what I can to polish the glass on the inside.

"All hands on deck!" the capitán shouts the order down the stairs. The van must have pulled up at the end of the dock with the new guests. I tuck the cloth into the back pocket of my shorts and quickly duck into the adjoining bathroom to peer at my face in the mirror. The serviceable mirror doesn't provide a great reflection; it's more like a mirror someone would take on a camping trip. Most female guests stop wearing makeup the first day. They just want to know their hair is combed and they don't have food stuck in their teeth. The men, who don't already have beards, simply want to shave so they can get a tight fit on their dive masks, and the reflection is sufficient for that.

I lean close and gently probe the sore spot with my fingers. It doesn't look too bad. Just a tad red on my otherwise smooth skin, but maybe that's because I've been fingering it. No one will notice during the chaotic arrival of the guests.

"All hands!" the capitán calls again.

I hurry from the cabin, pulling the door shut with a click and clamber up the steep steps. Besides the capitán, the dive instructor and me, a cook and an engineer round out the crew. It's a small but efficient operation. We all pitch in and help whether it's washing dishes or setting tables or serving dinner or breakfast or holding a wrench if the engineer needs help with the boat's engine. All of the staff are certified dive masters or instructors, and often take turns coming on the dives. Sometimes not all guests are scuba divers, but simply along for the ride. Other times, the boat isn't filled. On those occasions, the dive masters have an easy time of it with few divers in their groups.

I arrive up top with plenty of time to spare. The smells of town – the creosote of the dock, fish newly caught by those casting lines nearby, gasoline and tortillas – swirl in the wind. I'm grateful for the cool breeze, my cheeks and neck are warm from my work below

The guests are unloading from the dive shop van parked at the end of the dock. The van, like the boat, is nothing super fancy, but both are kept in tip-top shape with the same amenities as our competitors. Along with the adjoining bathrooms, our boat boasts an upper level sun deck; the common lounge has a large screen for movies as well as shelves of DVDs. Our dining room is unparalleled with its mahogany paneling. The capitán's bridge has all the modern bells and whistles.

I don't have time to snag a cap, so I finagle a spot in the shade. The crew wears navy t-shirts with the Calypso logo on the front. I fan myself with my hand, and then finger the sore spot on my forehead before I remember that I'm not superstitious. My hand drops to my side.

"You okay Catalina?" Manuel Salazar says. He's the dive instructor on the Calypso. He's worked on this boat for ten years. He stays with his family in town on the weekends.

"Right as rain," I say.

He touches the cross tattooed on the back of his hand. "No rain," he says. "Not this trip." He wags his finger at me. He leans towards me, squinting his eyes. "Bump your head?" he says.

"No," I say emphatically. "Just a pimple."

"That's only bad luck for you," he says laughing.

I poke him in the arm. "I'll show you bad luck. This time I'm getting the good ones."

Manuel snorts.

I hope I'm paired with a group of experienced divers on this trip. Leading dives is a lot more fun when I can spend time looking for octopus or damsel fish or seahorses to show the divers instead of constantly helping them adjust their buoyancy or grabbing their fins before they shoot to the surface. The Calypso advertises itself as a live aboard for experienced divers, but that doesn't always filter out those who haven't dived for a while or those who have only completed (twelve) dives locally and gotten their advanced certification.

Our winter trips to the Socorro Islands aren't for newbies. Although the Sea of Cortez isn't really for new divers either – with its cool water temperatures and strong currents – there are no guarantees new divers won't show up. I've seen it happen. In fact, the last trip I was put in charge of shepherding four recently certified divers who were not too familiar with buoyancy control. Much of my underwater time was spent in assisting them with adding or subtracting air from their buoyancy vest.

At least the Sea of Cortez isn't as bad as the Caribbean when it comes to inexperienced divers. Because the Caribbean is relatively close to the U.S. East Coast, people who haven't dived in years sometimes show up thinking they're still ready to get underwater safely. Others pick the

Caribbean as their honeymoon destination. They arrive at the resort boat with brand new certification cards and hangovers.

The first few times I led a dive at a Caribbean resort, I was terrified someone would die or be seriously injured on my watch. If you'd seen those dives, you probably would say I was doing more hovering than leading. Time and experience have calmed my nerves. Plus, I've learned to get to know the divers first before they take their first giant stride into the water. Lots of potential problems are headed off by helping divers adjust their gear and talking with them about their foibles. Most are up-front about any underwater worries.

I've never had a diver get lost or suffer from any serious ailments. But I know others who have led dives where someone following them panicked, shot to the surface and needed to go to the decompression chamber, or had a stroke or heart attack and died underwater or on board when all CPR attempts failed.

Please, grant me experienced divers this time, I pray. Just to cover my bases, I slide one hand into my shorts pocket and surreptitiously cross my fingers.

Chapter 2

I shade my eyes and look down the length of the dock, watching the guests mill about the back of the van while the driver unloads their gear. The distance disguises how experienced the guests are. Size, shape and age are not determining factors when it comes to diving.

"Too hard to tell about this group yet," Manuel says.

"Yeah," I agree. "But it's my turn with the experienced ones." I hope if I repeat my wish often, it will come true.

"We'll see about that chicle" Polo Guave says. He's the Calypso's engineer. He's the same height as me – 5 ' 6" – short for a guy but his oversized personality more than makes up for it. "I have a feeling I'm gonna get lucky this trip." His grin beneath his Calypso cap is wide.

"You don't even get a group," I laugh. "The only luck you'll have on this trip is if I let you join in with mine."

The capitán and Madelyn DeSoto, the cook, join us. Madelyn doesn't stay long; she's quiet, but never still. She jumps to the dock to help the passengers aboard. I like having another woman on the crew.

Maybe that's why I've stayed longer on the Calypso. I've been the only female on too many boats. Even though we share a cabin, we're not close. But Madelyn has had my back on numerous occasions when a male guest has drank too much and gotten out of line and I've done the same for her. I haven't always had that luxury. I've wanted to "deck" a drunk guest many times, and could have easily dropped them to the floor, but I've restrained myself and managed to slip away. The guests are always right is every boat's motto. The advent of online reviews has only served to harden that motto so that it might as well be written in stone.

Madelyn instructs the guests to remove their shoes, to come aboard barefoot. She indicates a plastic bin where the passengers can leave their shoes to be brought on board later. Most are wearing sandals that are easily removed. Some are already sliding them off in anticipation of Madelyn's instructions. They must be the more experienced ones. Only a few kneel and untie shoe laces.

The capitán welcomes the guests on board with an outstretched hand, assisting those who need help jumping the ever-changing gap between the gently rocking boat and the dock.

First on board is a couple who look to be in their early thirties. The woman is a whirl of motion. She ignores the capitán s outstretched hand, and instead steps lightly on board as if she's jumping into a dance.

"Hola!" she says, her voice full of cheer. "I'm Bertie."

She holds her right hand up to each crew member for a high five as if we're all on a team that's about to embark on a grand adventure. Let the games begin! Her straight brown hair swings just above her shoulders in a fashionable cut, no split ends there. I smooth the stray hairs that have escaped my ponytail. A simple silver wedding band encircles Bertie's ring finger, matching silver studs adorn her ears. Her teeth are impossibly white.

I'm prepared not to like her, but when she looks me in the eyes, her hand held up for a high five, I can't resist the sparkle I find there. I laugh and slap her hand. Her good-looking husband follows quietly in her wake. He's wearing loose athletic shorts and a gray t-shirt with a dive flag emblem on the chest. I don't catch his name, but I notice that he has nice feet with neatly trimmed nails.

They're followed by the chattering chaos of a family with three teenagers who appear to be friends with another family with teens, all seeming to crowd aboard at the same time with lots of laughter and jostling. I imagine they've been on other dive trips together. The second family includes a younger child in a sundress who's right in the mix with everyone else. There's no use assuming the young-looking girl with the swinging brown ponytail and freckles is not of age to be a diver. Her build is slight, but she could be eleven, twelve or even thirteen. I've been fooled by appearances before.

Among the last to board is an older couple; both have longish, wavy hair that's somewhere between blond and white depending on how the sun hits it. They've waited in a cluster with two women in their mid-thirties. Possibly their daughters. There's a family resemblance or it could just be that they all happen to have light hair and are athletic looking with slim figures. One of the younger women supports the man's elbow as he climbs aboard and calls him Dad. He shakes his head and frowns. "I'm perfectly capable of climbing aboard a boat," he mutters. "Done it thousands of times before." She doesn't comment, but she does drop her hand. And he jumps aboard landing on sure feet.

Names are a blur – except for Bertie's - but I'll learn them all during the week we spend together in the close quarters of the boat. I'll become particularly well acquainted with those I'm assigned to shepherd underwater. *Please God, let my group be experienced.* The older couple glance at me and smile. I blush and busy myself with loading the dive equipment and luggage onto the boat. I hope I didn't speak my request out loud.

Only fifteen passengers – not a full boat, the Calypso's ten guest cabins can hold twenty – but it's a good turnout for the less popular summer tour of the Sea of Cortez. I grapple with dive bags, stowing them in the pre-assigned spaces on the dive deck.

Before the guests go to their cabins – some just down the passageway, others below deck - they gather in the dining room for the capitán's official welcome. I enjoy this part of the trip. You can learn a lot about people and how the trip will unfold by how the guests interact in a room with strangers. Do they form tight circles with those they already know? Or do they mingle and exchange information?

The older couple sits with their hands and arms relaxed, their shoulders touching. Their faces are tanned. Maybe the better word is weather beaten. If they've been on boats as many times as the man says, they've been exposed to the salt air and the wind. When the two younger women sit with the older couple, the family resemblance is clear. One of the women has the same straight nose, blue eyes and dimpled chin as her father. The other takes after her mother with her brown doe eyes and apple cheeks.

The girl with the ponytail cruises about the dining room, peeking under tables. and knocking on walls. Searching for what? A hidden cupboard perhaps?

The capitán and her parents ignore her. He introduces the crew members. We nod and wave and quickly disappear down the passageway or the stairs to deliver the luggage to the cabins. At least Madelyn, Polo and I do. This trip might not be as popular as the one to the Socorro Islands but it's no less cheap and the guests expect stellar service. Luggage delivered to their cabins is a must. Manuel stays in the dining room to help the capitán collect diving certification cards and hand out forms to be signed.

I can hear the rumble of the capitán's and Manuel's voices. Although I can't distinguish their words, I know they're going over the boat's rules, dive schedules and menus for the week. We're almost finished delivering the luggage to the cabins when a babble of voices arises signifying the passengers are taking turns showing their current dive certification cards to the capitán and Manuel so that the certification numbers can be recorded. The two will also write down the number of dives each guest claims to have completed.

This is an honor system. Confirmation of dive experience will be obvious on the first dive. There's no hiding experience (or the lack of experience) underwater.

The guests are also signing waivers acknowledging diving is a dangerous sport and agreeing not to hold the Calypso or its employees liable if something goes wrong. On the Socorro Islands dive trip, there's lots of laughter and crude jokes at this point. No one expects danger from a sea lion or its pup in the Gulf of California.

Madelyn heads to the kitchen to finish up on a light lunch. The Calypso will slowly motor out into the harbor for our first dive. Then, the guests will be served a buffet lunch. We'll do a second dive before we continue the journey north into the Sea of Cortez.

I join the back of the group as the capitán and Manuel lead the guests out to the dive deck. Rows of upright, silver oxygen tanks line the backs of two long wooden benches. Below the benches are plastic bins with the guest's names written in sharpie where they can store their smaller dive gear like gloves, hoods, masks and snorkels. There's a camera table, a rinse tank for cameras and two freshwater showers to wash off the salt.

A separate hose allows guests to rinse their wetsuits (and other gear) and put them on a rack with hangers along with their buoyancy vests. Unrinsed gear quickly grows bacteria and stinks. Manuel shows the passengers the dive platform just below the dive deck where they can take a giant stride off the stern into the water. Folding ladders can be lowered from the dive platform for returning divers to climb back aboard. The Calypso also has two pangas (smaller rubber boats) that will be used for some dives.

Then, we all troop up the stairs after the capitán to the top deck where lounge chairs are arranged on the uncovered stern section for those wanting to lie out in the sun. A shaded bar is situated just behind the chairs towards the bow. Five bar stools are currently pushed under the ledge of the polished teak bar. The guests jostle each other and joke about dibs on the few stools. Bertie leans into her husband, whispering in his ear. The two laugh quietly together, then Bertie glances my way, catching me watching. She winks.

"Hope you'll join me for a drink someday Catalina," she calls. I smile. The capitán frowns, but continues the tour.

The crew is not supposed to drink with the guests, but the capitán has turned a blind eye before. We just need to be careful not to indulge too much, and to wait until after the last dive of the day.

The guests file in and out of the capitán's helm so they can be assured the Calypso has the latest technological gadgets necessary for an unforgettable trip. The boat tour done – only the crew cabins, snug behind the kitchen and the engine room are off limits - the guests are dismissed to check out their cabins and be back on the dive deck within fifteen minutes to gear up for the first dive.

The capitán starts up the boat's engines. Polo unties the heavy ropes from their dock ties and jumps aboard as the Calypso pulls slowly away from its mooring. I pause on the dive deck to watch our departure from the town, my gaze wandering over the tourists drifting in and out of the shops and restaurants. The wind has dropped as suddenly as it started this morning. Now, the colorful flags that waved so jauntily are limp on their silver poles. My view grows wider the further out the boat moves. Now, I can see the towering flamingo pink and white buildings of the resorts with their palm trees and jewel-toned pools. I imagine tourists languid on their lounges, diving into the pool to cool off.

Once we leave the harbor after our first dive, we won't see civilization for a week. I think of San Diego, further north, and lifting my gaze, I trace an airplane trail pointing in that direction. I've never made a habit of watching the town or resort or wherever it is the boat is leaving. I'm usually already at the bow, looking towards the horizon. I don't know why I'm looking behind us today. My heart has always been with the ocean; I usually can't wait to escape to the water and diving. I shake myself from my reverie. My focus returns to the water that parts behind us in a gentle wake, sending out small ripples that quietly lift the smaller boats moored in the harbor. We're on our way, and it's time to get back to work.

Manuel and I are busy on the dive deck, clearing away any items that might trip the guests as they make their way to the dive platform, making sure the dive weights are organized by size and situating the white board he likes to use to go over the dive site.

My neck glistens with sweat by the time the guests begin to trickle onto the dive deck. I'm not surprised that Bertie and her husband arrive first. He reminds Manuel and me that his name is Matt. Bertie needs no reintroduction. The two head directly to the pile of weights where they hoist a few uncertainly, and then set them back down.

"How much extra weight do you need?" I ask as I join them.

"That's the thing," Bertie says. "We don't know. This is our first cold water experience."

More weights will be needed to counteract the increased buoyancy of the heavier wetsuits. Bertie freely shares her body weight as does Matt. Finally, we settle on an amount they can try for the first dive. They can always adjust once they become more familiar with navigating the cooler water temperatures in the Sea of Cortez that average 75 degrees in the summer.

As soon as they step away, I'm busy with others who are struggling to figure out what weights they will need for an enjoyable dive. Sweat is dribbling down the back of my navy t-shirt when the older man with the long wavy hair appears.

"Can I help you?" I say. I've forgotten his name.

"Gordon," he says, "That's what you're wondering about, right?" He winks. I can't help but laugh.

"You know what weights you need Gordon?" I say.

He nods. "I've got it," he says, reaching for a stack of weights. He sets the stack by the older woman, and then returns three times for stacks he distributes to the younger women with them, keeping one stack for his own use.

I watch his actions noting his knowledge. When I turn back to Manuel, he's smiling because he knows exactly what I'm thinking. I smile and nod. There's no doubt that I want Gordon and his family in my group. I put my hands together as if I'm praying and lift my face to the sky. When I look over at Manuel, he's smiling.

Chapter 3

Bertie Clark surveys the crowded diving deck. At least there are only fifteen on this trip, and not the twenty the boat can hold. She knows from experience that most live-aboards conserve on space in this area, and the Calypso is no exception. The facing wooden benches are painted a serviceable green. Bertie supposes they're easy to wash down with a hose. An empty space divides the benches with just enough room for divers to waddle single file to the dive platform. Those waiting their turn will need to rotate their knees sideways so the other divers can maneuver past. The plastic bins for personal items are a nice size and slide easily under the bench. Bertie usually brings a larger dry bag on a boat for her clothes. But that's usually when they just go out for the day. For this week-long trip, her clothes are safely stowed in their cabin. Still, she'll need a safe space for her sunglasses and the small plastic purse where she keeps her lip balm, tissues and her cell phone. Sometimes, she needs to wipe her nose after a dive. She uses the phone as a camera. Matt, her husband, bumps shoulders with her.

"Excited?" he asks.

He's selected the dive destination. They agreed it was his turn. Bertie wasn't happy with his choice at first; she prefers dives in warmer waters. But after her initial doubts, she's studied up on the Sea of Cortez – or Gulf of California as others call it – and now, she's excited to descend below the surface and see some interesting creatures like sea lions, manta rays, whale sharks, as well as smaller species such as sea horses and angelfish. She nods and tightens her ponytail, smoothing any stray brown hairs away from her face. She learned on her first dive that hair can interfere with the seal on a dive mask. That entire dive, she struggled with water leaking into her mask and settling in a mini-pool just below her eyes.

"Totally," she says. The two exchange a quick kiss. Back home in Michigan, they're not big on public displays of affection, but something about being on a dive boat always seems to increase their libido. Others get sea sick, but not the Clarks. Bertie isn't sure if it's the rocking of the boat, the time spent underwater or simply the fact that they're on vacation and away from the busyness of their daily lives. She's given up trying to figure it out. She's learned to lean into the holiday, to allow her fun side to emerge.

The moment Matt locks the door of their home, and Bertie slides her arms into the straps of her dive bag, she becomes a different person. A person who's adventurous. A person who boards a boat without help and cheerfully greets the crew.

A person who leaves her stuffy name – Alberta – in Michigan and dons a nickname. Bertie is the one who travels to exotic locations and breathes underwater like a fish.

When Matt first suggested they take up diving and travel to Fiji, Alberta wasn't totally on board with the idea. Matt might have always dreamed of being a scuba diver, but Alberta had never even considered the thought. She was perfectly happy watching others explore underwater wonders. She was content sitting on her comfy couch and watching National Geographic ocean specials on television. After patiently listening to her protests, Matt sat her down at the computer and showed her pictures of Fiji.

The romantic grass huts and the pristine white sand pricked her interest. It didn't hurt that at that exact moment a winter storm was raging outside, rattling the windows and gusting down the chimney to nearly douse their cozy fire. Matt told her they could start their scuba certification in the local indoor pool, and finish in the turquoise waters of the island. Alberta wavered. She pictured herself in a bikini with a tropical drink in hand. They wouldn't dive all the time, Matt said. They could spend hours on the beach. Alberta could nearly taste the coconut in her Mai Tai. She told Matt she would think about it. What she meant was, she'd get back to him after studying up on diving and Fiji.

Once Alberta commits to something, she's all in.

She was an attentive dive student in the heated pool, she never felt claustrophobic when they practiced breathing underwater. She aced all the written exams. And she received her diver's certification card under the name Bertie. The moment the two settled into their seats on the flight to Fiji, she told Matt she wanted him to call her Bertie for the duration of their trip. Matt laughed and agreed. She's had Bertie as her dive name ever since.

She's still Alberta back home in Michigan with her family, and at work as a writer of school curriculum. She's Alberta when they travel to Chicago and take in the theater or the symphony or dine at the newest, most fashionable restaurants. But somehow, she just can't imagine being Alberta under water.

Matt is Matt no matter where he is. And Alberta loves him for it.

Fortunately, her passion for learning carries over even when she's being Bertie. Because of her studies, she can easily identify the different sea creatures they might encounter. When she talks about what she's seen, she doesn't mean to brag. She's not being competitive. Although others have misinterpreted her actions as such. She's just more educated than most. Bertie is blessed with excellent visual acuity and attentiveness to detail. Sometimes, she sees things underwater that others don't.

She's promised Matt that on this dive trip, she'll temper her enthusiasm. She'll wait for the dive master to point out creatures. She'll follow Matt's pre-trip instructions to "relax."

He taps her leg now. "Remember," he whispers. She nods and flashes him the underwater sign for okay, thumb and forefinger touching. Despite her earlier misgivings about the trip, she's got a good feeling about the Calypso. She loved reading the Odyssey in school. She doesn't mind the idea of being held captive on board. Plus, she felt an immediate connection with Catalina. She's hoping they're assigned to Catalina's group.

She's pretty sure the younger families will be kept together; they're friends after all. The adults have already told everyone about some of the dive trips they've shared. That means she and Matt will spend the week diving with the Bakers. It didn't take Bertie long to figure this out, and she made an extra effort to introduce herself and Matt to the family. They appear friendly enough. Bertie's sure she'll know lots more about them by the end of the week. It's hard to keep secrets on a boat this size.

The Calypso stops near a formation of rocks Bertie recognizes from her studies of the area. The jagged, free-standing cliffs rise out of the harbor like the broken- down walls of a giant fortress. Erosion has created a huge archway in one: El Arco, where the Pacific Ocean becomes the Gulf of California or the Sea of Cortez.

While Polo secures the Calypso to a mooring ball, Manuel calls for the divers' attention. He's standing at the white board with a black marker in his hand. He's already sketched out some of the site's features, a grouping of rocks and a longish looking reef. He's about to give a run - down of the dive site: what the divers could see and the depth and duration of the dive.

Bertie feels a flutter in her stomach, a tiny wave of anxiety that arises just before the first dive on every trip. She's learned she needs to be one of the last divers in the water; her nervousness only increases if she must wait on the surface for the other divers in her group to jump in.

The flutter was a surprise the first time she felt it while bobbing on the surface, her snorkel in her mouth, gentle waves slapping her tank. She nearly let the flutter morph into panic. Her thoughts giving over-size proportion to the ridiculous idea that soon she would be breathing underwater.

Fortunately, Matt distracted her by splashing a little water on her cheek. "We're going to love it," he said. "Just remember to breathe." His words and the splash were enough to break her train of thought. Now she knows to jump in last; all's fine once she sinks below the water's surface, the flutter vanishes, and she easily adopts a rhythmic breathing.

Now, while Manuel talks about the first dive, Bertie twirls her wedding band on her finger. She wore her engagement diamond on their first dive trip which she quickly learned was a mistake. Even underwater, the diamond twinkled and flashed, sometimes attracting the unwelcome attention of all matter of fish.

This trip, she's left all jewelry behind except for her wedding band and the simple earrings in their cabin. She looks around the group. Most, except Gordon and the young girl, are paying rapt attention to Manuel's talk. The young girl bounces from one foot to the next, only settling down when her father tells her to. Even then, she perches on the bench as if she's ready to rocket off at any moment. Gordon is using his dive vest as a pillow of sorts. He's leaning back with his eyes closed. A slight smile plays about his lips. Just beyond his head, the sun sparkles on the water like pieces of glass.

Bertie notices Catalina watching her. She imagines the dive master is sizing up the guests and Bertie in particular, wondering who the competent divers are. Bertie stops twirling her ring. She sits on her hands while Manuel finishes and asks for questions.

Chapter 4

I finger my sea star necklace – I admit it's my good luck charm - until Manuel announces the dive groups for the week. I smile and wink at Polo when I hear that I'll be leading Gordon and his family as well as Bertie and Matt. The other families want to be together. Polo and Madelyn will take turns helping Manuel with the larger group. They'll be needed to make sure the girl with the freckles and ponytail is safe. The minute Manuel started listed the names of those in my group I got to work committing them to memory. Six names will be a breeze to remember, especially since I already know three – Bertie, Matt and Gordon.

I've already noticed that Gordon and his wife are proficient at setting up their gear, checking the amount of air in their tanks as if they could do this routine in their sleep. They've helped their daughters who seem less adept. Matt and Bertie, also ready their gear in knowledgeable silence. Bertie spins her wedding ring. Is she nervous or excited? She notices me looking at her and sits on her hands.

My group will enter the water first. They're more experienced, and it's assumed they'll stay down longer than the other group. Also, the other group isn't quite ready. Some are just now pulling on their wetsuits and some are searching for their booties.

I maneuver along the crowded deck to where my tank is located near the platform. Gordon and his family have been assigned the spots nearest to me. I think his age got him that location. When we read the guest list, we didn't know he would be in such good shape. The Bakers take turns reminding me of their names. Gordon's wife is Ava; the daughters are Lauren and Lucky.

"You ever see that movie with Jaqueline Bisset?" Gordon asks me. "The Deep?"

I shake my head.

"It's an old movie Dad," Lauren says. "Older than her."

"Of course, you mention Jacqueline Bisset," Lucky smiles at her dad.

Ava laughs. "He wanted me to dive in a white t-shirt once."

Gordon grins. "I simply wanted to let Catalina know I've been diving since we used to throw our tanks over our heads like Nick Nolte does in the movie." Gordon lifts the hose connecting his buoyancy vest to his oxygen tank. "And we didn't have these either. If we wanted to inflate our vests underwater, we had to blow into a tube with our mouths. With all this technology, they've made diving about as easy and adventurous as climbing Mt. Everest these days."

Ava blows air through her lips in a short burst of laughter.

Bertie leans into the conversation. "Have you dived on the Wreck of the Rhone? The one in the movie? It's amazing."

"Many times," Gordon says. He slips his arms into his vest and buckles the straps around his chest and stomach.

Bertie starts talking about all the amazing and rare creatures she and Matt have seen on the wreck. Matt shakes his head.

"But you must have seen some wonderful things in all your years of diving," Bertie finishes with a smile.

I make a mental note to seek out sea life so Bertie can brag later about what she sees.

Gordon, Ava, Matt and Bertie all finish suiting up quickly. Bertie suggests the Bakers enter the water first since they are closest to the dive platform. Gordon is already pushing up from the bench and standing before she finishes speaking as if he can't wait to be immersed in the ocean. I've asked everyone to wait on the surface for this first dive, so we can all descend together. Until I'm more familiar with the group, I prefer to stay close.

Gordon and Ava make their way to the dive platform as if they're strolling down the neighborhood street, and not carrying fifteen extra pounds on their back. They help each other with their fins, inflate their vests, and then jump into the ocean with practiced ease. After briefly sinking underwater, they bob to the surface and wait for the rest of us. Lauren and Lucky are slower. Both need help to steady themselves as they shuffle to the back of the boat, navigating with the unfamiliar bulk of the tank on their backs and the extra weights in their vest pockets.

"It's been awhile," Lucky says. "But I think it's like riding a bicycle. You never forget."

Lauren jumps into the water, bobs to the surface, gives the all's well sign and swims over to where her parents are waiting. Lucky adjusts her mask, inserts her snorkel in her mouth, and with a hand holding both fast, she successfully leaves the dive platform. Matt is next, followed by Bertie. When I join them on the ocean's surface, everyone gives me a thumbs- up. I turn my thumb down, and we begin our descent to the sand at fifty feet.

Bertie swims head first to the sand as if it's a race. Matt follows more slowly. The others sink fins first. Gordon holds hands with Lauren, helping her on her descent. Or is that Lucky? It's hard to tell underwater as everyone is wearing a hood and a black wetsuit. I don't remember which daughter had the blue fins and which had the black. I remember Ava's yellow fins. She and the other daughter float downward like graceful feathers. That is if feathers sank rather than floated.

We don't wait long on the sand before Gordon and Lucky join us. I can tell now it's her that he's assisting. She's wearing a hood and mask like everyone else, and her lips encircle her regulator, but I do remember her eyes are blue. I make a mental note that she's the one with the blue fins that match her eyes. Lucky points to her ears so I know what delayed them.

The first fifteen feet of a dive descent can be the most difficult for some divers if their ear drums have a hard time adjusting to the change in pressure. She signals that her ears are fine now. After I run the divers through some drills, I point and gesture for the group to follow me. Immediately, Bertie is at my side. I'm not surprised. Bertie won't want to miss out on anything.

I fin for a short while, and then check behind me to make sure everyone is doing ok. All are certified divers. I can assume they know how to navigate underwater. When I ask them their air levels at the dive's midway point, I'll trust their reports. Still, some guests need help with their buoyancy and they appreciate my assistance.

This group looks good. Already, Gordon and Lucky are poking around the reef and Ava and Lauren are finning along with minimal effort. Matt and Bertie are hovering nearby clearly waiting for me to show them something.

I can see the second group descending just at the end of the forty-foot range of visibility- unusually poor clarity for this area. I'm hoping it's simply because we're not quite out of the harbor yet with its tides and sand. I'm sure the teenage boys are the ones who plummet downward like stones. Polo's not far behind them. I can already guess the earful he'll give me. I smile and continue on the dive.

I find eels in the rocks, and a stone fish which I warn the divers not to touch by crossing my gloved index fingers. Large schools of fish swirl above and around us, their silver fins flashing in the filtered rays of the sun that penetrates the water even to this depth. After forty- five minutes, it's time to head to the surface. The water temperature is 68 degrees. Bertie's lips are tinged with blue.

The three- minute safety stop is always a good place to really learn about a diver's experience. Air in the tank is low, giving the tank more buoyancy – almost like swimming with a float on your back. This is where many realize they need extra weight to keep them from popping up to the surface before it's safe. We haven't dived deep enough on this first dive for it to be a real problem if that happens. One of the reasons the first dive is relatively shallow. Too quick to the surface, and a diver could develop an embolism.

Bertie and Matt do yoga poses and blow bubbles during the stop. The Bakers hover together, holding hands. Every so often, Lauren or Lucky will float a little higher than the group only to be gently pulled down by Ava or Gordon. I think of the balloon bouquets my mother creates for her clients. The way they bob and float, their ribbons tugging against the weight that holds them fast.

When the three minutes are up, Bertie and Matt kick to the surface. The Bakers form a loose circle around Gordon and the family ascends as a group. The sun silhouettes their black-clad figures. Their bubbles surround them. And for a moment, they disappear in the sparkle as if they've floated into the air. I've never seen anything like it before. Then, the water churns and Lucky's blue fins flash briefly below the surface before she kicks towards the boat.

Chapter 5

Bertie takes a giant stride off the dive platform. She plunges briefly under the water, then bobs to the surface, her vest full of air to keep her afloat. She shivers when the water first rushes into her wetsuit, even though she knows her body will warm the water soon enough. Bertie thinks briefly of the turquoise water of the Caribbean, how easy it is to jump into that welcoming sea, almost like slipping into a bathtub at home. She pushes those thoughts away. They won't do her any good here.

Instead, she focuses on the fact that the group will be descending soon. She could be in the warmer Caribbean, but still her heart would be pounding at the thought of breathing underwater. This is the only time her brain recoils at the idea of leaving the surface air where it's natural for humans to breathe, where humans were created to breathe. Adventurous Bertie deserts and logical Alberta emerges. Matt treads water towards her.

"We're going to love it," he says. "Just remember to breathe." His words have become tradition.

Alberta takes measured breaths until Catalina gives the descent signal. Then, she inserts her breathing regulator, empties the air from her vest and convinces her brain that although..yes..her head is dropping below the surface of the water, she can breathe perfectly well. After a few breaths, she's calmly adjusted and now, as Bertie once more, she and Matt swim head first to the sandy bottom. The two have never had problems equalizing their ears. They fin in slow circles looking for sea creatures in the nearby reef while they wait for the others.

Being buoyant under water is one of Bertie's favorite parts of scuba diving. She and Matt have done enough dives that both are proficient at navigating just like the divers she used to watch on National Geographic.

Visibility is about forty to forty-five feet. Maybe fifty. Not as good as the eighty to one- hundred- foot visibility in the Caribbean, but Bertie is determined to remain positive. The books she studied before this trip promised better conditions, and hopefully they'll improve on other dives. She's not here to bemoan the poor visibility. Her fingertips are cold, and she can tell even with her gloves on that she's already getting one of her "dead" fingers where the skin turns ghostly white. But she's determined to enjoy this. Bertie's the adventurous one. Bertie's always ready for the new challenge. Alberta was left behind on the surface.

Since it's the first dive, Catalina gathers all the divers in a kneeling circle where each must demonstrate they know the scuba basics like mask clearing and regulator retrieval. Once that's completed, Catalina leads the group to the reef.

Bertie sees the eel peeking out of its crevice before Catalina, but patiently waits for the dive master to notice it. There's her promise to Matt to consider. She didn't know that vow would be tested so early. She consoles herself that she can always point out the eel to Matt if Catalina misses it. But she doesn't have to worry as Catalina shows the eel to the others.

When she's done looking at the eel, Bertie waves her hands to get Matt's attention. She removes her regulator and blows a bubble kiss towards him. He replies in kind. Behind him, Bertie sees Lucky grab Gordon's gloved hand as he's pointing at something. Lucky holds her dad's hand to her cheek before letting go. It's a sweet gesture, and something about it brings tears to Bertie's eyes. She quickly blinks them away as they'll steam up her mask and blur her vision.

Bertie turns around to find Catalina has finned ahead and is carefully searching the reef. She doesn't want to miss out on whatever creature the dive master will find so she kicks hard in that direction. Catalina turns up an octopus squished into the tiniest of rock cavities. Bertie has seen octopus before, but they never cease to amaze her. Catalina moves away so Bertie can get a closer look. She peers into the crevice forgetting all about the exchange between Gordon and Lucky.

The group follows a turtle at a respectful distance before it heads to the surface for a breath.

All too soon, Catalina signals for the group's own ascent. But then, Bertie realizes her fingertips and toes are numb. Once aboard the boat, she rinses off with the solar- heated shower soaking in the warmth, her fingers and toes stinging as the blood flows back into them. Bertie and Matt rinse their masks in the assigned tank, and then hang their wetsuits for the next dive before toweling off and heading into the dining area.

A buffet lunch is laid out in the dining room with an array of green salads, pasta salads and fresh fruits. Sandwiches cut into small triangles are stacked on a silver platter. Bowls of ice hold a variety of waters, juices and teas. Bertie and Matt sit with the Bakers at lunch. This is what often happens on dive trips. The people randomly assigned to dive groups become friends at least for the duration of the trip, while the others remain relative strangers.

The group talks about different dive trips they've taken, comparing visibility and fish sightings. Turns out the Bakers did a lot of diving when their girls were younger. Bertie and Matt are relatively new to the sport compared to them, having only been certified for five years.

No one can match Gordon's experience, not even Ava, as he was diving long before the two met. Gordon's even dived in the Red Sea while staying at an Egyptian resort. Bertie can barely contain her excitement at this revelation. She feels like an acolyte eager to learn all she can from a master. But before she can pepper Gordon with questions, Matt bumps her leg under the table with his and shoots her a warning look: their signal that Bertie is about to talk too much. Bertie forks a pineapple chunk into her mouth, the fruit cool on her wagging tongue.

Matt asks Lauren and Lucky how they liked the dive they just completed.

"Like riding a bicycle," Lucky repeats. "A little wobbly at first, but I'll get the hang of it again."

Bertie assumes Lucky is referring to the struggles she had with her buoyancy. She would never have mentioned it although she noticed the other woman sometimes moving underwater like she was bicycling. A sure way to burn oxygen and bring a dive to a quick end.

Bertie swallows the pineapple. "Is Lucky a nickname?" she asks, thinking of her own.

Gordon chuckles. "It's a long story."

Ava tucks into her green salad with a sigh. "If only I'd been awake."

It's obvious the older Bakers enjoy telling the story of Lucky's name. Lucky and Lauren shake their heads and look resigned to the retelling. Lauren excuses herself to the buffet table for a cookie.

"Ava was named after a movie star," Gordon explains. Matt looks confused, but Bertie knows right away that Gordon is referring to Ava Gardner. Bertie pats Matt on his knee, the signal that she'll tell him later. "So, when our first daughter was born, she wanted to carry on the tradition and name her after a movie star. Lauren Bacall."

Bertie says Bacall at the same time to show Gordon she's following along; maybe she also wants to prove she's educated about movie stars.

"When Lucky came along, Ava lost a lot of blood." Here Gordon wraps his arm around Ava's shoulders and gives her a gentle squeeze. She turns her face towards his and they kiss. Seeing older couples kiss always gives Bertie a warm feeling like the first sip of a good hot cocoa. She hopes she and Matt will be doing the same when they're old. Gordon clears his throat and continues. "Ava was in and out of consciousness for the next twenty- four hours. We nearly lost her." His smile in Ava's direction is watery even after all these years. "I couldn't leave our little girl without a name."

Bertie holds her hand over her heart.

"You hadn't already agreed on one?" Matt says, his voice rising. His fork hovers in mid-air with a teetering melon chunk he hasn't completely stabbed.

He's a pragmatic. Talking about upcoming events and reaching a consensus ahead of time is a big deal to him. Bertie wants to kick his foot but remembers its tender from the unfortunate chafing of one of his dive booties.

"No," Ava says. "We wanted to see our babies first. We figured they'd tell us their names."

Matt looks a little bit shocked. Even though Bertie and Matt don't have children yet, they've settled on names. Bertie thinks the Bakers' idea is romantic, but she knows Matt would have a hard time with it. Plus, she's known the names of her children since she was twelve. Emily if it's a girl. Evan if it's a boy. It won't matter if they're skinny, chubby, crying or quiet when they're born. It's Emily or Evan.

"After our second daughter was cleaned up, the nurses handed her to me in a tightly wrapped pink blanket" Gordon says. "She was a little fussy, so I walked around trying to calm her down. When I passed the window, a beam of sunlight touched her head. And that's when I noticed she had copper colored fuzz."

Bertie looks at Lucky to see if she still has the copper in her hair. Lucky's normally blond hair is dark with water from the solar shower. No one has showered in their cabins yet as there's another dive after lunch. Everyone's simply toweled off as best they could and pulled on t-shirts and shorts over their damp swimsuits. Bertie's shirt sticks to her bikini top. She's got two spreading wet spots on her chest, but so do all the other women. It's a dive boat and no one cares.

"The copper is long gone," Lucky says between bites of her turkey sandwich. Lauren has long finished her cookie. "Lucky for you," Lauren says, leaning back in her chair. The two exchange an amused glance that Bertie thinks is reserved for sisters with a history of shared experiences. She wouldn't know as she only has a younger brother.

"So, of course, I named her Penelope," Gordon finishes.

The table is silent while Bertie figures out how he arrived at the name Penelope. Ava sets her fork on her salad plate with a soft clink.

"Ohhh…Penelope…Penny…A penny is copper and lucky," Bertie says. Gordon beams.

"Penny is cute for a little girl," Lucky says, "but I simply cannot fathom using it as a grown woman."

"What about Penelope?" Matt asks.

"I always imagine Penelope as a helpless woman in a long frilly dress tied to a railroad track," Lucky says.

Bertie immediately pictures the woman as a steam locomotive bears down on her, the railroad tracks vibrating as the heavy engine draws closer, the steam swirling closer in a menacing cloud. She supposes she can't blame Lucky for sticking with the nickname. She wishes she would be brave enough to be Bertie all the time. What would her family think if she told them to call her Bertie?

"And I got to name Jordan," Lucky says.

"Jordan?" Bertie raises her eyebrows.

Gordon and Ava are shaking their heads. Lauren's inspecting her fingernails.

"Jordan's our sibling, but couldn't come on this trip," Lucky says quickly. "But what about you?" she smiles brightly. "Are you named after your dad?"

Bertie has a whole story ready about how she got her name; yes, her dad's name is Albert. She doesn't mention how her back- home name is Alberta. Matt has long since learned to go along with her tale and sits silently beside her.

Just as she's finishing up her story, her cell phone unexpectedly chimes inside the plastic purse she's brought to the table. On trips, she usually turns off her phone and simply uses it as camera. There's no wi-fi on board, but they are still in the harbor.

"We must be near a cell tower," she says. "Sorry."

Bertie reaches into the purse for her phone. She enjoys a week without cell service. She assumes others do too, and she feels warm and embarrassed at her error in leaving the phone connected to the outside world. She doesn't have a text or a missed call. The chime was the alarm on one of her apps. She's set the app to ding twice a day. Now, Bertie holds up the phone grinning, relieved somehow that the Bakers won't think she's been texting or emailing work. That she doesn't know how to disconnect on vacation.

"It's my app," she says. "Have you seen this one?"

The Bakers haven't.

"Oh wow. You might really like this. It's an app that reminds me I'm going to die."

"Soon?" Lauren's voice sounds squeaky. She clears her throat.

"What?" Bertie laughs. "No. No. Not soon. It's more a philosophical idea. You know, realizing you're going to end up dead someday helps you live more fully."

The Bakers are silent. They all stare at the table except for Gordon.

"Now that's a fine idea," he says. "Maybe I should get one of those."

Ava sniffles and looks like she's about to cry. She dabs at her eyes with her napkin. "Think I put too much pepper on my salad," she says.

Matt kicks Bertie under the table as if she doesn't already know the moment is awkward. She switches off her phone and slips it into her small bag.

Chapter 6

Bertie finds me at the boat's bow. I've been sitting here for a while, enjoying God's creation: the slap of the waves against the hull; the occasional spray that wets my face when the boat hits a wave; the salty smell and taste of the water on my lips. My eyes not quite closed, but not quite open either. A cap with the boat's insignia – a manta ray – shades my features. This is where I like to retreat at the beginning of the trip, before the younger crowd discovers the excitement of the dip and rise of the boat in the swell of the water.

We left the harbor a while ago after our second dive. The ocean is mostly smooth, and the bow is mostly steady. I lean against the boat, unsure of how long I've been out here. Polo knows where I am and to call me if I'm needed. Although I'm not shy, I do enjoy some breathing space.

The boat can get awfully small over the course of a week. Smaller on some dive trips than others, depending on the personalities and persistence of the guests. This group hasn't been together long enough yet for me to form an opinion about whether this trip will be a challenging one. I'm feeling optimistic though as I ruminate on the diving experience of my smaller group; we've already fallen into an easy dive routine under water. I anticipate an easy week.

Bertie's approach is quiet. I see her bare toes first. Her toenails are painted a pearl pink, one of her big toes has a small jewel embedded in the polish. It was the flash of the jewel in the sun that first caught my attention.

I imagine Bertie at the nail salon in Michigan, pondering her nail color choice. (yes, she's already told our group she and Matt are from Michigan). She tells the manicurist she's going to be on a boat; she's not going to be wearing shoes. I picture the woman suggesting the tiny jewel. I don't know Bertie very well, but she doesn't seem the type who makes flashy statements. Her earrings are tiny silver balls. Her wedding ring is plain silver, possibly platinum, I don't know enough about jewelry to tell the difference. If she has a diamond, she's left it at home. Probably nervous about thievery in Mexico.

When I see her feet, I look up. The sun is behind her, the wind plays with a few tendrils of hair that blow around her face, escapees from the messy bun swirled on top of her head.

"Mind if I join you?" she says.

The bow is not off limits to the guests. But I'm surprised Bertie's made her way up front so quickly. Usually, the adults prefer to enjoy the sundeck, the adjoining bar or the inside lounge.

I gesture for her to sit, and she lowers herself so that our shoulders are nearly touching. She tucks her hair behind her ears. I think about the way Bertie hangs at my shoulder on the dives, and I figure she's either someone who wants to see everything first, or she's someone who's already seen something before I have and she's waiting for me to point it out. If it's the latter, I appreciate her restraint. But I wonder how long she'll be able to hold back?

A single bat ray hurtles out of the water, followed by two more. The rays flap, fly a ways, and then flop back into the water with a splash. Bertie gasps and leans forward, shading her eyes with her hand.

"That's amazing," she says. "Bat rays?"

I nod.

"I've read about them," she says. "They're so much bigger than I imagined."

We watch the bat rays do their thing, bursting out of the water repeatedly, soaring into the air before dropping back to the ocean with a splash landing.

"No one knows why they jump out of the water," Bertie says. "I suppose there's a scientific reason for it."

"I like to think they're just having fun," I say.

Bertie laughs and settles back against the boat. "You've probably seen thousands of those rays," she says. She sounds somewhat envious.

"I never get tired of looking," I say.

Bertie nods. "I imagine not. When I look outside at home, I see our yard. Don't get me wrong, it's a nice yard. I always plant a variety of tulips before the first freeze. And I do enjoy the beautiful rainbow of colors in spring."

She's quiet. Then she says, "I like to think I'm adventurous. We travel. But it's not the same as actually living in a foreign country."

"I'm not sure I would classify the Calypso as a foreign country," I joke.

Bertie laughs. "Living on a boat in a foreign country, then. I'd like to know more about it." She shades her eyes again with her hand and looks at me smiling before turning her gaze back to the ocean. "Are you from Mexico?"

"Southern California." I say.

The waves slap against the boat. The wind teases Bertie's hair. I breathe deeply of the salt air while I think about my next words. Bertie's interest feels genuine, so I decide to answer in the same manner.

"I headed overseas right after college," I say. "Six years ago."

"Have you always been on the Calypso?"

I list the resorts and boats where I've worked, ticking off a finger for each one. Bertie has visited one and wants to know more about the other locations. She doesn't ask whether I would recommend it for a dive vacation, but instead is curious about what I experienced while I was there. I've had others ask me about recommendations, but no one has ever asked about my personal experiences. I share two brief stories with Bertie, keeping it light. We hardly know each other after all.

"So now you've worked your way closer to home," she says. "Is the Calypso your last boat? Are you nearly done with your nomadic life?"

Bertie's question catches me by surprise. I've never really thought of my life as nomadic. Nothing's really stopping me from going home. It's not like I'm being held captive by the goddess Calypso. I know I'm closer than before.

I remember my dad's face when I announced my plans to leave home and travel the world. His forehead wrinkled, and his eyes were sad. "How long will you be gone?" he said.

I hadn't really given the length of time much thought. And truly, at the time, I thought I would be gone no more than two years.

I originally wanted to skip college and work as a dive master right after high school. But my parents convinced me to get a college education first. "You're young," my dad said. "It's only four years." Four years seemed like forever to me at the time, but I promised to get a degree. I went to college and worked summers for a local dive shop.

"I'll be back before you know it, Poppy," I said, kissing his cheek. "You'll barely have time to miss me."

My mom was brisk. She grabbed a pencil, one of the pads that she made by stapling scraps of paper together, and started making a list. "Hat, sunscreen, bathing suits, shorts," she muttered as she jotted down items. "How many suitcases will you need?"

"Just my backpack and my dive bag," I said.

My mom tossed aside her list. "She's grown now," she said to my dad. "She's fulfilled her part of the bargain."

My dad grimaced. "I thought once she graduated she'd get a real job."

"Shush," my mom touched his arm. "She is getting a job." Then, she took me in her arms and hugged me. "Go with God," she whispered in my hair.

The two years somehow drifted into six while I logged more dives than I keep track of anymore. I've never been home. My parents came to visit when I was on a boat in the British Virgin Islands after I'd been gone for three years. They don't have a lot of money. The trip was an anniversary celebration. My brother couldn't make it, and then I moved to Australia which was too far and too expensive of a trip for him.

Now, I sit on the bow of the Calypso with Bertie and think about how all the weeks and months and years have slipped by like the never-resting water moving beneath the boat. And I wonder, am I like the boat, motoring along on the surface of life? Have I unwittingly become like Odysseus' crew who tasted the lotus and forgot the way home?

I hold my right hand loosely on my thigh, ready to tick off on my fingers the number of lasting relationships I've made on my journey. But I can't think of a single one.

Is Bertie right?

Have I inched closer to home because I'm feeling ready to leave this life behind?

I've always imagined being married and having children someday. I'm one of those people who is always looking for heart shapes in nature. I've seen clouds in the form of hearts, coral, seashells and once, the pattern on a turtle's shell. I suppose I could be like Manuel with his wife and children on shore. But I don't picture myself living apart from my husband and my kids. There must be some other way to have a foot in both worlds.

I don't know how to answer Bertie, so instead I ask her about her life in Michigan. We fall into an easy conversation about her family, how they eat dinner together every Sunday. We're both laughing about a story she's shared when Matt pokes his head around the corner and tells us it's time for another dive.

Chapter 7

Bertie closes the cabin door behind her with a soft snick. Matt is still napping, but Bertie wants to relax and maybe read a little on the sundeck. She's applied suntan lotion. The smell reminds her of summer days at the local pool. Gossiping with her friends and ogling at the lifeguard. She's smiling when she passes an open cabin door. She knows she should avert her gaze, but the door is open and maybe the occupants wouldn't mind if she gave them a quick wave on her way upstairs.

Gordon sits on a queen-sized bed with his head in his hands; his fingers are buried in his thick white hair. The covers are smooth except where Gordon hunches, there the blankets are bunched around him like a ring of small sand dunes.

"You don't have to do this." Ava's voice comes from elsewhere in their cabin. Bertie can't see her. "The doctor says you…"

At that moment, Gordon looks up from the floor. Bertie turns her face away and quickens her pace, unable to hear the rest of Ava's sentence.

She hopes Gordon doesn't think she's spying. She hears the cabin door click shut.

A wave of embarrassment heats her cheeks. Bertie is glad to reach the stairs and climb to the upper deck. She briefly wonders what Ava was talking about and why Gordon seemed so down. He's always so upbeat before their dives, telling one joke after another.

Her curiosity evaporates when she when she gets upstairs; a thin layer of clouds veil the sun. The breeze is cooler than she expected on this open section of the stern. The boat is moving towards where they will anchor for tonight's dive. Afterwards, they'll motor further north while the guests eat dinner. Dive boats usually move around so multiple dive locations can be experienced by the guests.

Despite the cool air, Bertie is determined to relax. The sun was hot earlier; she believes the clouds will blow away soon. She won't be dissuaded from her plan. She's come upstairs barefoot in a bikini with sunglasses, a book under her arm and a towel for the chair. She grabs the last empty lounge chair, spreads her towel and settles onto it. The younger members of the other families have pulled four loungers together and are laughing and chatting. The guys are shirtless in trunks and the girls all wear bikinis. Bertie takes it as a sign that once she's used to the temperature, she'll be fine.

The book she's brought has been highly recommended by her friends, and she's been looking forward to reading it. But, despite the well-written first two pages, she can't concentrate. The breeze chills her skin. Goosebumps pimple her arms and legs. She presses her back deeper into her towel, but no luck. Still cold, she stands and gathers her items. The girls in the group have donned t-shirts over their swim suits. They must have pulled them on while she was reading. Maybe the covered bar situated behind the sundeck will be a more protected spot. Bertie slings the towel over her shoulders like a shawl, wishing she'd thought to bring a t-shirt.

Lauren and Lucky are in the bar drinking and talking to Polo. Lauren sits on a bamboo stool, leaning her elbows on the dark wood bar. She fingers a tall glass with a frothy cream- colored drink topped with a tiny red paper umbrella. Lucky is perched on the stool next to her sister, sipping on a beer. Both are wearing t-shirts and shorts. Polo stands behind the bar.

"Mind if I join you?" Bertie says. The women nod and wave her over.

Bertie climbs on a stool, setting her book on the bar. She orders whatever it is Lauren is having. The women are silent while Polo mixes the concoction in a blender, the whir of the machine drowning out the possibility of more than a shouted conversation. When he's done, he pours the liquid into a tall glass, pops a bright yellow umbrella into it and slides the drink to Bertie. It smells of coconut, pineapple and rum.

"Very tropical," Bertie smiles, and takes a sip. She adjusts the towel on her shoulders. "It's a little chilly out there now." Bertie nods at the sundeck.

"Should have come up earlier," Lauren says. "We couldn't stand the heat and had to move to the shade."

Lucky laughs. "That's not how I remember it," she says. The sisters share a smile. Bertie wishes she had a sister she could share a drink and a joke with. She can't imagine sitting at a dive boat bar with her brother. He's not a very good swimmer or a risk taker. He's never left Michigan although he does often fish on the lake, and she has popped a beer with him on his fishing boat.

"Where's your husband?" Lauren says.

Bertie blinks at her question. She's still thinking about the beers she's shared with her brother.

"Your husband?" Lauren says again.

"Oh, right." Bertie blushes thinking about the interlude she and Matt had in their cabin. More than one place on the boat was blazing hot, she thinks, smiling into her drink.

The two sisters wink and laugh, and Bertie chuckles with them, sipping her drink and letting the towel slip from her shoulders. Then, Lauren comments on the book Bertie has laid on the bar. She's read it, and highly recommends it. Maybe Bertie will have an opportunity to read it sometime this week. Of course, she might be too busy in the cabin with Matt. She smiles and enjoys more of her rum drink, wondering how Lauren can be away from her husband on this trip. She noticed the wedding band on Lauren's hand right away, but hasn't asked her about it. Lucky wears no rings.

The group has been on six dives together so far. Matt and Bertie have done the full four offered each day, but the Bakers haven't always done every dive. They've eaten a few meals together, but the conversation is usually dominated by Gordon. Polo wanders out to the sun deck where he jokes around with the younger crowd. Their laughter floats towards the bar.

Now that the three are alone, Bertie asks Lauren about her husband.

"Curtis isn't a diver," Lauren says.

"And he doesn't mind you traveling without him?" Bertie can't imagine traveling without Matt. What would they talk about when she returned? He would pretend to be interested in what she'd done and seen, but it wouldn't be the same as sharing the experience with him.

"This trip is special," Lauren says without elaborating.

"Someone's birthday? Or anniversary?" Most of Bertie's drink is gone. She feels warm and relaxed just like she wanted. She's not usually an afternoon drinker. Unless of course she's on a dive boat.

"Just spending time with our parents," Lucky says. She changes the subject. "You and Matt been married long?"

Bertie's head buzzes a little, and she's easily distracted. It doesn't take much prompting from Lucky or Lauren to get her talking about how she and Matt met – at a tulip festival - how they eventually fell in love and he proposed – of course, back at the tulip festival. It was so romantic.

"What about you?" Bertie says to Lucky. "What's your story?"

Polo has returned to the bar at some point during Bertie's tale and refilled all the drinks. Bertie takes cautious sips of her second one, now that she knows Polo is heavy handed with the rum.

"I'm simply unlucky in love," Lucky says.

"That's not true," Lauren splutters. Bertie doesn't know how many drinks the two have downed. They could have been on their second or third round when she arrived. "Brett was a great guy."

"If you like cretins," Lucky mutters.

"You're too picky," Lauren says. "You always have been."

"I'm holding out for another Curtis," Lucky declares, raising her beer and taking a swig. She rubs her palm across her lips. "Maybe I'll get really lucky and find someone like dad."

"He's one of a kind," Lauren says somberly. Lucky nods. The mood darkens, as if more clouds have covered the sun. Bertie shivers. The towel has fallen to her waist, and she pulls it back up, adjusting it around her shoulders. Maybe her frozen drink has given her a sudden chill. She looks to the sundeck. The open area is brighter than the shaded bar. The younger crowd has dispersed leaving the lounge chairs huddled together, they've even pulled Bertie's chair into the mix. But maybe it has become cloudier and cooler after all. It's hard to tell.

The sisters clink their glasses in a silent toast, then quickly drain their drinks and stand. They're a little bit wobbly when they bid Bertie farewell. Polo rushes to assist them, but they wave him away. Linking arms, they disappear down the stairs.

Bertie wonders what the silent toast was about. She loves her own dad, but she would never want to marry someone like him. In fact, she picked Matt because he is the polar opposite of her dad. She remembers the familiar back of her Dad's head as he vanished into his basement workroom, already muttering about finishing his next project; too busy to come to Bertie's basketball game, or her brother's soccer tournament, always promising to attend the next one, to save time for the next family vacation.

Matt, on the other hand, doesn't like to waste time on boring projects. He prefers to hire professionals to fix up their own small home. So far, they've gotten rid of the popcorn ceilings and redone the bathrooms. People are working right now, under the strict direction of the kitchen designer Bertie found, finishing up their new kitchen while Bertie and Matt are on vacation.

Bertie loves that her husband is adventurous. And he's never shy about telling her or showing her how much he loves her. She feels warm again thinking about earlier this afternoon, and she lets the towel slip from her shoulders. She raises her glass to her lips in a toast to Matt, and then thinks twice.

She shouldn't drink anymore; she won't be able to participate in tonight's dive. Still, she's toasted to her husband, so she takes one tiny sip to seal the sentiment and then, sets the nearly full glass down and pushes it away. She adjusts the towel on her shoulders, opens her book and reads.

Chapter 8

Midweek, there's a talent show in the lounge for those who want to participate. Bertie has anticipated this possibility; her knowledge comes from previous trips on dive live-aboards. She's found that divers enjoy a party as much (if not more) than anybody. They don't mind having an excuse to gather and be silly. Bertie has packed a small ukulele and two plastic leis on the off-chance that she and Matt can use them on the Calypso.

Everyone, even the crew except for the captain - someone must stay at the wheel - crowds into the lounge, squishing together on the chairs and couches and sprawling on the carpet. The adults are all prepared with a drink in hand: not necessarily their first of the night. This is one of the nights when a dive isn't scheduled so the alcohol has flowed freely since dinner time and the room smells of beer, rum and coconut suntan lotion.

Despite the AC, Bertie feels warm. She fans her face with her free hand. When that doesn't cool her off, she holds her frozen mango margarita to her flushed cheek. Her eyes sparkle with excitement. Then, without warning, she slips from her perch on the arm of Matt's chair into his lap. Some of her drink sloshes onto her leg.

"Watch it," one of the men says with a smile. "This is a PG show."

Matt laughs and pretends to bite Bertie's neck. Bertie wriggles out of his grasp and returns to her seat where she alternates between sips of margarita and holding the frozen concoction to her cheek.

Jacqueline, the youngest on board, is the first act. She wears an electric-blue, one-piece bathing suit. She's twisted her usual ponytail into a bun that sits squarely on top of her head. She starts with a handstand, then progresses fluidly into a walkover. Her family cheers her on as she finishes with a bridge, her back held in a perfect arch. Almost lazily, she pulls herself into a standing position and finishes with a graceful bow.

Bertie is amazed at the girl's supple movements. She can't remember being able to move that fluidly when she was eleven or twelve. She was all elbows and knees as a girl. Bertie sips her drink and feels grateful Matt encouraged her to scuba dive. When she's underwater, Bertie believes she's as graceful as the demonstration she just witnessed.

The teenage boys perform a few incomprehensible card tricks, eliciting hoots and hollers among the youngest in the crowd. Bertie laughs and applauds with the rest. She can enjoy a goofy performance as much as anyone, especially when she's on her second (or is it her third?) margarita.

The teenage girls give a pleasant rendition of a popular song. They hit hardly any bad notes. Bertie's glad she's still young enough to recognize the song and actually know its lyrics.

It turns out Polo and Madelyn are quite the dancers. Madelyn wears a skirt that flares and swirls when Polo twirls her in the small space set aside for a stage. Madelyn's thick hair swings like a curtain around her face, a marked contrast to Polo's shaved head that glints under the lounge lights. Manuel passes on a performance, resisting the pressure of the guests, but Catalina shares a witty poem she's written about the boat and those on board. She's done a good job capturing the distinctive characteristics of the guests as they prepare for a dive. Everyone raises their glasses in a toast to her at the end.

Bertie and Matt go next. They don their leis – that's a much as Matt will do. His is a bright green and Bertie's is fuschia. Matt pulls over a chair to use as a drum. Bertie strums the ukulele and sways her hips while she sings the song Tiny Bubbles. It seems like an appropriate choice especially since she changes the words slightly to mention that the tiny bubbles are in the ocean while they are diving.

She spent many nights back home rewriting the lyrics of the famous song after their first dive trip when they had nothing to share on talent night. When the song is finished, Matt stands to bow with Bertie. Tonight, he holds her hand and twirls her (perhaps he was inspired by Madelyn and Polo). Bertie feels flushed and happy. She's not sure if it's the unexpected twirling, the rush of performing before a group, or the drinks she's consumed. Back at their shared chair, Bertie tips her glass and is surprised to find it's empty.

The parents of the teenagers and Jacqueline won't participate. They say they're not prepared. Nothing can change their minds, so Lucky and Lauren step to the front holding their drinks which they say are instrumental to their act. They both take a large amount of liquid into their mouths swish it around, and then swallow. With lips pursed, they begin a whistling duet. They're really quite good. Soon everyone is clapping along to the rhythm.

Bertie knows she should recognize the tune, but figures it must be from before her time. She thinks it was from a movie, but the alcohol blurs her brain and she can't think. The sisters finish with a flourish. Both down the rest of their drinks and clink their empty glasses together.

It's a grand finish that earns admiring whistles in return. Bertie wonders if it's the end of the show. But Gordon pushes up from his chair and holds out his hand in a grand gesture to Ava. He bows, and she lays her hand in his and rises.

The two seem to glide to the front of the lounge where the acts are being performed; he's wearing a t-shirt and wrinkled shorts; she's in a black t-shirt dress that flows around her knees. Despite their casual dress, their elegant movements stir Bertie's imagination. She can easily picture Gordon in a tuxedo and Ava in an evening gown. The two turn and face each other, holding hands. A hush falls over the lounge, even Jacqueline settles down at her mother's bare feet. Catalina leans forward where she's sitting on top of a low cupboard, resting her chin on her hand. Bertie has a feeling something special is about to happen.

Gordon's lips move slightly. Bertie thinks he's counting. At the same moment, the two start singing, their voices rising and falling and blending together in a powerful duet.

"Love me tender, love me sweet, never let me go, you have made my life complete, and I love you so. Love me tender, love me sweet, all my dreams fulfilled, for my darling I love you and I always will."

Bertie's eyes water as the two sing. Their voices fill the room and yet don't overpower it. She reaches out her hand for Matt's. A slow tear traces a path down her cheek and drips onto her plastic lei.

"Love me tender, love me sweet, take me to your heart. For it's there I belong and we'll never part."

The song seems to cast a spell over the small audience. Bertie feels as if she's entered into a magical space where Gordon and Ava are oblivious to those watching.

"For my darling I love you and I always will."

As the words fade away, Gordon leans forward and presses his lips tenderly to Ava's.

Chapter 9

We've motored further north into the Sea of Cortez. We're getting close to La Paz now. The women no longer wear makeup. Their hair is covered by a ball cap or pulled back in a ponytail when they're not diving. In between dives, both men and women relax on the boat in scruffy, loose t-shirts and shorts or bathing suits.

This is why I love being on a dive boat. There's no pretense. There's no hiding.

I've never been backpacking but I think being on a dive boat is somewhat like being in the backcountry except here you have gourmet meals, hot showers and flush toilets. Diving burns a lot of calories, so Madelyn always has healthy snacks available between meals.

Often, there's drama in such close quarters. I did see some of the teenagers arguing, and one of the girls ran off crying, but they're all playing cards in the lounge now and laughing so I assume all is well.

My diving group has fallen into a groove. It's funny how everyone sticks to their "place" underwater.

Bertie still hangs at my shoulder with Matt not far behind. Now that I know Bertie better, I no longer question her motives. She's confessed her embarrassing propensity to appear like a know-it-all. She says she's trying not to be labeled as such on this trip. She's begged my forgiveness in advance for any offense she perpetrates. As I said earlier, it's hard not to like her.

The other four take turns being buddies. On one dive I'll see Gordon and Lauren together, on the next it's Gordon and Lucky while Ava and Lauren pair up. The four still do what I've come to think of as their ceremonial ascent after the safety stop.

Watching them, I think of our family beach days, and I wonder if we did some things others might consider ceremonially odd. We did most everything together, except I was the only one to get scuba certified. My memories of those long beach days - the sun flattening on the horizon like a slowly deflating beach ball as we shook the sand off our feet - are encased in a hazy golden glow.

I remember a rhythm, an orderliness of sorts, to our end of day clean up; my brother and I rinsing the sand toys and loading the beach wagon; my father lowering the umbrella, brushing the sand from the cooler. Then, my mother leading the way as we followed in a line, first my father behind her pulling the wagon, then my brother pushing it from behind while I brought up the tail and watched for any items that tumbled out. I suspect time has worn away the edges of the truth. I'm not sure anymore if we even went to the beach together all that often.

After a dive, I ask Ava about the Baker's group ascent.

She laughs it off as nothing special. "We like to stick together," she says. She busies herself with rinsing her mask. When she finishes and looks up, her eyes are red. She tells me salt water seeped into her mask during the dive and stung her eyes. But I climbed aboard shortly after she did, and I don't remember them being red at all then.

It's not quite time for our second dive of the morning. Most of the guests are still in the dining room eating their second breakfast. Before the first dive, it's coffee, oatmeal or cold cereal. Afterwards, the guests climb back on board to the smell of bacon and fresh coffee. Madelyn's laid out a fully loaded buffet table of eggs, bacon, sausages, pancakes, fruit, pastries and juices.

I wander out onto the deck where the divers suit up, checking to make sure everything's in order before the rush to get ready. Gordon kneels on a bench, leaning between two tanks. His elbows are on the gunwale. He appears to be lost in thought. The gray-blue ocean that surges beyond him is empty. A few thin clouds float in a faded denim sky. No heart shapes in the sky today.

It's unusual to find him alone. Whenever I've seen him, one of his family members is hovering somewhere nearby. And I don't mean to disturb him, but he calls my name when I stuff a wayward dive bootie into the appropriate bin.

"Catalina," he says while I'm working the bootie into the plastic container. I'm trying not to breathe too hard; the bootie has that funky stink rubber gets when it's not rinsed well. Gordon's voice startles me, and I jump.

"I guess you're surprised to find me without my posse," he says, lowering his voice. He looks towards the dining room. "Good. They're still eating."

His smile barely tilts his lips. "I can't seem to get a minute alone."

"I'm sorry to bother you," I say. "I'm done here, so I'll leave."

"No, no," he says. "Have a seat." He waves at the opposite bench. I sit down, unsure what he wants. He's such an experienced diver, maybe he has a complaint about my leadership underwater. I compose my features and sit up straight.

"Relax," he says, "you're doing a great job. I can tell you love your work."

I release the breath of air I didn't know I was holding.

"Thanks," I say, pulling my knees up and wrapping my arms around them in a hug.

"How long have you been at this?" he says.

We talk awhile about our dive experiences, discovering we've dived in some of the same locations. Of course, Gordon's experience is vastly greater than mine. He begins to regale me with stories of his early years of diving.

"But I never did what you're doing," he says. "I didn't have the guts to do something like this on my own." He shakes his head. This time, his smile slowly blooms on his face, crinkling his eyes and showing his teeth which are brilliantly white against his tanned skin. "Your father must be proud of you."

"Yeah," I say, even though I know my words aren't true. Gordon doesn't need to know that my father thinks I'm wasting my college degree.

Gordon lifts his ball cap from his head; he rakes his fingers through his flattened mane of hair before re-settling the cap.

"Still", he says as if I hadn't spoken, "I've lived a great life." He looks past me out to sea. "Just look at this beautiful world." He waves his hand at the water. "All that life teeming below the surface. All those sights we've seen that others only dream about or watch on television. The unbelievable freedom we've had breathing underwater."

Gordon's words remind me of my own passion for the ocean. I nod in agreement.

"I have no regrets," he declares.

We're both silent.

"I bet you won't have any either," he says with a chuckle, breaking the somber mood.

Then, Lucky steps out of the dining room. "There you are dad," she says; her voice sounds like an exasperated school teacher's. "We've been looking for you."

Gordon winks at me. "I've been here all along Lucky girl," he says

Chapter 10

Our second dive this morning is a drift dive. It's important that after each diver jumps into the water, he or she grab the rope that trails behind the boat. That way, we'll be able to gather on the surface together. We'll descend at the same time and approximate rate of speed or the different underwater currents will carry us in varying directions.

Lauren and Lucky have regained their dive confidence. They assure me they'll be fine. If a pair drifts too far from the group, they can always kick to the surface and inflate their safety sausage to wave above the ocean's surface and signal they need help. The boat will send a panga to pick them up.

While we're diving, the Calypso will motor to the spot where the current carries us. We won't have to swim back fighting against the current, using up our precious air. Manuel goes over the dive parameters for the day. After drifting for about fifteen minutes, both groups will drop below the current and explore an underwater cave. This time, his group will be entering the water first.

The dive deck is exposed to the sun, but there's little warmth to be had this morning. Thin clouds I saw earlier have stitched themselves together in a gray blanket that lets through the light but nothing else. We're far enough out that land isn't visible; only the undulating ocean swirls around us, the spray of small white caps breaking its monotonous gray. An occasional wave spurts against the side of the Calypso, spitting salt water onto the dive platform. The boat rises and falls, rocking on the swells that pass beneath it. I survey my divers, but none appear affected by the tilting of the boat; no one is lifting a hand to their mouth or leaning over the side.

Instead, my divers are huddled in towels that they're clutching across their chests.

All except Gordon, whose already pulled his wetsuit up and over his shoulders. I watch as the rest reluctantly don their cold, damp wetsuits with a series of groans and complaints, slowly drawing the clammy legs up to their waist but leaving the rest unzipped. Eventually, Lauren stands and grimaces as she slips her arms back into her sodden wetsuit.

"Brrrrrr," Gordon clutches his arms across his chest, shivering and clattering his teeth together before smiling at his daughter. "Good thing you come from hardy stock."

"Ha!" she grits her teeth as she pulls the zipper up, encasing her body in the cold suit.

"You can always skip the dive," he says.

"Not on your life," Lauren says. She covers her mouth with her hand as if she's a little girl caught swearing. "Sorry, didn't mean to say that." She plops on the bench next to Gordon and reaches for his hand, giving it a squeeze.

"Don't worry about it princess," Gordon plants a kiss on her hand, and then drops it to adjust his booties.

Somehow, Ava manages to scoot even closer than she was before to her husband. I imagine she's trying to soak up some of Gordon's body heat.

Bertie displays her own displeasure with the feel of the wet rubber on her skin by showing me a crying face as she pulls her wetsuit back on. I smile and shake my head. Matt is behind her and doesn't see her expression. Putting on a cold, damp outfit isn't my favorite either. I imagine it's like choosing to jump into refrigerated Jello when you're already feeling chilled.

It's not like diving in the tropics, where you become overheated between dives and you welcome the feel of the cool suit – that is if it hasn't dried out yet. Sure, I was warmer in my towel than I am now, but I know I'll be warm again in a few minutes after we jump into the water. It defies logic, I know. The fact that jumping into cold water in a cold wetsuit will eventually prove to be warmer.

But sometimes experience outweighs logic; why else would we willingly sink underwater and breathe as if it's the natural thing to do?

While my group is busy suiting up again, checking air pressure and squirting lens cleaner into their dive masks, Manuel's group enters the water. They all successfully hold onto the rope and descend below the surface at the same time. Hopefully, all is going well underwater. Madelyn is helping him today.

When it's our turn, Lucky and Lauren quickly take turns jumping into the water and grabbing the rope. Next are Ava and Gordon, followed by Matt and Bertie. I join the group, and then give the signal to let go of the rope and descend.

We all drift down at about the same rate of speed into the current which isn't moving as quickly as some I've experienced but its pull is still evident. It would be impossible to hover by a reef without holding on to the coral.

My divers have all proven to be skilled. I don't worry about them underwater. I'm grateful Manuel assigned me this group, and I do a little happy spin in the current. Drift diving is a favorite of mine. There's nothing like being pulled along by a current. It feels like flying underwater, requiring no effort except breathing. I think of birds, wings spread on an unseen rush of air. Apparently, Bertie and Matt feel the same, as their arms are outstretched like they're superman and superwoman. I cruise by them and execute a somersault.

As I'm upside down, I notice that only three divers are behind us.

Gordon is missing.

I turn and kick hard back against the current. As Ava, Lauren and Lucky pass me, I signal to them. Where is Gordon? Somehow- even after all of Ava's words about how they like to stick together - they've gotten separated.

Gordon is without a buddy.

A dangerous situation despite his years of experience.

I kick and use my arms to move against the current and not far up ahead, I see Gordon. My heart's pounding from relief and my burst of speed. I thank God I noticed he was missing when I did. I'm grateful the current wasn't so swift after all.

Gordon is hovering just above the current the rest of us are riding.

When I rise out of it, the water around him isn't moving much. It almost seems still compared to the stream that was pushing us along. His back is to me, and he's not aware of my presence when I come up behind him. He's upright and staring off into the distance at something that seems to fascinate him. As I move around him, I can see his face and I get the impression he's smiling.

But that can't be, because his regulator is in his mouth, his bubbles rising at a slight angle to the surface. I search the area where he's looking, thinking he must see something amazing – maybe a whale shark. Those tend to hang on the surface.

I remember Gordon telling me he'd like to see another of the gargantuan creatures. Sightings of them can be rare. Still, if there's a huge whale shark in the water, I don't see it.

By this time, my heart's pounding has slowed to its normal beat; the inhale and exhale of my breath is noticeable to me once more. Gordon still hasn't noticed me. I reach out and touch his arm. He startles and turns slowly towards me. The look of disappointment in his eyes surprises me.

Did I miss something?

I look over his shoulder. I still see nothing. Not even the flash of a huge tail or a giant shadow moving in the water.

I form my gloved fingers into the ok sign, asking Gordon if he's all right. He responds in kind. He points to his ears. Gordon hasn't experienced problems with clearing his ears before, but that doesn't mean it couldn't happen to him. Pressure in the ears is painful and no joke. I point my thumb up. Does he want to ascend? Gordon shakes his head, signaling that he wants to continue the dive. I doubt we'll be able to catch the rest of the group. I figure they're long gone in the current (as slow as it was) by now. Fortunately, they're all experienced divers. If they don't see the cave, and drop out of the current, they know how to get to the surface on their own to deploy their safety sausages. In fact, Bertie and Matt are certified as rescue divers.

But when I turn around, all of them are hovering near us. They must have kicked against the current after me. Bertie and Matt are searching the nearby waters for the sea creature that caused Gordon to separate from the group. Gordon's dive reputation is such that I imagine they assume like I did that he's seen something unusual. The Bakers don't look beyond Gordon, although none of the women approach him.

Bertie finally looks at me. I shrug my shoulders. We've all used up some oxygen working our way back to Gordon. I signal for the others to give me a report on their tank levels. Based on what they tell me, I figure we'll be fine drifting to the cave. We will have to cut our bottom time short at the cave though. We descend again, taking our time for Gordon's ears; all of us keeping in the same current.

Bertie and Matt execute forward and backward somersaults. They signal for me to do the same. I would normally join them, but something about the incident with Gordon has put me off. The Bakers drift along, arms and legs akimbo, almost like rag dolls.

I point to distant hammerheads headed in the opposite direction. A turtle flies by on a faster river of water. Soon, we reach the coordinates of the cave where we'll do some exploring. We drop out of the current and onto the sandy bottom. The yawning mouth of the cave is before us, large enough for the Calypso to fit inside or a Cyclops to keep his herds. A roundish opening in the ceiling that's not quite big enough for a diver to squeeze through lets in rippling light.

Despite the spaciousness of this cave, not everyone likes swimming into enclosed spaces. If Gordon and Ava opt out, I'm not going to leave them outside by themselves. I can't put my finger on my uneasiness; it's just a sense I have.

When I was certified as a dive master, my instructor told the class that the most important thing we should remember was to trust our gut. "If something feels wrong, don't discount your feelings," the instructor warned. "Everything might look right. And everything might be as it seems. But, your gut is your spidey sense of observation. You might have 'seen' something that can't be explained."

I took her words to heart.

My parents liked to tell stories of how they knew not to drive down a particular road, so they took a detour. Later, they learned about a multiple car accident with fatalities. They knew not to take me to the beach one Saturday; they resisted my fierce protests. That day, a surfer got bit by a Great White Shark. She didn't die, but she required multiple surgeries and was left with a limp and an impressive scar. They had plenty of other less dramatic stories, about how God's angels had protected us, so I learned at an early age to trust my instincts: my gut.

During my years as a dive master, those instincts have saved several divers from potentially disastrous mistakes. I'm not saying those divers are alive because of me. But I like to think I saved them from a potentially panicky situation. And hopefully, helped them retain their love of diving.

Now, everyone decides to go in the cave. I remind them of our shortened time, and then I lead the way inside trusting that everyone will follow. Also, Manuel's group is just outside the cave exploring the reef so I'm hoping if anything untoward happens, he or Madelyn will take care of my people.

The rest of the dive is uneventful. The Calypso meets us at the agreed upon end of our drift. Only two divers from Manuel's group got separated from the others in the current and had to be rescued by the panga.

The Bakers perform what I've come to expect as their group ascent. As usual, Gordon ascends in the center of his family, the women holding the three points of a triangle around him. They rise together as if they are a giant amoeba emerging from the sea to start life on land.

Back on board the Calypso, Bertie is bubbling over with all she's seen on the dive. She and Matt hang their gear, and then head into the lounge where she wants to check out a fish book. The Bakers are unusually quiet. Lucky rubs her face and sighs before bending to pull off her dive booties. Lauren holds her mask by the rinse bucket. But instead of rinsing, she stares at the horizon apparently lost in thought. Ava rubs Gordon's back and whispers in his ear. He shakes his head. He gives her a quick peck on her cheek, and then stands to shimmy out of his wetsuit.

I still feel unsettled as I step out of my wetsuit and take care of my gear. I remember how happy I was when Manuel assigned me the experienced group. Maybe my joy blinded me to something. Or maybe the close quarters of the boat, the 24/7 of life together is simply exposing cracks in the Baker family dynamics. I've seen that happen time and again in my years of working on dive live-aboards. Days spent together with not many distractions can be a challenge for some families. I decide that must be the case with the Bakers. I dig in the general boat bin for a bottle of ear wash.

"Want some Gordon?" I hold up the small white bottle.

"What?" Gordon rubs his head with his towel.

"Ear wash?" I say.

"My ears are fine," he says.

"We have some," Ava reaches into her bin and retrieves up a clear bottle with what appears to be a homemade remedy. "Gordon's been making this stuff since forever," she says. "You can borrow some anytime if you want." She narrows her eyes at Gordon and squeezes his hand. He leaves for the cabin without saying another word, his towel slung over his head.

"Gordon," Ava calls. "Your towel."

Wet towels, wet dive gear, wet anything are not allowed inside the cabins. The constant drip of ocean water would eventually ruin the carpets, imbuing them with that same funky smell as the unwashed bootie. Gordon flings his towel behind him and disappears inside.

Ava leaves the bench to pick up the towel. She drapes it over Gordon's tank.

"Sorry about that," she says. "He's having a hard day." At my quizzical look, she adds, "He's not used to his ears bothering him on a dive," she says. She follows Gordon inside.

Lauren and Lucky are desultory in getting out of their dive gear. Lauren unzips her wetsuit and begins to take it off only to realize, she's still wearing her dive booties. Lucky attempts to disconnect her regulator from her tank without first clearing the air from her vest.

When I go inside to have a snack – the next dive isn't until after lunch - the two sisters are still bumbling about the dive deck.

Chapter 11

Bertie waves Catalina over when the dive master peeks into the lounge. She's wondering what fish they saw on the dive. She's found a picture in the fish book, but for once she isn't certain about whether it's the correct one. Matt argued about it with her for a little bit, then left for their cabin saying it wasn't worth fighting over a fish.

But Bertie wasn't ready to give up. When it comes to knowledge, Bertie can be as determined as a parrot fish pecking away at the structure of a reef, loud enough for divers to hear the hammering underwater.

Catalina leafs through the book, until she reaches the page of photos of various damsel fish. Bertie recognizes the specific fish they saw right away. Then, Catalina flips to the pages with the white eel and black leopard ray that also showed up on the dive. The two discuss the gorgonian sea fans and rainbow- colored sponges.

Ava passes by the windows of the lounge, presumably on her way to her cabin. When she's gone, Bertie speaks in a lowered voice, "What's up with the Bakers?"

"What do you mean?" Catalina says, looking up from the book she's holding.

"They always stick so close together," Bertie says. "I've never seen buddies so attentive underwater like they are; they're usually never more than one or two feet apart. I was shocked when Gordon got left behind."

"I guess they didn't think he would have problems clearing his ears," Catalina says.

Bertie shakes her head. "That's the thing. I don't buy that ear trouble excuse."

Catalina shrugs. "Even experienced divers sometimes make mistakes."

"Yes," Bertie agrees. "I've read all the articles. That's how they die."

"Don't worry," Catalina says. "I'm confident it won't happen again. You done with this?" She holds out the book to Bertie.

Bertie closes the fish book, and then returns it carefully to the shelf where she found it. She debates whether she should mention what she overheard when she passed Gordon and Ava's cabin, Ava's mention of a doctor. Maybe Gordon has a medical condition that affects his diving. Bertie opens her mouth, but then she remembers Matt's admonition to not appear as a know-it-all. She promised him she would chill out on this trip. Surely, the Bakers disclosed any medical condition of Gordon's on the first day when they all filled out their forms. Gordon's situation is not her business.

"Okay then," she says. Catalina is the dive master after all. Bertie is simply a guest. She inhales, lifting her hands over her head, then exhales as she brings her arms down to her sides with her palms up. As she does so, she imagines her worries about Gordon evaporating into the air.

"Just reminding myself to breathe," Bertie says. "Sometimes I forget I'm on vacation." To prove to herself and Catalina that she knows how to relax, Bertie plops onto the couch, swinging her bare feet up and arranging a pillow behind her head.

"Should I leave you to your nap?" Catalina says.

Bertie laughs and waves her hand towards a chair. "I hope you'll relax with me," she says. "That is if you have time."

Catalina settles into the chair, crossing her feet at her ankles. "Are you enjoying the trip?" she says.

Bertie looks at the ceiling. It's paneled with clean, white wood. She briefly wonders how often it must be painted to stay so fresh. Someone must have eaten popcorn in the lounge earlier, the smell of butter lingers. Bertie digs a lost kernel out of the cushions.

"It's different," Bertie says, rolling the kernel around between her thumb and fingers. "I'm getting used to diving in colder water. And putting on my clammy wetsuit when it's not dry." Bertie shivers dramatically and makes a face.

Catalina laughs. "It is more of a challenge than diving in warmer waters."

Catalina tells Bertie about learning to dive in San Diego. She describes maneuvering past the surf, descending into murky waters and the need for a dive light even during the day. Soon, their conversation switches to life back home with younger brothers and Bertie's job.

Bertie's stomach rumbles when the smell of tacos drifts into the lounge. Catalina excuses herself, and Bertie joins Matt at the buffet lunch of make-your-own tacos with carne asada or chicken. His cheeks are flushed from his nap, his hair rumpled.

After lunch, Bertie and Matt relax on the upstairs deck. The afternoon is warm, the sun shaking itself free of the earlier cloud blanket. Bertie feels lucky to have snagged two lounge chairs on such a nice day. Usually, the deck is busy with the teens. They must be off somewhere else.

Bertie sighs in contentment. This time, she's not cold in her bikini. She lies with her hat over her eyes and her arms resting alongside her stomach. She always eats too much on these dive trips. She always feels inordinately sleepy afterwards. Of course, Bertie's researched the subject of diving and calories. She was happy to discover that diving unexpectedly burns a lot of calories even though the underwater activity doesn't feel like it requires much effort. She's not sweaty or sore after a dive, like she is after a run, so it doesn't make sense. But she's never gained weight on a dive trip, so she doesn't feel badly about cleaning her plate or going back for seconds. The sleepiness makes sense as well. She's just worked out after all. Plus, she's on vacation!

She's drifting in and out of sleep. Manuel will let them know when to get ready for the afternoon dive. Her lounge shakes, someone bumps against it. Bertie hears a murmured apology. She stays beneath her hat as a second person swishes by; the edge of a towel brushes her thigh. Bertie's too sleepy to protest or care.

There's the sound of lounge chairs scraping on the deck, then the flap of towels in the wind and the squeak as the chairs settle under the weight of a reclining body. Low voices blend with the vibrating of the engines. The boat is motoring to the next dive location. Every so often, the wind floats a phrase in Bertie's direction.

"a sign maybe," says one voice sounding somewhat hopeful

"determined," says the other.

"wish he wouldn't."

Bertie dozes off. She awakens as the two speakers pass near her lounge with a rustle of clothing. "Someone will have to distract her," one says. The other sighs. Bertie shifts. Her throat feels dry. She groggily wonders who needs to be distracted. Maybe it's Jacqueline, the youngest on board. The girl participated in a few dives, but she seems to mostly snorkel now. Bertie assumes her parents realized the girl's not ready for the more advanced diving in the Sea of Cortez.

"Dive time!" Manuel calls from the dive deck. Bertie shifts her hat off her face and onto her head. She blinks, then sits up and stretches. Matt's gentle snores rise from his chair. Bertie leans over and tickles his bare chest. "Wake up sleepy head," she says.

He pulls her down for a snuggle.

When Bertie and Matt arrive on the dive deck, Jacqueline is sprinting around the boat passing from the bow to the stern in dizzying loops. Bertie wonders what the plan is to distract her. She seems like a normal girl cooped up on a boat for way too long. Still, Bertie remembers why she and Matt haven't had children yet. They're not ready to give up on their diving for the time it takes to raise a child to the age required for dive certification. There'll be plenty of time for children. Bertie just turned thirty.

None of the Bakers are on the dive deck.

"It'll be just the three of us," Catalina says. She's already wearing her wetsuit but hasn't donned her booties yet. Her tanned feet are small. Her nails are bare of polish. She wears a silver ring on the middle toe of her left foot. Bertie didn't notice it before. Catalina must not have been wearing it.

"We'll be diving near the boat," Catalina says. "You can go in by yourselves if you want."

Bertie and Matt exchange looks. Matt shrugs his shoulders letting her know she can choose. They're more than capable of diving without Catalina. Bertie does enjoy leading. But she also wants to take the opportunity to find underwater creatures unique to this dive location. And Catalina will know where to find those creatures.

The other times the Bakers didn't show, they joined Manuel's group. With more people surrounding the dive leader, Bertie couldn't always be in the front of the group. Sometimes, she was even the last to see the fish or other sight the leader pointed out. Then she would only have time for a quick glimpse. If she lingered too long, the group was already circled around something else. And she didn't want to miss out on seeing whatever it was.

A smile blooms on Bertie's face at the thought of having Catalina on a private dive. Matt always lets her be in front.

"We'd love to have you lead us," Bertie says. Matt nods in agreement.

Jacqueline and her dad jump off the back of the boat, landing with a splash. They snorkel towards the reef on the starboard side churning the water with their fins. Bertie guesses the snorkel trip is the distraction. She's happy when Catalina leads them in the opposite direction. She's even happier when Catalina finds an octopus and two moray eels for them after poking around in a rock.

Chapter 12

Manuel tells the divers they'll be dropping to a seventy- foot depth where there is a rocky outcropping. He comes close to promising hammerhead shark sightings but in the end, offers nothing iron-clad. I've seen schools of hammerheads at this underwater mountain before. Still, the ocean is huge, and conditions aren't always perfect. There's no 100 percent guarantee of animal sightings in scuba diving. Gordon takes one look over the stern where the boat is moored this morning, and then declines to get in the water.

"Waste of time," he says with certainty.

Lucky and Lauren are already suited up and ready to go. Ava isn't as far along. She unzips her wetsuit and steps out of it. The younger women shrug their shoulders. They adjust the straps on their vests.

"You'll be sorry when we tell you about the sharks," Lucky says.

"Ha!" Gordon says. "You'll really live up your name if you see anything down there." Still, he steadies them as they shuffle to the dive platform and helps them put on their fins.

Lucky and Lauren jump in followed by Bertie and Matt. I'm close behind. The other group has already descended, holding onto a rope Polo fixed from the boat to the mooring on top of the rock. The rope will help us get below the currents bedeviling the surface and the shallower depths. Without it, we might get swept away.

Today's current is significantly stronger than the one we drifted in the other day. As we pass through it, gripping the rope, our bodies fly like flags on a windy day. The water below the fastest stream is moving at a slower speed. Still, when we let go of the rope, we are forced to hold onto whatever rocks we can find on the stony peak of the mountain.

Visibility is no more than twenty feet. Maybe twenty- five at the most because of the swirling sand that clouds the view. Hammerheads could be swimming by in droves, but I can't even see a shark-shaped shadow despite my best efforts at searching the water around us. I lead my group of four in a tight circle around the mountain, before giving the signal to ascend. It's not worth staying down any longer. I can't see Manuel's group. I assume they've already returned to the Calypso.

We take turns grabbing onto the rope to aid in our ascent. Because we've spent time so deep, we still must carry out a safety stop. I spend the time watching as the four hang onto the rope like pennants, heads bent towards their dive computers, no doubt eagerly awaiting the beep releasing them to the surface.

We climb back on board, cold and wet for no good reason. Just because everyone knows there are no guarantees, doesn't mean they accept disappointments lightly. Repeated complaints litter the dive deck with the discarded booties and wetsuits. The divers head to their cabins to get warm. The crew changes out the mostly unused tanks with fresh ones. Madelyn heads to the kitchen where I imagine she's refreshing the coffee and tea table with hot water. The capitán turns the boat to Sea Lion Rock, leaving behind the choppy waters and hopefully the poor visibility.

Sea Lion Rock is usually a hit with the divers. Of course, sea lions need to be in residence. I finger my sea star necklace as we approach. When I hear the sea lions barking, I drop my hand and smile.

"Good thing we're not superstitious, hey, chicle?" Polo bumps his elbow against mine.

"Yeah," I say. "Good thing."

Polo likes to tell stories about the Sea of Cortez. His favorite is about El Lavadero, Las Animas. Las Animas is named after the church bells which ring to summon lost souls and El Lavadero means the washing machine. The dive site is often referred to as the washing machine of lost souls.

Before we dove at El Lavadero one morning, I overheard Polo telling Bertie that the thousands of silver jacks schooling in the water are the lost souls. She twisted her ring and looked spooked while our group waited its turn to descend at the site. I thought maybe she wouldn't come, but she did. Afterwards, she told me that when she saw the mass of circling jacks and thought of them as lost souls, she felt more sad than scared. I knew what she meant. I always say a prayer when I see the swirling fish, the sun glinting on their silver scales.

Polo tells divers of other legends, myths I don't believe about curses and sea lions. The capitán warns him at the beginning of each trip not to scare the divers with his stories of sea lions luring ships to the rocks with their unearthly barking. Maybe old-fashioned ships would founder on the rocks, imagining that the noises were those of tame dogs stranded with their masters. But the Calypso's modern systems keep us well away. When

Polo tells the story, his brown eyes grow serious as he warns his listeners not to look into a sea lion's eyes which are almost the same color as his.

"They seem harmless like me," he says. "But they'll steal your soul."

"But not your body?" I joke. "I can still swim back to the boat?"

"Maybe," he admits, "but you'll be a soulless wretch."

I think he half believes his own stories. He's reluctant to dive at Sea Lion Rock. I also think he's got his legends mixed up with Greek mythology. I've tried to point out the similarities to him. And he's read the Odyssey, but he won't listen. He says there's no connection between the sea lions and the Sirens.

"I can listen to the sea lions bark all day and I've never gone crazy," he says.

Now as the Calypso approaches Sea Lion Rock, I ask if he's diving today.

"Nah," he shakes his head. "It's Madelyn's turn." I wink at him. He laughs and turns away.

Unlike Polo, the divers are excited to swim with the sea lions. The boat's close enough to the rocks that Jacqueline can use the SNUBA that her parents have restricted her to after her first two nearly disastrous dives on this trip. My whole group is suiting up for the dive.

Gordon has never dived with sea lions. He's in a jovial mood, joking with Polo about adopting a sea lion cub to raise as a pet. He's heard Polo's stories, and he's enjoying teasing the engineer about bringing a cub on board for Polo to care for until we return to the harbor. Bertie tells us all how we can tell the difference between sea lions and seals. She goes into detail about the ear folds even though Matt taps her leg with his glove.

Gordon starts calling her Professor Clark. Bertie's laugh is infectious, and we're all smiling before we jump into the water and descend.

I find two sea lion cubs nestled into an unwater rock niche. We kneel in a semi-circle near them. The cubs are curious and venture out of the safety of the rocks to check us out. I've cautioned the group to remain still. Soon, the cubs grow confident we won't hurt them. They swim around us, not going too far from their rocks. Gordon blows bubbles from his extra regulator at one of the cubs.

The cub inches close, snagging a piece of the regulator in its teeth. It chews on the rubber mouthpiece much like I imagine a curious baby would. When we swim away from the cubs, two adult females join us, swooping and darting among the group. Gordon and Bertie mimic their moves. But they're no match for the swift sea lions. Gordon returns to playing with the cub, allowing it to gnaw on his extra mouthpiece again.

A deep, distant barking reverberates through the water. The male sea lion is headed our way to check on his herd. I don't believe in Polo's stories, but I also don't want to be underwater with a one-ton protective male. There's no telling what he might think of us or do to us. By the time I get everyone's attention and signal for our ascent, the male arrives.

Despite his bulk, he executes wide, speedy circles around us. The sound waves of his barking travel through the water and vibrate deep within me. Gordon gently extracts the mouthpiece from the cub. He can replace the dirty one with a clean one on the boat. The male circles closer. Ava grabs Gordon's arm, and points to the surface. He seems reluctant to leave the cub, but he doesn't resist his wife's pull. We all ascend. Thankfully, there's no need for a safety stop as we've not been too deep during the dive.

I don't tell Polo about Gordon and the sea lion cub he played with. But Polo hears about it from Madelyn. He's full of warnings when he finds me on the bow where I'm leaning against the boat, my Calypso hat pulled low, my eyes closed. He doesn't wait for me to look up at him, before he launches into a passionate lecture about how I needlessly endangered my divers by my careless behavior.

"You're their caretaker," he declares. "Their shepherd. What do they know? They're sheep."

I keep my eyes closed, hoping he'll go away, but he bumps me on the shoulder with his knee. I remove my hat and look up at him.

"My divers are fine," I say. "Gordon's fine. In fact, he was the most playful I've seen him be underwater."

"Playful like a sea lion cub," Polo says, his eyes dark.

"Stop it." I close my eyes and lean back against the boat. Polo hovers for a few minutes, but when I don't move, he finally leaves.

Chapter 13

The sun is a globe hanging low on the horizon. Its final rays streak the clouds with brilliant oranges and golds. I pause in my preparations for tonight's dive to gaze at the glorious sight. I never tire of watching the sun set over the ocean, often casting a shining path over the waves; I'm thankful for another day at sea.

When I was little, I'd cry at the sight of the sun disappearing, the light slowly fading beyond the curve of the water past where I could see. I was sad we would soon be packing up and leaving the small section of sand we'd claimed for the day. Our fun at the beach was over. I mourned its loss until my mother held me in her arms and assured me we would return just as the sun rose every day.

"Little girls who live on the other side of the world want to play at the beach," my mother would murmur in my hair. "It's their turn, and we must share."

I wonder if my mother is watching the sunset now as I am. I wonder if my parents have spent the day at the beach.

Manuel's voice calling the divers to the briefing breaks my reverie. I join the others at the whiteboard. Tonight's dive will start at the sandy bottom, then we'll fin to the reef, and finally, all return to the sandy bottom and kneel in a circle. That's where we hope to encounter Manta Rays.

We'll start the dive before the sun slips away for the night, entering the water while there's still enough light to see under its surface. Part of the fun of a night dive is experiencing the amber glow of the water fade to black. Watching the daytime fish disappear into their nooks and crannies for the night, before their predators begin to hunt.

I remember my first night dive in San Diego. I entered through the surf with some friends just as the sun was setting. A few surfers rode the waves just north of us. The beach was clearing out, the seagulls squabbling over the detritus on the day. I could hear the distant bark of the sea lions at the base of the bluffs just south of us. We had enough reflected light to swim out beyond the waves, and then adjust our fins and masks before our descent. The twilight water was shadowy, the half- moon a pale light peeking just above a line of palms behind us. We would use the beach bathroom light as our guidepost when we resurfaced.

I was nervous and excited when we dropped below the surface. When the daylight faded, it felt like a thick black curtain had been dropped around us. I couldn't see anything beyond the beam of my light or the beams of my friends'. The silence felt absolute. I was hyper aware of my breathing and the noise of my bubbles. My heart began to race. I concentrated on slowing down my rapid breaths. I matched the relaxed, slow pace of my friends. I tried not to worry about what could be swimming towards us, just out of sight in the inky darkness. I trained my light on the familiar bed of sand dollars. I watched an octopus swim with its unique pulsing movement. My heart skipped when a soup fin shark swam nonchalantly into and out of our light beams.

My favorite night dive was in the Caribbean. I was working at a dive resort then. We motored out to a dive site before sunset, and then slipped into the warm water just as sky faded to lilac then mauve. Turtles pushed lazily through the water to the reef where they settled into their sleeping nooks for the night. Brilliantly colored fish that darted about freely during the day vanished into the shelter of the coral. At full dark, different sea creatures emerged. It was like a city street with the day's busy traffic gone and the shops locked up for the night. The night crowd was edgier; the reefs like the alleys shrouded in shadow.

When Manuel finishes his briefing, the divers return to their bench space and finish suiting up quickly.

Tonight, all in my group are diving. Bertie and Matt check to make sure each of them has a flashlight secured to a wrist and a spare secured to a vest. Gordon checks the flashlights for his family. Since the drift dive, the Bakers have been sticking together underwater, swimming as a group of four when they're all in the water. It's impossible to tell who the buddies are, but I don't mind.

As long as no one gets left behind again.

Gordon asks if we might see any sea lions tonight. The Calypso has moved away from Sea Lion Rock, but we can still hear faint barks if the wind is blowing towards us. His question makes me think of Polo. I don't believe Polo's stories, but I can't help looking into Gordon's eyes when I tell him no; I can't help searching to make sure he still has his soul. I feel foolish when he returns my gaze with a smile.

The tip of the sun is touching the horizon when my group slowly sinks below the surface. We waft through the last golden glow before darkness. I love the twilight feel of the water, the ripples of sun on the ocean's surface above us, the fading shafts of light penetrating the liquid around us, the shadowed space below us.

Sometimes I think of Persephone descending into Hades, the light fading behind her. It'll be dark soon, but unlike the unfortunate Persephone who must live in Hades for half a year, we'll all return to the lights of the Calypso, the warmth of our showers and hot toddies at the bar.

Once on the sandy bottom, I lead the group to the reef where they spread out and examine all the nooks and crannies. Octopus usually leave their reef nooks and come out at night, jetting through the water like pulsing heartbeats. The water slowly darkens; the divers switch on their lights. The visibility is about sixty feet. Manuel's group is a swarm of lights just at the edge of the reef about fifteen feet away.

Gradually, the cluster of lights moves towards the sandy bottom, and I turn to lead my group in that direction as well where we hope more than one Giant Manta Ray will appear. Giant Manta Rays are the world's largest rays with a wingspan of up to twenty-nine feet. They can weigh up to 3,600 pounds. Despite their size, the rays, like whales, eat krill. Tonight, we hope one or more will feast on the phosphorescent krill ensnared in our light beams. My group and Manuel's kneel on the sand like supplicants waiting for a priest, presenting the swarming krill as a sacrifice in the beams of our lights.

The first manta flies out of the darkness around us and swoops over Gordon's head. Ava tips sideways in surprise, but Gordon rights her. I can hear Bertie's exclamation of delight as a second manta enters the circle. It turns somersaults as it vacuums up the krill.

I check the dive computer on my wrist. Time literally flies when divers are enthralled with the manta. We've been kneeling for thirty minutes. Another large shape emerges out of the darkness. Manuel captures a third manta with his light. He briefly flashes his light on his gloved hands, so I can see his two thumbs up signal. I know he's hoping this experience will make up for the aborted Hammerhead Shark dive.

Matt hugs his body to signal that he's getting cold. The initial excitement of the mantas keeps the divers warm, but after kneeling for so long, the cold begins to feel like it's seeping into your bones. He points at Bertie whose lips glow ghostly white. He points up, towards the Calypso. The boat is moored not too far away. I can see the blurry outline of its lights. I give them the okay signal, dipping my light to my hand.

I've lost sight of the Bakers. They've somehow become mixed in with the other group. It's difficult to keep track of where individuals are with most of the divers in black. Many of them have shifted around in the circle, trying to get the best view of the mantas. The lights are like search beams on an opening night, glowing in the vast expanse of the ocean.

Still, it's possible to count the individual lights; I know how many are on the dive.

The manta rays keep feeding, swirling above us, sometimes skimming just over our heads. Finally, Manuel signals the ascent, waving his light to get the divers' attention. The group begins a slow rise to the safety stop, lingering as long as possible in the magic of the mantas, many still shining their lights at the krill.

We're hovering fifteen feet below the surface, some hanging onto the boat's mooring rope to stay down. I count lights again, before turning my light to my computer. A beep, beep, beep, and I know it's time to ascend. I'll wait for all the lights to return to the surface before I do. It's my turn to stay underwater to make sure all return safely to the boat.

Not my favorite assignment.

Being left behind to hang alone just below the surface in the night ocean is creepy. Don't get me wrong. I love the ocean. But I also have a vivid imagination fueled by my study of Greek mythology. It's easy to picture monsters of the deep inhabiting the blank space just outside the reach of my light. I do my best to concentrate on the divers. To forget whatever might be lurking in the absolute black just past my sight.

All the divers are close to the surface, when a steady light pierces my gaze. Instinctively, I cover my mask with a gloved hand. But it's too late. My sight is washed out.

I'm not mad.

This has happened before. Divers don't mean to rake their light across another's face. Often, they're managing too many things, like their buoyancy, and they forget about the direction their light is pointing. This time, I guess a diver might have been wishing for one last look at a manta.

Maybe the diver thinks I'm one because the light stays focused on my face. My glove is an imperfect shield. My eyes are closed but I can see the brightness in the edges of my mask. The light bounces off the plastic and reflects on my eyelids. After what seems like a long time, the light vanishes.

I move my glove. When I open my eyes, two glaring white spots are in front of me. I'm blind to the life, real or imaginary, below me, and the divers above me.

I bob to the surface. My pupils are still adjusting. The boat lights are too bright, and I must avert my eyes. The black-clad divers ascending the boat ladder are blobs. My night vision hasn't fully returned by the time I swim to the ladder where I await my turn as the last diver in the water. I take deep breaths through my snorkel while I tread water, floating above the waves slapping the boat. All appears dark below.

I'm tempted to shine my light into the depths, to reassure myself that the monsters are imaginary and not real. But I resist the temptation, telling myself I would rather not see whatever is down there. That is, if I could see anything with blurred vision.

"Ignorance is bliss," I murmur. My words echo in the mouthpiece of my snorkel. I can feel the rough spots in the rubber with my tongue.

In the past, I've chewed on it, using it to soothe my nerves while I waited in the dark. But my nervous habit grew too expensive – I've replaced a lot of snorkel mouthpieces - so I've quit doing that for the most part.

The dive deck is mostly empty when I finally set my fins on the dive platform and climb the ladder. I'm shivering as I maneuver onto the dive deck. I don't blame anyone for rushing to their warm showers as soon as possible. Of the guests, only the Bakers are still hanging around the benches.

Manuel is towards the front of the deck, wiping off the marks he made on his white board noting the location of the reef and the sandy bottom. Polo is winding up the hose the divers use to rinse their vests and wetsuits. Lucky and Lauren are peeling off their wetsuits; their heads are covered with towels.

Ava approaches and peers into the water behind me, shining her light onto the dark surface beyond the dive platform.

"Where's Gordon?" she says.

Chapter 14

My heart stills.

"What do you mean?" I say. The taste and smell of the ocean is strong in my mouth and nose. I'm still wearing my tank and vest. I reach a gloved hand to push my hood back.

"Isn't he with you?" Ava says. "We saw him just behind you when we finished our safety stop and did our final ascent."

"Where's Dad?" Lauren and Lucky join their mom at the back of the boat.

I'm in the middle of their loose circle. For a moment, I imagine I'm participating in their ceremonial ascent instead of Gordon. The sisters are wearing their towels like prayer shawls. The water in their hair drips onto the towel. The waves slap against the side of the boat, and it rocks without warning. I stumble and nearly fall. Lauren reaches out a hand to steady me. The weights in my vest feel heavier than usual in the pockets.

"Wasn't he with you?" I say. "I saw the four of you together."

Water droplets slide down my face. They roll into my eyes, and sting. I blink, wiping the drops with the back of my glove. My mind races.

I remember seeing the Bakers together at the reef. I remember seeing them kneel on the sandy bottom. I remember the first manta skimming over Gordon's head. I remember him ducking.

"You always ascend together," I say. "It's what you do." I talk as if they would forget the ceremonial ascent they've done on every dive.

Ava looks away. Lauren clears her throat.

"Dad wanted another look at the manta," Lucky says. "We all saw you still in the water, so we thought it would be okay."

Manuel approaches. "What's going on?"

"The Bakers don't know where Gordon is," I say. My voice is rough in my throat. I can't say he's missing outright. Surely, he must be somewhere on the Calypso. I alternate between feeling hot and shivering with cold in my wetsuit.

Ava descends to the dive platform in her bare feet; her flashlight beam shines high above the water; her white hair glows with a light of its own against the black sky. Lauren and Lucky begin running barefoot along separate sides of the boat, yelling their father's name over and over. As far as I can see, the ocean is an unrelenting black. No light bounces back from under the water. I'm caught in a state of disbelief, unmoving on the dive deck.

"Are you sure he's not on the boat?" Manuel asks Ava. She turns to look at him; her flashlight beam illuminates his knees. She's holding onto the handles at the top of the dive platform ladder. No one's pulled it up yet, and the bottom rungs are covered with water. Manuel's voice is calm. "Maybe he's in your cabin already? There was a lot of confusion earlier. Everyone was racing to get out of their dive gear."

Manuel beckons to Ava, and she allows him to help her back onto the main dive deck. I hardly notice as Manuel helps me out of my vest and sets it and my tank aside while he talks with Ava. Usually, I stand taller without the extra burden. I pull off my gloves, stretch my hands over my head and shrug my shoulders. But now, I slump under the possibility of a different burden.

What if I did lose Gordon?

What if he's alone in the night ocean?

The monsters of the deep awaken in my imagination, and I'm hard pressed to push them aside.

Ava shakes her head when Manuel suggests she leave the deck to check her cabin.

"Polo!" Manuel's voice is sharp. "Check the cabin." Polo runs inside still wet from the dive. He's removed his booties, but his wetsuit hangs open at his waist. I imagine water dripping on the dining room carpet, creating little puddles where bacteria can grow.

Madelyn is in the kitchen preparing hot drinks. Manuel sticks his head into the dining area and calls to her. "Get ready to dive." Manuel, Polo and I can't return to the water just yet. It's too soon after our dive; we must wait on the boat for any nitrogen bubbles caught in our bloodstream to dissipate.

Was it only minutes ago that we were under the water watching the manta ballet?

Time slows to the slap of the waves, and the sound of Lauren and Lucky shouting Gordon's name over the black waters. It's a clear night but without the moon, it's nearly impossible to distinguish the horizon. Later, thousands of stars will pepper the sky, but it's too early for more than one or two.

I remember my gut telling me to check the waters below me. If only I'd listened to my spidey sense, instead of passing it off as my crazy imagination.

The capitán appears on the dive deck. Polo must have found him and told him to come downstairs. Gordon must not be in his cabin.

"Polo's on the helm," the capitán says. "Who did the count tonight?"

Dive boats count divers as they return to the boat, a relatively new practice. In the past, a few divers got left behind when the boat motored away from a dive site. Manuel tells him Polo got an accurate count. He shows the list with a check next to Gordon's name. The capitán frowns. He pulls his shirt off. He'll go in with Madelyn. The two suit up as quickly as possible. Manuel and I set up fresh tanks for them. He gives them the coordinates of our dive, so they can began searching for Gordon in the right spot.

Ava's been standing this whole time, her dive light creating a glowing puddle on the deck. At the sight of the capitán and Madelyn preparing to jump into the water, she collapses onto a bench. Up until that point, I too was hopeful Gordon would be found on board. We could all have a hot toddy in the lounge and toast whoever found him.

Instead, Lauren and Lucky shout their father's name at the unresponsive ocean. I imagine they're hoping Gordon has surfaced somewhere near the boat. Polo switches on the boat's search beam. It begins a slow sweep of the ocean around the boat. Those who have left the dive deck to shower, return at the sound of the commotion. They're dressed in warm clothes and sweatshirts. Some have knitted caps on their heads. I shiver again. Manuel hands me a towel.

The guests fan out through the boat looking for Gordon. Even the cupboards are opened as if Gordon might have decided to crawl into a dark space and hide for a while.

We've practiced for this. The capitán runs us through regular drills. We know what to do if a diver gets lost. I first discussed this possibility when I received my dive master certification. Still, now that it's happened, I feel helpless. Those drills and discussions involved theoretical divers. Not someone I know. Not Gordon.

My head hurts.

The capitán and Madelyn jump into the water. I watch their lights as they descend below the surface. Then, I help Manuel launch one of the pangas, so he can search the water's surface. It will be like searching for a needle in a haystack – an extremely large haystack. I tell myself that Gordon's experience will prove to be his salvation. If anyone knows what to do in the ocean, it's Gordon.

Polo and I will stay on the boat. I join Lauren and Lucky in scanning the ocean for a glimpse of Gordon's head, the flash of his dive light or his inflated safety sausage bobbing above the surface. I raise my voice with theirs. Shouting Gordon's name until my voice is hoarse.

The Calypso is a hive of activity and loud voices, but after a thorough search, the guests settle down to wait. Some, like me, pray. They've taken up stations around the perimeter of the boat, some on the lower deck, others joining Polo on the upper deck.

The search beam passes a wide bright circle around and around the boat. A few bat rays fly in and out of the light. A swell lifts the boat every once in a while, clacking the oxygen tanks together and setting the wetsuits hanging on the rack to swaying. Ava, Lauren and Lucky establish a silent vigil at three points on the deck. Ava faces the stern, Lauren looks out over the starboard side and Lucky gazes aft. I think of all the times they held the three points of a triangle around Gordon on their dive ascents. I pray Gordon will be restored to their center. A slow hour passes while the capitán and Madelyn search the dark depths.

At the ninety-minute mark, I move to the dive platform to watch for the bubbles of the returning divers. Finally, I see their lights and bubbles just below. Their three-minute safety stop feels like thirty.

Madelyn surfaces first, followed by the capitán.

Gordon's not with them.

Chapter 15

Bertie is there when the captain insists the Bakers take a break from shouting and looking for Gordon. He assures them the crew is doing everything possible to find the missing man. He personally escorts them to the dining room and waits while they slide into a booth. Madelyn silently places hot drinks before each.

Hot drinks for everyone else are set up on a table by the stairs leading to the upper deck. When Bertie prepares her own drink – adding a larger dollop of rum than usual - she hears the captain radioing the coast guard. She says nothing about what she heard when she joins the Baker women in the booth. Between her drink and the Baker women's she can smell the rum wafting in the steam rising over the table. She assumes Madelyn poured a good portion of the alcohol into each of the Bakers' drinks.

Matt passes by the window every so often. He's pacing around the Calypso like some of the other guests. Bertie knows her husband can't sit still in a crisis. When his grandpa died, he roamed about his parents' house, wandering down the hall to his old room, through the kitchen and back out into the living room so many times, his mom finally told him to go outside.

"He'll wear out the carpet," she said. Then, as now, Bertie stayed behind, perched on the couch with Matt's parents. She's good at providing comfort. She can be still and listen. She always has a tissue ready.

Tissues seem to be in short supply on the Calypso. So, Bertie leaves the booth and searches for some. She sees Catalina and Polo launch the second panga while she's looking. She finally finds an unopened box in the back of a lounge cupboard behind a stack of board games. She brings the tissue box to the booth.

The other guests avoid the Bakers. It's like an accident on the freeway. People walk slowly by the family with quick glances and murmurs, but they don't stop. They look through the window, like Matt, as they pass. Bertie isn't afraid to stop. She's spent most of a week with the Bakers. She feels as if she knows them. She can't imagine how they must be feeling about Gordon's disappearance.

Someone must have dropped the ball somewhere. When Madelyn and the captain surfaced without Gordon, everyone was waiting on the dive deck. Bertie imagined the bow lifting out of the water with all that weight at the stern.

No one said anything when the two climbed out of the ocean onto the dive platform. The squeak of the captain's wet booties, and the clank of Madelyn's regulator as it swung against her empty tank resounded as loud as thunder. Catalina helped the two break down their gear in silence.

Bertie never thought it was a good idea for the Bakers to dive as a foursome. It's too easy for assumptions to be made about who's watching out for whom. It's better and safer for two to pair up as buddies. Then, you know who to watch out for and who's watching out for you.

But now's not the time to judge the Bakers. Sometimes accidents just happen.

Bertie wouldn't want to lose Matt underwater. She imagines for a moment that she's the one who's lost her husband. She's the one slumped at the table while the search light swings by the window. Tears spring to her eyes. She pulls a tissue from the box.

Matt would never get lost. She's a good buddy. Not perfect, but good enough not to lose track of him. She realizes she's being judgmental again. She dries her eyes, thankful Matt is safe, and pushes the tissue box closer to Ava.

"Can I bring any of you another drink?" she asks. The Baker women stare at her blankly.

Bertie not only feels badly for the Baker women, she also feels sorry for Catalina.

Gordon's an experienced diver who shouldn't need careful supervision. But, still, Catalina must be feeling somewhat responsible for losing him. Bertie wonders if she should have told Catalina about the snippet of conversation she overheard between Ava and Gordon in their cabin after all.

She wishes she and Matt hadn't ascended before everyone else. She wonders, as a certified rescue diver, was she not looking closely enough? She thinks back to the manta skimming over Gordon's head. She thinks about Ava tipping over, Gordon righting her. She thinks about the Bakers mixing in with Manuel's group. She remembers briefly thinking that was so unlike them and then, the manta executed a flip right in front of her and she lost her train of thought.

Bertie assumes the captain told the Baker women he was calling the coast guard. She pictures hearing those words about Matt and the tears well again. Bertie dabs with her tissue. The boat is moving in ever-widening circles.

The Bakers' silence spreads to the rest of the boat. Bertie can't remember hearing the Calypso so quiet before. Usually, the teenagers and Jacquelyn can be heard moving about, calling to each other. Now, even they are hushed. Lauren and Lucky lean in to flank their mother, their shoulders touching. The group tableau reminds Bertie of the many times the Bakers gathered for a group ascent.

Except this time, Gordon is missing.

Bertie is uncharacteristically quiet as well. She's never been on a dive boat or trip where a diver has disappeared. She knows that a diver without oxygen underwater would eventually pass out. She knows what happens to a drowning person, water flooding the previously open airways. Surely, Gordon would kick to the surface for air. Surely, he would use his inflated vest to stay afloat. Surely, he would inflate his bright orange safety sausage. He's an experienced diver. Probably the most experienced on this boat. She won't think about the predators that inhabit these waters. The sharks and the Humboldt Squid. Bertie shudders.

"Does Gordon have a whistle?" Bertie asks, breaking the silence.

Lauren looks confused.

"Sometimes divers attach a whistle to their vest," Bertie says.

"He does," Ava says. "Bright orange like mine."

Lucky grimaces. "He loaned it to me yesterday when he saw I'd lost mine."

Ava pats Lucky's hand. The two exchange an inscrutable look.

"He's probably bobbing on the surface waiting for us to find him," Bertie says. "Gordon is experienced. If anyone could be calm in this situation, it's Gordon."

"Gordon certainly knows what to do," Ava says.

Lauren sniffs. Bertie reaches across the table to nudge the tissue box closer.

Chapter 16

So far, there is no sign of Gordon on the water's surface. I say "so far" because I'm holding onto a glimmer of hope. But even I know finding someone bobbing in this vast ocean will require the same amount of luck as winning the lottery.

That's why divers carry safety sausages – giant inflatables that stick up over the water like those waving blow-up figures car dealers use to grab your attention. Still, Gordon could be down in a trough while the Calypso motors past him. I try not to think of inflatable life boats that have drifted unnoticed at sea for months. I try to be positive. I concentrate on the fact that the capitán is following the current we think Gordon might be drifting in as best we can. The coast guard will be arriving soon to help with the search.

In the meantime, the crew moves around the boat gripping mugs of coffee. Some of the guests are curled up on the sundeck recliners under blankets dragged from their cabins. Others are stretched out on the couches in the lounge. Somehow, it feels wrong to lie down on a bed, your head on a pillow, the covers pulled up while the Baker women slouch in a dining room booth.

Bertie sits with them. She slumps, her usually straight posture lost to the past hours. Her hair hangs in messy locks around her face. I haven't seen it loose since the day she first stepped on board.

I carry my own mug of coffee that's long grown cold. Still, as I stand barefoot in the dining room doorway, I take nervous sips. Lucky looks up, and I avert my gaze. Leaving the doorway, I return to the dive deck. A soft breeze that smells of seaweed and salt cools my warm cheeks, lifting strands of my hair off my neck. The boat rises on a swell. I sway. Coffee sloshes onto my hand, dripping onto the deck.

I'm sick to my stomach.

I wish I was seasick. I wish I could simply lean over the deck rail and vomit out the queasiness that roils in my stomach because my gut's not cooperating with my irrational hope. My stomach tells the truth of the situation that Gordon is gone forever – thanks to me.

He was in my group. I was his leader. He was my responsibility. How could I lose him? How did I let my spidey sense get overwhelmed by imaginary fears for my own safety?

I step wrong on something hard.

More coffee spills out of my tipped cup at the stabbing pain that cramps the ball of my foot. I grimace and curse. I can make out the white form of a small shell on the deck. Grabbing the shell, I fling it over board not caring if a guest collected the shell and wants to keep it. I don't bother to watch for the splash.

I collapse on the bench, rubbing my sore foot. The search light methodically drifts by, a circle of brightness that briefly illuminates the water, then moves on. A single tear slides down my cheek, followed by another, and another until I lift the hem of my sweatshirt to blot my damp cheeks.

Once, when I was twelve, I lost my brother.

Just like every other summer, we'd spent most weekends at the beach. We'd leave our house where the neighbors were bracing for another hot day and drive to the coast where the marine layer seemed stuck like glue to the sand. We didn't let the gloomy skies bother us or send us scurrying home earlier than usual.

Still, when August rolled around and the sun finally appeared at the beach, we all felt happier. My father bought us ice cream when earlier he'd complained it was too cold. My mother emerged from under her sweatshirt, showing off her turquoise swimsuit.

I'd always gotten along with my mother before that summer. But something had changed between us, and now she irritated me like sand in my swimsuit. She seemed to constantly complain to my father about my sass and my attitude. But instead of quelling me or sending me off in a quiet sulk, her words only spurred me on to further unhappy interaction with her.

On the day I lost my brother, I finally couldn't stand to be around my mother anymore. I needed a break, or I would explode. I knew exploding at my mother wasn't a good idea; I'd already suffered my father's wrath when I lashed out at her before. So, I grabbed my surfboard and sprinted to the ocean. I blinked away the tears that stung my eyes. I wouldn't let her words get to me.

The sand was hot, but the soles of my feet were calloused so I barely felt the burn on my skin. I was eager to plunge into the cool water, to paddle out on my own away from my family, especially my mother. I was awakening to my own opinions and I needed time to let the water calm me.

"Don't go out too far," my father yelled over the sound of the crashing surf. "It's better if your brother keeps to the white wash."

I pretended I didn't hear him.

I didn't look behind to see whether my little brother was following me. But he was a fast runner, and he splashed his board down into the water next to mine.

I ignored him.

I ducked under one wave and then another, pushing myself out past the surf with strong, confident strokes. I doubted he would follow me. But when I climbed onto my board, straddling it with my legs and waiting for a wave to surf, there he was grinning at me, his head bobbing next to his board, wet as a seal's.

"Surprised you, huh?" he said, before climbing onto his own board.

I narrowed my eyes at him. "Dad doesn't want you out this far," I warned. "You need to swim back now."

"You're not the boss of me," he said, angling his board away from me.

We bobbed in the ocean for a while waiting for the next set. Me fuming and him grinning. I could see our father pacing on shore. His hand shading his eyes. My brother might not be as good a surfer as I was, but he was a strong swimmer. Let him learn a lesson, I thought.

I paddled towards a rising wave. I dropped into it and rode towards shore as easily as a seagull skimming on an air current, my mood lifting. At the end of the ride, I stepped off my board into the water, ducking under to immerse myself.

As soon as I surfaced, I felt a heavy hand on my shoulder. I shook the water out of my eyes, pulling my surfboard towards me.

"Where's your brother?" My father had waded out into the ocean. The water swirled around his bare chest. A clump of seaweed bumped against his skin before loosening and floating away.

My heart clenched, but I waved my hand vaguely towards the horizon as if my brother's whereabouts were none of my concern.

"I told you…" He shook his head and walked further out into the water. I debated whether to paddle out and catch another wave or head towards shore. Before I could decide, a wave rose behind me, and I quickly dove under it, losing sight of my father. When I resurfaced, I scanned the ocean but couldn't see my father or my brother.

Our umbrella seemed small and far away on the beach. I squinted, but I couldn't make out my mother lounging in its shade. I caught the next wave, riding it as far in to shore as I could. The spot our family had staked out was deserted.

I stretched out on my towel, pretending I wasn't worried. But it wasn't long before I sat up and searched the ocean and the sand for signs of my family. A few minutes passed before I saw my mother walking further down the beach. It looked like my brother was with her. As they drew closer, my father emerged from the ocean carrying a broken piece of what looked like my brother's surfboard.

I braced myself for the lecture I knew was coming. But neither of my parents said anything.

They simply packed up our belongings even though sunset was hours away and loaded the car. Their silence spoke volumes to me.

Later that night, I crept into my brother's room and told him I was sorry I'd lost him.

"Don't worry about it" he said. "I always knew where I was."

I wonder now if Gordon knows where he is even though we can't see him.

Chapter 17

The rescue chopper arrives with a clatter. The coast guard boat is still on its way. I watch as the helicopter moves slowly around the Calypso. It shoots a bright beam of light at the waves where it dances a weird duet with the Calypso's search light, the circles coming together like the sign for infinity, and then splitting apart.

I count five of the largest bat rays I've seen flying up out of the water and through the merging lights, one after another. A magnified voice with a Mexican accent calls Gordon's name over a loudspeaker. The guests who were asleep on the sundeck and in the lounge file to the deck railing where they line up to watch.

Now that the professionals are here, the tiny spark of hope I thought was quenched flames to life inside me. I set my mug in the kitchen and join others at the lower deck railing. When the helicopter hovers over the boat, my sweatshirt is plastered to my body with the wind, others lose their ball caps overboard. They disappear into the darkness, until the helicopter and boat lights circle back. Then, my heart leaps for a second when I see a hat on the waves. Gordon? I lean further over the rail, until I realize, the object is only one of the lost caps.

Bertie comes out to stand beside me. I know she thinks for a moment the lost cap is Gordon because I hear her gasp. I know when she realizes it's not him because she puts her arm around my shoulder. I'm grateful for her presence.

"It'll be okay, Catalina," she murmurs. "No matter what."

Her words bring another welling of tears. I hope she's right. I backhand the tears. Bertie offers me a tissue. I wipe my nose which has also turned into a faucet. I notice the Baker women are also on the dive deck. Bertie gently nudges me towards the three. When Ava reaches out her hand and takes mine, I lean into her, wetting her shoulder with my tears.

After a while, the rescue boat shows up with more lights and another magnified loudspeaker. The rescue boat stations itself a short distance away to cover more area of the ocean in the search for Gordon. By now, the noise of the chopper, the whirling blades and blaring loudspeaker so loud when it first arrived, is a normal part of this awful night.

We resume our pacing about the boat, peering out into the darkness as the helicopter swoops overhead. The arrival of the boat gets me to thinking that I haven't tried hard enough to find Gordon. After all, a rescue boat wouldn't arrive if a rescue weren't possible.

Now that both the helicopter and the boat are here, I'm certain that if I just keep looking long enough, I'll spot Gordon's head bobbing on the surface. He'll wave. I'll call to the capitán to stop the boat. I'll lower the ladder for Gordon to climb aboard. And when he does, we'll all be waiting on the dive deck to welcome him with a round of applause. He'll grin. "Well," he'll say, "here's another fine dive story. It reminds me of a movie." Ava will laugh. Lauren and Lucky will smile, and the capitán will turn the boat back to our last dive site.

But a helicopter can't fly forever, and eventually the one over the Calypso banks back towards its home base. The silence after the helicopter's departure seems ominous. The flags at the stern whip in a wind I didn't notice before. Choppy waves litter the water when the Calypso's search beam goes by. Spray slaps my face if I lean too far over the rail. My eyes ache with the strain of the search. Not many besides the crew are still moving about the decks. Even the Bakers and Bertie are back in the dining room booth.

The rescue boat circles the water in the opposite direction of the Calypso moving further away, until the loudspeaker becomes fainter. Eventually, I can hardly hear the rescue boat, but when the speaker either stops calling Gordon's name or moves completely out of range, the hush is profound.

No one could survive ocean temperatures in the mid- to -low seventies for this long. Not even Gordon. Hypothermia would lead to confusion and loss of consciousness.

I watch the night swallow the rescue boat's lights with a heavy heart. I feel the Calypso swinging around. We're headed back to the harbor. And the horrible truth sinks in, finally snuffing my hope.

Gordon is gone for good.

I'm exhausted. My well of tears is dry.

I think numbly of Gordon's body washing up on a beach somewhere. Perhaps body parts will be missing. I shudder at the gruesome thought. I remember Gordon's passion for the ocean. I pray he's sunk to a soft sandy bottom where he can rest in eternity. I picture coral growing on his skeleton, creating a new colorful reef where gorgonian fans and bright sponges thrive. I imagine divers visiting the site. Intense rescue efforts haven't turned up a single body from a recently lost flight of hundreds. So why shouldn't Gordon be granted the same peace? The thoughts briefly comfort me.

The capitán or someone switches off the Calypso's search beam. The boat is dark with only its running lights.

I wrap a dry towel around my sweatshirt and head to the bow. I see a few dark shapes in the dim light of the dining room. Guests asleep in the booths. I don't know if it's the Bakers. I assume Ava wouldn't want to return to her cabin alone.

At the bow, I sink down, leaning my head against the boat. My thoughts are scattered.

I review our last dive, going over each step multiple times.

What did I miss?

When I was certified as a dive master, our instructor told us we might someday face the possibility of a diver dying on our watch.

"Scuba is an inherently dangerous sport," she said. "We're humans breathing air underwater. It's possible, but not natural.

"In the end, divers must be responsible for their own safety. The safety of their equipment, the safety of their buddy's equipment, how they handle unexpected situations underwater.

As a dive master, you do what you can. But no one is perfect."

I remember her words, and still I wonder: what did I miss?

I pull the towel tighter around my body. The sky lightens to a gun metal gray. Soon, a thin band of light appears. It widens until the sun glides up and over the horizon.

The start of another day.

I look out over the vastness of the sea. And for the first time in my life, I'm numb to her charms.

Chapter 18

Bertie's on the upper deck with Matt when the Calypso motors past the giant rocks where they all did their first dives and pulls into the harbor. Bertie remembers the anxiety that washed over her while she and Matt waited to do a giant stride off the dive deck. She remembers Gordon treading water next to her before they all descended below the surface. She recalls his reassuring grin; the deliberate lowering of one eyelid in a wink that made her smile and temporarily forget her nerves. If she squints, she can almost imagine Gordon's ghost bobbing at the surface, ready for the next dive. Her eyes mist.

As the Calypso pulls into the dock, Polo jumps off and winds the thick rope around the heavy cleat bolted to the dock to secure the boat. Three men in uniform wait in a tight grouping. Bertie assumes they're the local police the captain mentioned earlier. The captain addressed the guests in the dining room telling them the police would have questions for them about Gordon's disappearance. He apologized for the delay. He assured them he was aware everyone must be anxious to disembark as quickly as possible. As compensation, he told them hotel rooms at a local resort would be paid for; the dive shop van would shuttle them to hotel as soon as the police finished. The guests who did not dive with Gordon would be questioned first.

Now, the captain shuts off the motor. He passes Bertie and Matt then descends the stairs from the upper deck to greet the officials. Bertie feels no urgency to leave her spot on the railing. Instead, she looks out over the shops and restaurants that line the harbor. The colorful pennants along the street, hang limp. The late morning heat rises from the concrete and asphalt in waves.

She really has no desire to spend a day in town shopping; she's not one to poke around in kitschy gift shops buying cheap souvenirs to bring back home. She's sad about Gordon. She's sad for Ava, Lauren and Lucky. She wishes Gordon's tragic disappearance had never happened, and the Calypso was anchored at a dive site right now instead of at the dock in the harbor where the boards smell strongly of creosote and fish.

If it wasn't for Gordon vanishing, she thinks they would be exploring a shipwreck. Manuel mentioned one when the Calypso first motored out of the harbor, the day he reviewed all the dives they might do depending on the currents and the weather.

But wishing won't change anything; Bertie heaves a big sigh, and then follows Matt down the stairs to their cabin.

They pack their duffels which doesn't take much time at all; swimsuits, t-shirts and shorts don't take much space or need careful folding. Bertie doesn't have any resort clothes, but she can make do with what she has. She debates whether she should leave the leis and the ukulele. She doubts she'll ever use them again. They would remind her of the talent show night when Gordon and Ava sang their duet. Bertie sets the props on rumpled bed covers, and then zips her bag. Matt doesn't say anything about her decision.

For a moment, the two are silent, holding their duffels and surveying the tiny cabin. The space smells like suntan lotion and wet swimsuits. Bertie is surprised at the overwhelming nostalgia she feels for the place. It's just a plain cabin on a dive boat. Not that much different than any of the other dive boat cabins they've occupied on other trips.

A queen-sized bed with built in drawers dominates one side of the room; a compact stack of shelves for their odds and ends nearly fills the rest of the space. The door to the bathroom is ajar. She can see the steel toilet and sink. The drain in the middle of the floor for the shower water. Bertie looks out the small porthole. She's disappointed she can no longer see the ocean. Instead, another boat moored near the Calypso blocks even her view of the harbor.

Maybe she's feeling emotional because being on a dive boat is like going to summer camp. Bertie remembers all those years of camp she attended while growing up. The whispered conversations in the darkened cabins under the pines, the water fights on the lake while canoeing, the goofy camp songs and bad food, legs lumpy with bug bites and the forever friends she made.

Now, she can't remember a single name. Looking out the porthole, she thinks of all those times she peered out the dirty window of the bus ferrying her home. She remembers the mashed- up feelings of exhaustion, homesickness and sadness swirling inside her.

Gordon's disappearance has added another layer to the sadness. She thinks of all the meals and conversations they shared with the Bakers. How she admired the evident close connection between the four. How it reminded her of her own family. Bertie doubts she would have stayed in touch with the Bakers after this week. But she hopes she and Catalina will remain friends. She vows to make a concerted effort to keep in touch.

Matt picks up his duffel and exits to the hall. Bertie sweeps the cabin with a last glance. The two head up the stairs to the main deck. The police are meeting with the two families who they don't know well, the ones who were in Manuel's dive group. Bertie assumes they won't have much to say. Like summer camp, she's already forgotten many of their names, except of course Jacqueline's. Who could forget her name when she was constantly roaming about the boat, loudly complaining about how bored she was?

The guests have piled their bags just outside the dining room, the captain explaining earlier that the police might want to search the bags. No one objected. And why would they? Let the police see their wet swim suits and stained t-shirts and shorts. Matt and Bertie drop their duffels by the jumble of bags.

Matt returns to the sundeck with a book he's been hoping to finish. Bertie finds Catalina on the dive deck. The dive master is looking out over the harbor, appearing lost in thought. Bertie wonders if she, like Bertie, is remembering their first dive in the harbor.

Bertie sinks onto the bench beside Catalina. The sun is hot on her shoulders; the water laps against the side of the boat. Mariachi music drifts from one of the restaurants in town. And now, Bertie catches the scent of tortillas frying in hot oil.

Maybe it wouldn't be so horrible to get off the Calypso and find a shady patio where she and Matt can sip margaritas and forget about what happened for a little bit. The boat rocks gently and bumps against the dock when the families disembark. Their voices and laughter are loud as they proceed down the dock, and for a moment Bertie imagines they're all just getting on board the Calypso, just starting off on their adventure. But the voices fade, and Bertie still sits on the bench beside Catalina. Her face is sweaty. Her t-shirt sticks to her back.

For once, Bertie is at a loss for words, so she silently squeezes Catalina's hand. The other woman gives her a faint smile.

Matt appears on the dive deck and signals that it's their turn to meet with the police. Bertie turns towards Catalina and envelopes her in a hug.

"Let's stay in touch," Bertie says. Catalina nods, but Bertie can tell she's not really listening. "I mean it," Bertie says. Matt's waving for her to come into the dining room, but she holds up a finger. "Give me your number." She fishes in her plastic purse for her cell phone and powers it up. As soon as the screen lights up, the death app chimes.

"Guess you've got messages to answer," Catalina says. "Vacation really is over." Her attempt to smile at her joke is lost on Bertie because she's staring horrified at her phone. She can't believe she ever downloaded the stupid app in the first place. She'll absolutely delete it as soon as possible. She shudders as she recalls her conversation about the app with the Bakers. What was she thinking?

"Bertie," Catalina says. "You okay?"

Bertie wrenches her gaze from her screen. She stares blankly at Catalina before she remembers she wants the dive master's phone number. By the time she types Catalina's name and number into her phone, Matt has vanished from the doorway. Bertie assumes he's already talking to the police. She hurriedly returns her phone to her purse.

"I'll say a proper goodbye later," she promises.

The dining room is quiet without the chatter of others, the clink of silverware and glasses and the quick movements of Jacqueline darting in and out of the space.

Matt is already sitting with the police looking perfectly at ease in the same booth where Bertie passed tissues to the Bakers. In fact, Bertie sees the very same tissue box still on the polished mahogany table top. She believes the box is empty. Apparently, no one has taken the time to throw it in the trash.

Bertie takes a deep breath. Throwing back her shoulders, she strides towards the booth. A police officer rises to shake her hand and introduce himself. His skin is cool against her sweaty palm. He seems friendly, but are his dark eyes scrutinizing her? She slides into the booth next to Matt.

"I was just out on the dive deck," she says. "It's hot out there."

She hopes he doesn't think her palm is sweaty because she has something to hide. Bertie has never been questioned by the police before. She takes that back. She did get pulled over once for speeding. The officer did ask her questions through her open car window. Obviously, this is different. Bertie wipes her sweaty palm on the side of her shorts.

The officer holds the dive forms Bertie and Matt filled out when they first arrived on the boat. He peers at their handwriting. He has no trouble figuring out Matt's name, but his eyebrows squinch when he attempts to pronounce her name.

"It's Bertie," she says. No need to confess her actual name is Alberta. She shifts in the booth. She knows she's not being investigated. She knows she's not facing arrest. Still, her stomach flutters just like when she jumps into the water for the first dive of a trip.

Setting aside the dive forms, the officer pulls another sheet of paper towards him. He reads from a list of questions: Did you know the Bakers before boarding the Calypso? Did you know Gordon? Bertie and Matt answer no. Bertie is feeling better at the easy questions.

When the officer asks what the Bakers were like, Bertie feels comfortable enough to offer more information than a short no. She tells the officer that the Bakers are a very close family. She tells him how Gordon enthusiastically shared his passion for diving with not only his family but with the others on the boat. She tells him about the moving duet sung by Gordon and Ava. Her stories fade when she notices the policeman's pen resting on his paper, his eyes wandering about the cabin.

At her silence, the officer returns his attention to Bertie and Matt. He picks up his pen. His expression grows serious. "Did you notice anything unusual about the Bakers or Gordon either on board the boat or in the water?" he says.

Matt quickly says no. Bertie considers her answer. She never mentioned the conversation she overheard when she passed Gordon's cabin to Catalina. She decides it's not relevant to the officer's question. Maybe Gordon simply had a headache that day. Maybe Ava was warning him not to dive. Why stir up something out of nothing?

"Did you notice something?" the officer's gaze is riveted on Bertie. She shakes her head.

Matt rubs his face with his hands. His beard looks rough and prickly. He didn't shave this morning. His eyes are red. He and Bertie didn't sleep much either last night.

"Gordon was the most experienced diver on board," Matt says. "Poor guy must have had a heart attack or something."

Bertie feels tears welling at the thought of Gordon dying alone. She reaches for the tissue box. Plunging her hand inside, she feels one last tissue which she extracts and uses to blow her nose.

"At least he died doing what he loved," she says. The sentiment doesn't make her feel any better. She and Matt are both trained rescue divers. She wonders again if they could have saved the older man.

As if he read her thoughts, Matt rubs her back. Bertie gives him a watery smile.

The officer rustles the papers before him. "Anything else you'd like to add?"

Bertie shakes her head. The officer picks up his pen and makes a note. "How about you sir?" the officer turns to Matt.

"No, nothing," Matt's answer is short.

"I won't keep you longer," the officer says.

Bertie and Matt slide out of the booth. Now, she's eager to leave the Calypso where it seems like Gordon's ghost is everywhere. She makes a quick detour to the dive deck looking for Catalina to tell her goodbye. But the dive master is gone. Feeling disappointed, she joins Matt and Polo who are waiting for her by the gunwale. The duffels are on the dock next to their larger dive bags with their equipment.

Matt steps off the Calypso onto the dock. He holds out a hand to help Bertie, but Polo already has a hand at her elbow. She's glad for the assistance. Her legs are wobbly after being on a boat for nearly a week. The dock feels like its swaying beneath her feet.

She slides her arms through the straps of her dive bag and picks up her duffel. Matt has done the same. He's already headed towards town. But, Bertie turns for one last look at the Calypso.

Catalina waves from the upper deck. Bertie waves back. Not the proper goodbye she wanted, but she's already off the boat. There's no point in turning back.

As they leave the boat behind, Bertie can't help but drag Gordon's ghost with her. She spins the wedding ring on her finger and worries over the clues she must have missed; the hints she didn't follow that Gordon was a diver in distress and that maybe the Bakers weren't so honest after all.

Chapter 19

Polo finds me on the dive deck where I'm not doing much of anything.

I came downstairs after puttering around on the upper deck, straightening the lounge chairs, wiping the bar with a damp cloth and waving goodbye to Bertie. I feel sadder than usual watching them go.

I don't often watch the dive guests as they head back to their normal lives. I'm usually busy stripping the beds and wiping down the bathrooms in preparation for the next boatload of divers. But I'm still leaning on the railing as Bertie and Matt load their dive equipment and duffels into the dive shop van and disappear into town. I feel the loss of their presence almost as keenly as Gordon's which is silly because Bertie gave me her phone number. She's not dead. She's simply returning to Michigan.

In the distance, I can see the sun glint off an airplane departing from the nearby airport. The pull of home is strong. I'm exhausted and heartbroken. I don't know if I can get excited for another dive trip on the

Calypso; I can't picture jumping into the water in the same spot where we lost Gordon.

I can't help but wonder if we left the search area too quickly. Maybe we didn't give Gordon the chance he deserves.

I sit on the bench and pull out the bin assigned to Lauren. It's empty. Ava's is the same, but I find a penny in Lucky's bin. I stare at the piece of copper in the palm of my hand, remembering how Gordon gave the coin to his daughter before the first dive. She was nervous after not having dived for a number of years. I remember Gordon smiling and pressing the penny into her hand for luck. She dropped it into her bootie. I wonder if the penny was in her bootie the night Gordon disappeared? I slip the coin into my pocket. If I see Lucky before she leaves, I'll give it to her.

I pull out Gordon's bin. Nothing in there but a bright orange plastic whistle. I search my memories of the night dive. Was Gordon wearing a whistle on his dive vest? A whistle isn't mandatory, but it can be an effective tool for a diver's safety. A whistle blown on the water's surface could be louder than a shout if a diver is lost. I stand, put the whistle to my lips, and blow.

A sea lion pops its dark head up, breaking the water's surface, and my heart stills. I run to the rail; all logic is gone.

"Gordon!" I shout. The sea lion dives under the water, disappearing somewhere under the Calypso.

"Chicle," Polo says, his hand on my back. "It's just a sea lion. Gordon is gone."

Tears well in my eyes. I turn to Polo, unashamed of my grief. He unties the bandana he always wears knotted around his neck and hands it to me. I wipe my cheeks.

"It's not your fault," he says. "No one blames you."

"I'm surprised you don't think the sea lion is Gordon." I say. My voice is accusatory, remembering his dire warnings after our visit to Sea Lion Rock.

Polo smiles and holds his hands with the palms up. "Maybe it is," he says.

I can't tell if he's serious or if he's joking around. And despite myself, I kind of like the idea of Gordon as a sea lion. It's not too different from my hopes that his skeleton will be the start of a new coral reef. I turn my back on the harbor, leaning against the rail.

"Has something like this happened on the Calypso before?" I say. Polo has worked as the boat's engineer for a long time. I don't know how long, but he was on board years before me.

Polo shakes his head. "No, but I've heard of other deaths on other boats." He joins me on the rail. "Usually there's a body," he adds.

I shudder at the thought of bringing Gordon's body out of the water, hefting it up the ladder. Would we stretch it out on one of the benches? When would we stop blowing air into his lungs and realize it was too late to save him? I picture pulling off his wetsuit and booties, toweling his body dry and carrying it to his cabin. I don't know why, but the thought of his body drifting off into the deep is a more comforting thought.

The sun is bright on the dive deck, and I shade my eyes to peer into the dim dining room. I can make out shadows sitting around a booth.

"It's the Bakers," Polo says. "The capitán asked me to knock on their cabin door when the officers were ready to talk to them."

We're silent while the wind blows snatches of the conversation towards us. I can hear the deep baritones of the investigating officers, the lighter tones of the three women and sobbing over the lapping of the water against the boat.

Manuel appears on the dive deck. Normally, he would question why we were lounging around when there's work to be done. Normally, we would jump to our feet. We would busy ourselves with the myriad of tasks that need to be done before the next round of divers appear at the end of the dock.

But today, we remain still. He nods at us without speaking. He fiddles with the white board, fingering the marker in the silver tray, wiping the board with a clean cloth.

When the dining room conversation ends, Manuel drops the cloth into the white board tray. He rounds the outside corner of the dining room. Polo and I follow. The capitán and Manuel are already at the gunwale when we arrive. We join them, standing in a line similar to the one we formed on the first day we greeted the passengers. Gordon's whistle dangles from one of my hands, I finger the warm penny in my pocket with the other. Ava emerges from the cabin first, followed by Lauren. Lucky trips on the door's high threshold, but the capitán is ready to steady her. The women pause. I get the feeling they're not quite ready to leave the Calypso.

I hold out the whistle to Ava. "I found this in Gordon's bin," I say. Ava takes the whistle from my fingers with a nod.

Then I withdraw the penny from my pocket. Holding it in my palm, I offer it to Lucky. She looks bewildered.

"I found this in your dive bin," I say. "It must have fallen out of your bootie."

I can tell the moment she remembers as the confusion flees and a single tear slides down the side of her check.

"It's yours," she says, refusing to take it from my hand. She's the first off the boat, stepping lightly onto the gunwale and jumping onto the dock before Polo or Manuel can help her. Lauren follows quickly.

Ava lingers to thank each of us; her brown eyes are unfathomable pools of grief; her fingers clutch the plastic whistle. My own eyes grow misty when she holds my hand and expresses her gratitude. The capitán assists her off the boat. The four of us watch as the women traverse the dock. Someone has already loaded their dive equipment and personal luggage onto the van. The capitán lifts a hand in farewell as they climb into the van, and the door slides shut. I slip the penny into my pocket.

Manuel goes inside the dining room for his turn with the police. The boat's crew is being interviewed last, so the guests can be on their way. I'm not sure what to do with myself or these unsettling feelings. I fiddle with the penny.

It's too hot to sit outside. I don't want to go to the cabin I share with Madelyn. I peek into the kitchen where Madelyn is busily scrubbing the breakfast dishes. She's singing, but I can't make out the words over the clatter of the pots. The room smells like bleach. The counters are wiped clean. A mop and bucket are ready for use. I don't want to be roped into a kitchen chore; I quietly back away from the door and wander into the lounge.

The room smells stuffy from the guests who sacked out on the couches during our search for Gordon. Decorative pillows are scattered around, some on the floor. I search the cupboards for room spray. I find a can that promises lavender breezes and I spritz the room with a good dose. I think I read somewhere that the scent of lavender is supposed to calm your spirit or at least improve your mood. But when I'm done, and the room smells like a garden, I'm still in a funk – unsure of whether I can or should lead a dive group again.

A few games are out, so I mechanically collect all the pieces and then store them in a cupboard. I return the pillows to the couches, punching them into shape and then punching them some more. Maybe if I ran the vacuum, the noise would blot out the thoughts whirring in my head. But I don't get out the vacuum from the supply closet.

Instead, I head to the cabins recently vacated by the guests. The teens were bunked in cabins below deck. I don't even want to go below and glance into what I'm sure is a total mess. I pass the cabins where their parents stayed. I stop at the door to Gordon and Ava's cabin.

This is where I've been going all along, but I pause with my hand on the doorknob. What feels like a cool breeze whisks down the hall, raising goosebumps on my arms and legs. Luckily, I'm not superstitious or I might think the breeze is Gordon's ghost. I finger the penny in my pocket, and swing open the door.

The covers of the queen-sized bed are rumpled. A pile of wet towels hold the bathroom door ajar. The air smells like antibacterial hand wash. I step inside. I don't know what I'm looking for, but I move to the bathroom where I open the small cupboard behind the mirror. The shelves are empty of course. Back in the bedroom, I scan the dresser drawers and small shelving area – both also empty. Finally, I sit on the bed. I hardly know what I'm doing when I lay back and rest my head on the pillows.

Did Ava and Gordon know this would be his last resting place when they first came aboard the Calypso? I study the ceiling and wonder what Gordon was thinking when he lay here in the bed.

I jump when the door to the cabin slams shut. But then, I put my head back against the pillow, taking deep breaths in the stillness. Sun spills onto the bed from the round porthole. I watch the dust motes float in the spot of sun. My eyelids are heavy, and I drift off to sleep.

I surface from a deep slumber when the door opens, and Manuel calls my name. I think at first that Manuel is talking to me in my dream. That perhaps he's telling me who's been assigned to my dive group. It takes a while for the room to come into focus, for me to realize where I am.

"Catalina," Manuel says again. "The police are waiting."

I blink my eyes and sit up. I'm groggy when I swing my legs off the bed. My hair has come loose from my ponytail. I push the heavy strands out of my face with one hand while I search the pillows for my ponytail holder. Manuel is silent, watching from the doorway, while I scrape my hair back into the restraint.

When I stand, he says, "What are you doing in here?" I shrug my shoulders. He steps aside to let me pass him. And when I do, he picks a silver hair off my shoulder. We both stare at the strand for a moment, before Manuel brushes it from his hand. I watch it float to the floor.

"I was sleeping," I say, covering a yawn. I know that's not what he's asking, but since I hardly know myself why I was in Gordon and Ava's bed, I can't give him another answer. He shakes his head, and I follow him to the dining room where the officers are waiting to speak to me.

As soon as we enter the dining room, I'm desperate for a drink of water. My throat feels parched like I've been breathing oxygen underwater for a very long time. I take a detour to the coffee bar where Madelyn always keeps bottles of water on ice in a large silver bowl. The ice is melted, but several bottles float in a pool of cold water. I grab two.

When I arrive at the booth, the officer stands and holds out his hand. I hold up the two dripping bottles to show why I can't shake. He shrugs and indicates with his hand that I should take a seat. I slide into the booth opposite him. It occurs to me that I should offer him a water bottle, and I hold one up.

"Would you like one?" I say in Spanish. I'm nervous about his questions. I'm nervous he'll judge me and pronounce me a poor dive master. But it's not like I'm buttering him up by offering water. The guy simply looks thirsty.

He accepts the proffered water. We both crack open our bottles at the same time and take a swig.

"Catalina," he says, looking at a stack of papers in front of him. Then, he looks up at me. "Do you mind if I call you that?"

"Not at all," I say. I swallow more water from the bottle. I set the bottle on the table and rest my wet palm beside it. When I raise my nervous hand to smooth my hair, my palm print can be seen in the beads of moisture on the table.

The officer nods, considers his paperwork, and then leans back against the booth. "You've been on the Calypso for two years?"

"Yes, that's right," I agree.

"You've been a dive master elsewhere?"

"For four years," I say. My throat is dry again, and I put the bottle to my lips.

"Is this the first time a diver has died on your watch?" he says. His eyes seem to pin me to my seat like a bug. I shift. The back of my thighs feels sweaty; my skin sticks to the cloth of the booth.

"Yes sir," I say. Adding the sir seems like the right thing to do at this point. I'm horrified when tears prick at my eyes. I drink more water and fight against the moisture welling in my tear ducts. I brace myself for the judgment I know is coming.

The room is silent while the officer shuffles his papers. He clears his throat.

"The Bakers have told me that Gordon got lost on purpose," he says. I'm trying to wrap my thoughts around his words when he adds, "He came on this trip to die."

Chapter 20

I'm stunned by the officer's words. Gordon wanted to die? The Bakers stepped on board the Calypso knowing from day one what Gordon planned? The dining room is silent while I process this information.

I picture Ava and Gordon confidently setting up their dive equipment. I think of Lauren and Lucky, unsure on the first dives, their father helping them.

"What?" My voice comes out with a squeak.

"Apparently he was diagnosed with a terminal disease," the officer says. "He was determined to die on his terms."

I swallow hard. I'm still thinking of the time we all spent underwater and on board the boat. My mind is grasping at threads trying to pull together the narrative the officer is sharing.

"Did his family try to stop him?" I say.

"That's what they say." The officer folds his hands, settling them on top of his papers. "Of course, they knew about his disease and his desire not to fight it, but they say they did all they could to convince him otherwise. They told me they were hoping just as much, if not more, as the rest of you that he would be rescued that night."

In the silence, I can hear Madelyn banging around in the kitchen, slopping the mop across the floor, and then knocking it against the bucket. I hear footsteps as another crew member walks across the deck above. Manuel cruises by the window. He stops and asks if I'm ok, giving the underwater sign with his forefinger and thumb forming a circle. I nod.

I lift my water bottle for a sip, but discover that it's empty. The officer waits in the booth while I leave for another water bottle. I fish the last one out of the silver bowl where it's bobbing on the surface of a pool of water. The ice is completely melted. Water droplets run down my hand. I wipe them on the side of my shorts and return to the booth.

"I understand you were the last one in the water with Gordon that night," the officer says. He leans forward, his brows nearly meeting. "Were you aware of what Gordon was planning?"

Water goes down the wrong pipe, and I cough and splutter for air. His words send a chill through me. What proof do I have that I wasn't helping Gordon end his life? I haven't forgotten that I was the last one in the water. I haven't stopped thinking about what I could have done differently to save Gordon's life. I haven't stopped blaming myself for his disappearance.

But it never occurred to me that I could be thought complicit in his death.

I close my eyes and inhale several deep breaths, exhaling through my lips until my heart slows to a more normal pace.

When I open my eyes, I speak with a voice that trembles. "Officer," I say, "I was the last one in the water after the dive. I can't deny that. And believe me, I feel horrible about what happened. Gordon was in my dive group. But, I didn't know that Gordon hadn't come aboard the Calypso. If you check the boat's dive log for that night, you'll see that Gordon's name was checked off the list as a returned diver. I didn't make that mark."

I lean back against the seat. Despite my deep breathing, my heart is hammering in my chest again. I feel like I did that night when my imagination was running wild and I was picturing all sorts of monsters of the deep in the dark waters just below me.

Could I be stripped of my dive master's certification? Or worse, could I be arrested and put in jail?

"I've seen the log," the officer says flicking the papers with his finger. "No one admits to putting that check beside his name."

"At least two of the guests snorkeled that night," I say, scrambling for an explanation. "Maybe the person in charge of the list accidentally checked Gordon's name when they returned instead."

"I've considered and investigated that possibility," the officer says. "But even the person in charge of the list can't be sure it was in his possession the entire time."

"Are you suggesting someone deliberately checked Gordon's name?" I say incredulously.

The officer straightens the stack of papers. "I've heard from the guests and the crew that the boat was chaotic that night. No one seems to be sure of anything."

The night's become a blur to me. I distinctly remember Ava asking me about Gordon when I first returned to the Calypso. I remember her face when she realized Gordon wasn't emerging from the water behind me. I remember Lauren and Lucky crowding around me and the feeling of dread that weighed me down, a feeling I'm still battling. But the rest of the night is a kaleidoscope of images. The Bakers shouting Gordon's name, the Calypso's search light, the clatter of the helicopter, the fading loudspeaker on the rescue boat. I couldn't begin to coherently piece together a time line of events. Maybe I could if I had a good night's sleep.

"You didn't answer my question," the officer says. "Were you aware of what Gordon was planning?"

"No." My answer is short and emphatic.

The officer nods and makes a note. "What were your observations of the Bakers?"

I chew on my thumbnail while I consider the officer's questions. It's a bad habit I thought I'd broken. When I realize what I'm doing, I sit on both of my hands.

"Gordon and Ava were experienced divers," I say. "Lauren and Lucky were a bit rusty in their dive skills, but they regained them quickly. I was happy to have them and the Clarks in my dive group."

"Any particular reason?"

"It's easier to lead a group of experienced divers," I say. "I had a particularly challenging group the previous week – lots of newbies – and Manuel was nice enough to give me the easy group this time around."

The officer is silent, waiting, I presume, for more information.

"They did have an unusual way of ascending after a dive," I offer. I tell the officer about the Baker's group ascent. "But they did it every time, so I just assumed it was something they did. Divers can be quirky."

The officer asks some questions about the Bakers on board the Calypso. Did I notice anything unusual or overhear anything? I shrug my shoulders and shake my head. The officer thanks me and tells me I can go. He stands while I slide out of the booth.

I can feel his eyes on my back as I step outside onto the dive deck. I'm sure he's weighing my answers and deciding whether to charge me with dereliction of duty or complicity in Gordon's death. I don't know why I headed out to the dive deck. I just know I need some air. There's the sharp scent of diesel outside as the boat that was moored next to the Calypso pulls away from the dock. Its dive deck is lined with metal tanks. People are milling about the deck, readying for a week-long trip.

The Calypso's dive deck is clean. Bins are neatly tucked beneath the benches. Hangers are restored to the metal rack where dive guests hang their wetsuits and vests. The camera table is wiped dry and the rinse bucket is turned upside down.

Looking at the Calypso's dive deck, I remember my conversation with Gordon, his remark that he has no regrets. At the time, I thought nothing of his words. But now I wonder, should I have noticed an underlying meaning? I think of the drift dive when Gordon was nearly left behind, of my spidey sense the rest of the dive that something was off.

I have no proof the Baker women deliberately left Gordon. And even if they did, I don't feel badly about not mentioning the incident to the officer. Their grief was palpable after Gordon's disappearance. I'm having a hard time believing they were faking while they were shouting Gordon's name. If that means I'm complicit in Gordon's death, then so be it.

I lean against the boat in the shade of the overhang, waiting for the officer to come outside and arrest me. I'm so done with this life. The freedom I've experienced underwater is gone, vanished with the disappearance of Gordon.

I'm sickened by the thought that he used the ocean that's given me so much life to take his own life, that he spoke with me dishonestly on this boat, and that he presented himself as a healthy diver. I picture him frolicking with the sea lion pup. I feel betrayed and used. I don't know how I can trust another diver I've just met, another group of strangers.

I honestly don't believe I can take a giant stride off the dive platform with the same enthusiasm I once felt. I dig Lucky's penny out my pocket and drop it in the tip jar by the white board. It rattles around in the recently emptied jar, and then settles on the bottom.

I hear footsteps behind me and I turn. Manuel is standing nearby. I'm surprised to see him. I thought he would take advantage of this extra time at the dock to see his family.

"I'm leaving soon," he says, as if he can read my thoughts. "I wanted to check on you," he says. "The officer told you about Gordon?"

I nod. "I can't do this anymore," I say.

"Maybe you just need some time off," Manuel says.

"No," I say. "I'm done." I look out past the cliff-like rocks where the harbor opens into the ocean, and then back to Manuel. "I'll stay for two weeks. Give you time to find another dive master. But that's it."

Manuel slips his hands into his shorts pockets and rocks back on his heels. "I hate to see you leave over this," he says. "We all know that diving is a risky sport. But we love it anyway." His voice is fierce. "You're a good dive master. Guests could die underwater for any number of reasons."

"I know that," I say. "But knowing it and experiencing it aren't the same." My gaze slides towards the airport. "I'm going home," I say.

Part II

Chapter 21

Gordon holds his mask and regulator against his face. He executes a giant stride into the ocean, the splash covering his head as he sinks. Then, he bobs to the surface, touching the top of his hood to signal he's okay. Ava, Lucky and Lauren quickly follow him into the water like dominos. I hesitate on the dive platform, the tips of my black fins dangling over the open sea.

The sun's low on the horizon behind the group; a watery path that leads from the dive boat into the distant beyond shimmers with gold. I can't see below the mirror-like surface to the darker depths. The wind is no more than a soft sigh; it's as if the Calypso is floating peacefully in a bath. The Bakers gently push aside the golden water with their gloved hands, their kicking fins, and buoyant vests keeping them afloat. Gradually, Ava and her daughters drift into a semi-circle around Gordon. There's an open spot for me. But I've still not fully committed to the dive.

Shadows obscure their faces. I can't see their expressions. But I know they're looking at me. I'm their dive master. They're waiting for my lead.

While I pause, the dark head of a sea lion pops up in the water. The animal slides into the circle, and I'm shut out. I watch as the Bakers turn their attention to the new arrival. The circle grows tighter. I imagine their fins churning underwater, moving them ever closer to the sea lion and each other.

It's clear they've forgotten me hovering at the edge of the dive platform. I'm like a statue, unable to move or speak. Without warning, the sea lion dives beneath the surface, the tip of its tail showing briefly; its movements are so smooth there's barely a ripple on the water. Then, Gordon follows. His fins kick up above the surface like the sea lion's tail. And he's gone with the smallest of splashes. The water smooths over as if Gordon was never there.

Twilight approaches as the sun slides below the horizon, the gold fades, and the Baker women swim back through the now shaded water to the boat where I'm still stuck, the tips of my fins hanging off the edge. Sweat trickles down my back and fogs my dive mask until I'm no longer certain of the details of what I've witnessed.

I'm disoriented when I swim back to consciousness.

I stare wide eyed at the unfamiliar shadows of the studio I've lived in for the past eight months. Sometimes, the headlights of a passing car will light my window and remind me I'm no longer on the Calypso. Other times, I'll lay in the darkness while my cottony brain struggles to disconnect from the dive platform. My bed seems to sway in an ocean current. But no matter how I wake, my skin and my cheeks are damp with sweat and tears.

Water dreams are supposed to be about rebirth and life.

But, mine are all about death.

In other dreams, Gordon and I are suspended in a darkness so impenetrable I can't see anything but the pinpoints of our dive lights. He's not much more than a shadow. But I know it's him.

I feel safe at first.

I imagine this must have been what it was like in my mother's womb. A warm, familiar liquid of muffled sounds. We float and bob like twin corks. Then, Gordon's light blinks out. I grab for him. But my fingers slide through the liquid and come up empty. I swing my light wildly around. But see nothing.

I'm alone.

Except for the possibility of monsters sharing the nightmarish space.

I've called and called for Gordon. But have gotten no answer. I've watched as Gordon descended into Hades.

I've told Nate about my dreams.

He holds me in his arms and smooths my wild, damp hair from my forehead. He assures me it's only natural for me to dream about Gordon. His death was a traumatic event. He's a scuba diver himself so he understands the risks of the sport. He tells me the dreams will fade with time. And they have become less frequent. He never says he's tired of hearing about my nightmares. But I stop talking about them. How will they ever go away if I continually obsess over them?

When I first got home, I did some research on the prognosis for someone with Gordon's disease. It wasn't pretty. I came to understand why Gordon might choose to end his life, even though I didn't agree with it.

I used to talk on the phone with Bertie for hours, both of us searching for clues we missed during that week on the Calypso. Of course, I told her about Gordon's choice. She was shocked. But then, she filled me in on a conversation she overheard between Ava and Gordon. I understood when she told me she thought nothing of it at the time.

Another time, she recalled a snatch of conversation she heard on the sun deck about the need to distract someone. She assumed the speakers were talking about Jacqueline. "Remember how squirrely she was?" Bertie said. I just remember her being a busy girl.

Bertie couldn't say for sure if the voices were Lauren and Lucky's but given what happened with Gordon the night of the Manta Ray dive, she guessed they were.

"Maybe he was planning to off himself during the drift dive, but you saved him," Bertie said. I winced at her word usage. "So, they distracted you somehow on the night dive."

Until that moment, I'd forgotten about the diver's light blinding me underwater. It had seemed so normal at the time, just a typical accidental use of a dive light. We both speculated the light was pointed by one of the Baker women. But we had no proof. Nor could we figure out who put the check by Gordon's name on the list of returned divers. We agreed the Baker women seemed sincerely worried about Gordon the night he disappeared. Maybe they regretted helping him once they were back on board the Calypso.

Eventually, I put a stop to our speculations. It wasn't doing me any good.

Now, Bertie and I talk about normal things. I tell her about my studies, the struggles I'm experiencing returning to school after six years for my masters in Greek Mythology and Art. She talks about her work deadlines. I talk about Nate, she tells me about Matt. We make plans to visit each other. I talk about boating with her on Lake Michigan. She talks about diving with me off the San Diego coast and maybe traveling to Catalina Island to dive in the kelp beds. But I haven't done any diving since I returned home. I left my dive equipment at my parents' house, tucked next to the box of my childhood possessions. The only thing I brought to the studio was my dive light. I don't know why. Maybe it's because I believe it will illumine the monsters in the deep.

I haven't even been to the beach.

But it's been more difficult to put a stop to my dream conversations with Judy. She's studying the psychology of dreams at the local community college and usually badgers me until I confess I'm still dreaming about Gordon.

I think it's because she catches me when I'm at my weakest, waiting at the local coffee shop in a semi-circle with strangers anxious for their morning coffees. She's on the other side of the counter, creating lattes and mochas, steaming milk and scooping ice. We struck up a conversation when she first started working here a few months ago. She saw me with my textbooks and laptop, and we became friends, bonding over our studies.

This morning, when she slides my latte across the counter, she notes the shadows under my eyes.

"Another dream?" she says, taking a quick break from working to lean towards me.

I cradle the warm cup in my hands and take a sip. "No," I say. I cover my yawn with the back of my hand.

She shakes her head as if my yawn is proof I'm lying and returns to the orders that are lining up.

I weave through the waiting crowd, the scattered chairs, and tables, finally settling at a small, round table for two in the back corner of the cafe. I sip my chai and retrieve my laptop from my shoulder bag. I'm taking online courses to complete my master's and earn my teaching certificate. Nate says he'll put in a good word for me at the local high school where he teaches chemistry and coaches boy's lacrosse.

The cafe is cozy this morning with the smell of roasting beans and warm muffins; the line swells and subsides with those getting drinks to go. Two young mothers are ensconced on the overstuffed couches. The low table in front of them is littered with scattered crayons and papers they brought to occupy their preschoolers, but the little girls are sprawled on the lone rug with their Barbie dolls.

Others at various tables shuffle papers back and forth and check their phones. A few wear headphones and type on their laptops. Later, when the clouds lift, someone will open the French doors onto the patio where there are tables under a bougainvillea- covered trellis. On warm days, misters keep the patio cool; heaters are available to warm the patio in the winter. Really, the only time I've seen the patio vacant is during the infrequent rainstorm.

When I first got back to Poway at the end of last summer, I was like a dog with its tail between its legs. I didn't want to go anywhere or socialize with anybody. My parents let me stay with them.

They still live in the house where I grew up. It's a three-bedroom, two-bath ranch with a wide lawn in front. They've made a few changes; now, the back yard has a concrete patio with a built-in barbeque. An above-ground hot tub that looks like a wine vat is positioned near the master bedroom which has been retrofitted with French doors. My old room is done up in neutral shades of gray and white; there's a double bed, a small dresser and a chair. Two round aqua pillows on the bed provide a pop of color.

Despite the changes with the house, my parents look the same. They have a few more lines around their eyes and mouths, but their hair is still thick and dark like mine. They've stayed in shape. I imagine my mother could still fit into her turquoise swimsuit.

I might still be there if it wasn't for Bertie. She constantly encouraged me to get out on my own, to meet new people. She's become the friend I didn't know I was missing while I traveled for six years.

"You're becoming a hermit," she said once during a video chat. "What is happening with your hair?"

I looked in the mirror after that call. My hair cascaded in wild tangles about my face. Even I cringed at my pale reflection. I got serious about finding a rental. I spent very little of my salary and tips while I worked as a dive master, so I had enough money to support myself until I got a teaching job.

I found a small studio apartment in Poway above someone's detached garage. From my kitchen window, I have a view of the rock-strewn foothills to the east. The view is better in the winter, when the large birch drops its leaves. Now that it's spring, bright green leaves filter the view. I love the sound of the breeze fluttering the leaves. Sometimes it reminds me of the hissing of the ocean as it parted against the bow of the Calypso.

Poway grew while I was gone, but it's still got enough country in it that I can hear coyotes howling at night. And I know there are rattlesnakes nesting in the rocks I can see from my window. Some slither into people's yards. One afternoon, my landlord showed me the rattler he'd killed in his rose bushes by chopping off its head with a shovel.

I house-sit for my landlord in exchange for a low rent, and I help my mother with her balloon business "An Elegant AffAir." She started it after I went off to college for my bachelor's degree. The business helped pay for a portion of my education and my brother's. Now, it's grown large enough to keep two occupied. Spring is an especially busy time of year with graduations and school dances. We just finished decorating bars for St. Patrick's Day. It's amazing that bars still want balloons. I can't imagine the décor survives too late into the evening of drinking.

My mother owns two vans. Sometimes, I drive to one location while she heads to another. I've gotten used to the questions about the logo on the side of the van featuring a woman with flowing dark hair and soulful eyes in a ball gown you might see in Renaissance paintings blowing what many believe are bubbles. They're actually brightly colored balloons. Bubbles are clear. People also ask if I'm the model for the woman. I'm not. But depending on my mood, I might say I am.

My mother was excited to have me back in town for the World Balloon Convention. I wasn't planning to attend, but my mom looked so sad when I said no, I changed my mind. I even went to one of the parties dressed in a costume my mom created out of balloons.

I sent a picture of myself to Bertie. She got a good laugh out of seeing my head popping out of an alligator's mouth. My mom wanted to have my head inside a shark's open jaws in a nod to my past career, but I refused.

They say time heals all wounds. I'm still waiting for that time.

I mostly drive by the ocean these days on my way to and from client locations. I've seen the sunset from the freeway a time or two. It's been easy to avoid trips to the beach during the fall and winter. My parents joke that I got my fill of the ocean during the past six years. They laugh and tease that the Pacific is too cold for me now. They're happy I'm home, and my dad has made no secret of his pleasure that I'm pursuing a real job.

I've never told them about Gordon or the Bakers.

I open my laptop, closing my ears to the bustle of the coffee shop, the whir of the grinder and get to work.

I'm deep into my studies when Judy pulls over a chair and sits down.

"Break time," she says with a sigh. She sets a large glass of ice water on the table and leans forward. "So, what's the latest dream?"

Chapter 22

Bertie slides her sensible black work pumps under her desk, then pulls on her snow boots. She dons her heavy coat and wraps a wool scarf around her neck. She's so sick and tired of this winter. It seems to have gone on forever this year. And now, the forecast is predicting yet another storm moving through with more snow. She can't wait to turn the page on her calendar from March to April. Maybe then this winter will be over.

She trudges out the school district headquarters building to the parking lot. The air smells damp with the promise of snow. Fortunately, today was clear and warm enough that ice didn't freeze on her windshield. No need to get out the scraper. Something, however small, for which to be grateful. Bertie tries to hold onto that thought when she gets into her car. But it's difficult when the leather interior of her Volvo is as frigid as the air outside. Bertie starts the engine and waits while the car warms up. Matt's cooking dinner tonight; he's promised to make his specialty, pork roast with baby red potatoes, something Bertie's looking forward to enjoying.

She's also anticipating further discussion of their next dive trip, and she's hoping they can settle on a spot tonight. She's eager to begin her research, to start fantasizing about swimming in warm, tropical waters this time around. This is what keeps her sane during these long winters now, the knowing that the whole world is not covered in snow.

Maybe their next trip should be after Christmas. January or February would be a good time to take a break from this bone- chilling weather. Although, Bertie remembers the last time they returned from a tropical vacation in January. When she closes her eyes, it's easy to visualize climbing the stairs from the island tarmac to board the plane. She recalls the beads of perspiration dotting her upper lip. And the fronds on the palm trees drooping in the still, humid air as if even they were too hot to move. On takeoff, she remembers looking out the window as they circle over the island, climbing higher and higher over the clear, turquoise waters and reefs where they spent a week diving. And then, hours later, the back-to- earth arrival at their home airport in the midst of a snowstorm.

Bertie recalls the leaden skies and the wet spit of snowflakes on the small window. She opens her eyes to the gray skies out her windshield and shivers just thinking about the way the airplane skidded just a little on landing. She can't decide if the anticipation and the break are worth the re-entry. Maybe it would be better to stay strong and push their way through the winter. She's done it her whole life.

Before, Bertie enjoyed the Michigan seasons. She'd go to the lake in the summer, be excited for the leaves to turn colors in the fall, sled, ice fish and skate in the winter and welcome the spring by closely watching for the first tulip to push its head up out of the soil.

Before, she also believed her family was close. But that was before she met the Bakers. Before Gordon disappeared.

Bertie settles her hands on the steering wheel, staring blindly at the stark landscape through her windshield.

A tap on her window startles her. It's her boss' assistant signaling for her to roll down her window.

"Alberta," the assistant says, her breath makes white puffs. "You forgot this." She hands the folder she's holding in her gloved hands through the open window. "I know you wanted to work on it tonight."

Bertie takes the folder, setting it on her laptop case on the passenger seat. The assistant waves and heads to her own car. Bertie heaves a heavy sigh as she drives out of the parking lot. She'd forgotten her plan to work tonight. She's facing a deadline. She was so looking forward to spending time looking at pictures of island destinations. She even anticipated calling Catalina to talk over potential dive sites.

Her thoughts are elsewhere when the signal light turns red. The file folder slides off the seat, scattering papers on the floor, when she slams on the brakes. Before, she would have found a safe place to pull over where she could retrieve the papers and return them in an organized fashion to the folder. Now, she just keeps driving. She'll scoop them into a pile when she gets home.

She scans the landscape as she drives. The bare tree branches Bertie enjoys so much at the first of winter, now remind her of ghostly arms grasping for the sky. The snowy fields are still white, but the snow along the side of the road looks dirty and worn. Even the thought of ice skating or ice fishing no longer excites Bertie. She watches the road closely for spots that seem glassy so her tires won't slide on unexpected ice patches.

Since she's become friends with Catalina, Bertie pays attention to the weather in San Diego. In fact, she's loaded the San Diego weather on her phone, and she knows that it will be 65 degrees there today. Thirty degrees warmer than here! Maybe she and Matt should move to San Diego, then she could enjoy nice weather year- round. Before, she would never have considered moving.

Before the dive trip on the Calypso, Bertie believed she would always live in Michigan near her family. After all, it's important that they spend Sundays together like always: brunch with Matt's family, and dinner with hers. It doesn't matter that the menu is always the same or that the conversations follow similar patterns. They're family.

The truth behind Gordon's death shocks Bertie. It still does. She can't imagine her family supporting a decision like the one Gordon made. And she's right. His choice offends their Christian sensibilities when she tells them. Not that they go to church all the time, but they do show up for Easter, Christmas, weddings, funerals and baptisms.

Gordon's death compels Bertie to engage with her family in a different way. She realizes their conversations aren't as deep as she thought. She wonders if it would be possible to have an honest exchange with her parents and her brother. She's not sure that if she were dying, she could be open with her desires like Gordon was with his family.

When her father leaves the table after one Sunday dinner, hitching up his jeans under his Michigan State t-shirt, Bertie follows him down into his basement workshop.

He pauses on the bottom step and turns to look at her. "What are you doing?" he says in mild surprise. His eyes are obscured by the glare from the single light bulb on his wire-rimmed glasses.

"Can't I spend time with my dad?" Bertie says.

He's silent, considering her for a while, then continues down into his workshop, the bald spot on the top of his head reflecting the light. The space below is shadowy at first, lit only by that one bulb in the stairwell. For a moment, Bertie is reminded of the descent on a night dive. She knows not to hold her breath on a descent, but she does now. She feels like something big is about to happen. Then her dad presses a switch, there's a snap, and the room is flooded with light. Bertie exhales. The workshop smells of wood, solder, and some sort of oil.

Bertie looks around the space for a place to sit, and finally dusts off an old rusted stool. She prays it will hold her weight. The workshop is well organized. A bright light is strategically placed over the clean workbench. Tools hang neatly on hooks within easy reach. Bertie's dad pulls out his own stool and settles into work on his current project. At first, Bertie peppers her dad with questions. He answers with grunts, finally switching on a country music station.

Bertie leaves her stool to peer over her dad's shoulder. He appears to be shaping something out of wood. But when Bertie leans too close, he shifts on his stool blocking her view.

After that first Sunday in the workshop, Bertie persists in her efforts to spend time with her dad, following him down on numerous Sundays. Her dad has worked down there alone for years. She hopes it won't take that long for him to accept her presence. She remembers the Bakers, their family jokes and laughter. The life-altering secret they'd shared.

When she tells Matt the frustrating results of her workshop visits, he advises her to give up.

"He is who he is," Matt says. "Just like your mom."

Bertie thanks him for his philosophical advice and perseveres in her efforts. As far as she can tell, Gordon's disappearance hasn't spurred Matt to engage in different ways with his family.

At least her mom is easier to spend time with, if only Bertie could fit into her schedule. Now, that she's retired, her mom is busier than ever with volunteering at the garden club, working out, and taking painting classes through the local school district's adult education program. Her brown hair is cut in a short, easy-to-care-for style, her horn-rimmed glasses are up-to-date, and she favors earrings that dangle. Despite all the working out, her figure is plump. Bertie guesses it must be the cooking classes her mom is taking at the cookware shop in the nearby strip-mall.

"Once you have children," her mom says, "I'll have plenty of time. My friend Susan takes care of little William nearly full time while her daughter works." Bertie's mom pauses in her cooking, or painting, or sketching, holding whatever utensil she's using suspended in the air. "Of course, I won't do that. But I probably could work out something part-time." Then, she smiles at Bertie, blows her a kiss and returns to her project.

Bertie's brother and his wife usually come to dinner every Sunday. But it's difficult to get her brother alone. Finally, Bertie realizes that just because the experience with Gordon changed her, her family is the same as they've always been. The closeness she thought they had was simply a figment of her imagination.

Maybe Matt's been right about her family all along. At least, he's been quiet about it and supportive these past months.

Bertie pulls her car into the garage at home and kills the engine. She loves coming home at night to the cozy two-bedroom cottage she and Matt purchased a couple of years ago. It's one of the smaller homes in an up-and-coming neighborhood of tree-lined streets, only four blocks from the river and not too far from her parent's gabled two-story home, the house where she grew up.

Bertie grabs up the spilled papers, stuffing them back into the folder and her briefcase. She could grow to love another place. Maybe she'll spend some time online tonight looking for jobs in San Diego. She pushes a button, closing the garage behind her and opens the door into the kitchen; the smell of roast pork welcomes her. Matt sits at the kitchen table with his laptop. Sometimes, he can work at home. Despite the weather, he's wearing an old t-shirt, shorts and flip-flops. He looks up with a smile at her entrance.

"Aloha babe," he says.

Bertie beams back at him; she's certain he's checking out dive sites in Hawaii. Suddenly, all's well. Work can wait. Further discussion with her family can wait. She drops her briefcase by the door, steps out of her boots, hangs her coat and scarf on a hook and saunters in her socks towards the table.

Chapter 23

Now that I'm almost done with my latte and I'm fully awake, I resist Judy's efforts to extract details of my dreams. She looks disappointed when I tell her my dreams aren't as frequent.

"I've decided not to talk about them anymore," I say, draining the last of my tea. "Gordon made a choice to take his life. I'm not responsible for his death. I refuse to let him haunt my dreams and my conversations."

I speak firmly as if my tone of voice will not only convince Judy to drop the subject, but also myself. And I do feel the tiniest shifting in the burden I've been carrying since Gordon disappeared last summer. Maybe I can be free of these nightmares someday after all. Maybe I can breathe underwater again someday. Maybe all I needed to do was say the words out loud.

"I'm not responsible," I repeat. "I refuse to let him haunt me."

Judy leans back in her chair. She told me once she was named after the movie actress Judy Garland. I'm only familiar with the actress as Dorothy in The Wizard of Oz. The Judy I know is looking at me now with her brown eyes narrowed. Her brows are pulled into a V pointing at her perfectly straight nose. Her glossy, impossibly jet-black hair is swirled into a messy bun on top of her head. I asked her once if it was dyed, and she said it wasn't. Her brows are the same jet-black, so I suppose the color is possible. A tiny stud sparkles in her nose, matching the two in each ear lobe.

"I have a big paper due at the end of this month," she says. "You know I was hoping to analyze your dreams to prove my hypothesis."

"Haven't I given you enough?" I say.

"You really don't want to talk about them anymore?" she says. I shake my head.

"And you no longer feel responsible?" she says. This time I nod. I wish these movements of my head truly meant that I was free.

She slurps the tiny amount of water left in her cup. "Well, then, I'll figure something else out. I suppose I can write about your cure."

There's a surge in the background noise. A line is forming at the coffee counter. The coffee grinder whirs into action; the air grows more redolent with the smell of coffee. Judy pushes back her chair and stands. "Looks like break's over. You want to catch that movie we talked about?" We agree to text later.

I leave before the lunch crowd. I have a balloon job to set up. Although my mom says this is the busiest time of year, it seems like we've been constantly on the go selling air since I joined her last fall. At first, she and my dad made all sorts of jokes about me being an expert with tanks of air. I pretended to join in the mirth and thanked God when they stopped. I don't need reminders about my work as a dive master.

This afternoon we're constructing a congratulatory arch at the local high school for an awards banquet. Other balloons will decorate the tables. I love setting up balloons at the school because I hope to see Nate.

We met at winter formal, and we've been dating for a few months now.

I was helping my mother set up a much larger balloon arch for the formal when Nate wandered into the gym. He told me later that the boy's lacrosse practice he was coaching was over. He'd heard noises from the locker room and was curious about the sounds.

The arches can be difficult to set up. Most high schools prefer to use a balloon arch built on a metal frame as it's cheaper to fill the balloons with air and attach them to the frame then to fill all the balloons with helium and construct a floating arch. My mom inflated the balloons at home. I helped her transport them in the vans. Despite the preparations, tying the balloons can be time consuming. Nate might have heard me using a few choice words.

The winter formal theme was Under the Night Sky. The committee asked us to build an entry arch of black balloons. Gold balloons representing stars were yet to be hung from the rafters. A large silver moon balloon would be filled with helium for the photo backdrop. My mother's vision was to also add some shooting stars to the mix with a trail of balloons of varying sizes in what's known these days as an organic display. We still had a lot to accomplish when Nate Xavier arrived.

He was wearing long shorts and a hoodie with the high school logo emblazoned across his chest. A tattoo bisected his tanned calf. I couldn't make out the design. His blond hair stuck out from under his ball cap. I would never have pegged him for a chemistry teacher. He looked nothing like my high school science teacher who seemed ancient and who always wore a white collared short-sleeve shirt with pens in his pocket. I learned Nate was new to the campus, having recently been hired when the previous chemistry teacher unexpectedly retired.

"They're trying to get him back," Nate said as he helped us decorate. "So maybe I won't be here too long."

I got a closer look at the tattoo when Nate climbed the ladder. It was an interlocking chain of small x's. I liked the simplicity of it. I also like that he followed my mother's shouted instructions without complaint.

Soon, some members of the decorating committee filtered into the gym, one boy and two girls. The boy wore ripped jeans and a black t-shirt with a cartoon caricature I didn't recognize; the girls wore flannel shirts on top of leggings.

"Hey Mr. X!" the boy yelled when he saw Nate. "Didn't know you liked latex." The three laughed and took pictures with their cell phones of Nate on the ladder. When they caught sight of me, they nudged each other and whispered. Their antics didn't bother me, and Nate descended the ladder in an unruffled manner. After we were done decorating, he caught up with me in the parking lot and asked for my number. It was hard to look away from his blue eyes.

And I haven't tried very hard since.

Today, my mother comments on how slow I'm moving setting up for the awards banquet.

"Hoping to see someone?" she says with a wink.

I blush and return to my work inflating balloons for the tabletop decorations from the tank and twisting them together. I haven't told my parents I'm dating Nate. But my mother's not blind. She probably saw Nate follow me out to the parking lot the last time we were here.

We work in silence for a while. My mother's fingers dance over the balloons she pre-inflated at home, twisting and shaping them into the most fantastical creations. My efforts are definitely clumsier. But I like to think I'm improving.

"I've always been proud of you Catalina," my mother says out of the blue.

Her words catch me off guard. I look at the balloons in my hands, at the scattered ones I've popped that surround me.

"No, not about that," she says. "Although I'm grateful for your help and I love these times we spend together. I'm happy you're pursuing your teaching degree." She considers the balloons she's holding. "I hope it's what you truly want."

I open my mouth to speak. This is the first time we've talked like this. I don't know what's spurred her on today. I'm not sure how to answer her. But before I can say anything, my mother speaks.

"You must have loved scuba diving to be gone so long," she says. "I missed you, of course, but I always knew how happy you were around the ocean."

She ties a weight to the balloon bunch she's holding, and then releases them into the air. They bob and sway at just the right height above the table top. Not too high that they can't be seen by those who will be seated, but not too low so that they disrupt the flow of conversation.

"Maybe you can love teaching just as much," she says.

"I can, and I will," I tell her. I'm fumbling with my balloons; my hands seem to be all thumbs.

"Scuba diving's not a career," I say. "It was time for me to become serious."

My mother shakes her head. "Now you sound like your father. I don't know what brought you home, but I wonder why you no longer even go to the beach."

"I don't have time for it," I say. "Between balloons and studying, my life is full."

She studies my face. I can tell she's waiting for me to say more. I don't, so we go back to our work.

"I used to think I knew you well," my mother says. She starts on another table display. "But I suppose all mothers think that of their babies."

I hate that her voice sounds sad. I'd like to believe she'd understand what happened with Gordon, that she'd still be proud of me. But I'm not ready to take that risk, so I stay silent. When we finish, my mother surveys the room with a satisfied smile.

As we're packing up our gear, Nate appears.

"Want to get dinner?" he asks me.

"Her life is full," my mother says smiling as she leaves for the parking lot pulling the wheeled tank behind her.

"I'd love to," I say.

Chapter 24

Bertie senses a difference in Catalina. Maybe she missed the boat on her own family dynamics all these years, but she believes she knows her friend well. They've talked about personal beliefs and emotions that she's never broached with her family. Catalina feels like someone she's known for years.

She remembers how depressed Catalina was when she first returned to Poway. Then, Catalina talked as if her life was over; she spoke about never enjoying the freedom of being underwater again. How could she? Someone had died on her watch.

Bertie likes to think she's the one who sparked the teaching flame in her friend. Catalina was so knowledgeable about the fish and other creatures in the Sea of Cortez. Why not teach children to share her enthusiasm for the environment? Bertie wasn't surprised when Catalina decided to pursue her masters and get a teaching degree. Now, it sounds like a certain friend could help her get a job.

Bertie smiles thinking about Catalina's new love interest. She remembers when she and Matt were first dating. The passion and excitement of seeing her hunky new boyfriend. Some might think that passion dies with marriage, but that hasn't happened to Bertie. Although, she's been a grump lately with the bad weather. Constant freezing cold and snuggling under heavy blankets is such a turn off for her.

The longest winter ever is not the only thing keeping Bertie down in the dumps. She got a brief lift after talking with Matt about their next dive vacation. She even felt somewhat energized when she perused job boards in San Diego. But she can't help but being bummed out about her family and how they're not cooperating with her newfound desire to go deeper.

But she's not ready to give up. This Sunday, at dinner, she has an announcement that she hopes will demonstrate her own growth. She just needs to find the right moment.

Her mother cooks a familiar dinner of roast beef and baked potatoes. She roasts the accompanying vegetables instead of steaming them. A new method she learned in her cooking class. Bertie is quiet at the dining table while her brother tells the same juvenile story about her first bra that he's told a million times. And, no surprise, her parents laugh, adding their own stories about her awkwardness in middle school. Bertie's smile is indulgent.

She has high hopes for her announcement, but the timing isn't right. Her mother slices her famous apple pie, passes around generous pieces and suggests getting down the old photo albums from the attic. Bertie's parents recently converted the attic into a small bedroom that's easily accessible. Photo albums and memory books line the shelves her father made in his basement workshop.

Bertie's gaze wanders past the window, nothing to see there but wide-snow covered lawns and giant bare trees, to the china buffet that displays the crystal glassware and china her mother only gets out for special occasions. Light sparkles on the wine glasses and champagne flutes from the chandelier overhead. At least twice a month, her mother takes down each glass, wiping the dust with a special cloth so the glass won't scratch. When the family chuckle about Bertie's clumsy youth dies down, Bertie suggests her mother get out the crystal and china for next Sunday's dinner.

"Why not?" Bertie says. "Life's short. Let's treat every Sunday like a special occasion."

This isn't her special announcement. And although she's never thought of asking about the crystal and china before, she thinks it's a great idea. No, it's a fantastic idea. This is a change she believes for a moment her mother might get behind.

But her mother laughs nervously. "That's our wedding china," she says.

"It's beautiful," Bertie says. She's still excited about her idea. "I'll come early and help you get it out."

Bertie looks around the table. Everyone becomes very interested in the crumbs left on their dessert plates, moving the bits about with their forks. The candle her mother lights in the center of the table every Sunday, switching out the color and scent seasonally, starts smoking, spewing fumes of cloves. Her mother wets her fingers and pinches the wick dousing the flame.

"That's a nice offer sweetie," her mother says, "but we're happy using it at Thanksgiving and Christmas."

"Don't forget Easter," Bertie's dad says. He tosses his napkin on the table, and pushes back his chair. Dinner's over and he's headed to the basement.

Despite the chilly reception her spur- of- the- moment suggestion receives, Bertie decides to forge ahead with her planned announcement.

She's talked over her plan to ask her family to call her Bertie instead of Alberta with Matt and Catalina for weeks. Maybe that's the jump start she needs to show her family she's serious about changing things up. She might give up following her father to the basement; she might stop trying to fit into her mother's schedule. They and her brother might still be the same as always. But she's different. She's no longer Alberta.

She hasn't been the same since the Calypso.

Every change starts with a small seed or bulb, Bertie thinks. Just look at tulips. You plant the tulip bulbs underground, and there they stay all winter while the ground freezes. The dirt above them might be covered with snow, but it is still dirt. Underneath, the bulb is changing and growing. In the spring, the ground thaws, and a tulip emerges in glorious and splendid color from that dirty bulb.

Bertie's done with being Bertie on dive trips and Alberta in Michigan. It doesn't matter that her family is frozen ground. She's ready to push through the soil and emerge as Bertie. She's eager for her family to embrace the person she's become.

Bertie inhales a deep breath and speaks in a casual voice before her father can depart using the casual tone she's practiced in front of her bathroom mirror.

"Hey," she says. "I was hoping you all could call me Bertie from now on." She explains how she likes being called Bertie, that the name fits her well, and that she already goes by Bertie on dive trips. Her voice sputters to a stop at her family's reaction.

It feels as if she's dropped a nuclear bomb on the table. Her mother stops clearing the table and stands with her hands full of dirty plates; her brother and his wife stop talking about their boat. Her father, whose mind is clearly already on his latest basement project, stops pushing back his chair from the table so abruptly, it nearly falls to the ground. At her mother's gasp, he grabs for the chair and catches it. He's careful in returning it to its proper position, sliding it just so under the table. He picks up his napkin and folds it.

"Why would I do that?" he says, when the napkin's back on the table. His fingers curl around the chair's carved wooden frame.

"We've always called you Alberta. It's a perfectly wonderful name." He sounds insulted as if she was questioning his name: Albert. "Next thing you know, I'll be asking everyone to call me Bert." He snorts.

Her family piles on, trying to make Bertie feel badly about ditching the name they've always called her. Bertie's mind isn't changed; she's stubbornly quiet, her mouth set in a line, her fingers gripping her napkin in her lap.

Then, her brother reminds every one of the time Bertie asked to be called Princess Leia. Her mother's ready to get the photo album of that Halloween when Bertie dressed as Princess Leia. Only then, does Bertie break her silence diverting her mother by asking about her latest project. Her dad, obviously feeling that it's safe to leave the table, disappears down the basement stairs.

Unfortunately, her mother sets down the plates and pulls pictures from a handy buffet drawer of the baby bonnets her friend knitted for each of her grandchildren, even the ones who live in another state.

Matt squeezes Bertie's hand sympathetically under the table, so that her hand releases the napkin. Bertie's eyes mist at his touch. But before the tears can fall, she grabs her water glass and gulps what's left.

Someday, her father and mother will be gone. They won't vanish into the ocean depths like Gordon, but they will no longer be here to host Sunday dinners. She loves them, but as Matt says, her family isn't going to change. They're happily set in their ways. Bertie's the one with a choice. She can continue to interact with them like always. She can slip into the role of Alberta on Sundays or she can be that brave tulip in the face of resistance.

She fakes a watery smile at the photos. She listens to her mother's gushing. The flow of conversation washes over her. Her heart feels constricted, the tears threaten again.

Afterwards, she and Matt clean up in the kitchen like always. Next Sunday, it will be her brother and his wife's turn to do the dishes. When they're done and all the pots and pans are back in their assigned place, Bertie and Matt bundle up against the cold and say their goodbyes. Bertie can hear the whir of the sander in the basement like always. The smell of sawdust mixes with the lingering scent of the roast. Her mother hugs and kisses her on the cheek.

"See you next week Alberta," her mother says.

Bertie's brother smirks at her before saying his own goodbyes.

Bertie settles into the Volvo with a shiver, pulling her coat tightly about her. Matt sets the Volvo's heater to high as they drive away.

"You've always been Bertie to me," Matt says when they're almost home. "I knew it when we first met."

Bertie can't stop the tears. She dabs at her cheeks with her wool scarf. She wonders how she knew to pick Matt while she was still Alberta.

Chapter 25

This afternoon, Nate is picking me up for what he calls a surprise date. We agreed on a morning meet-up, but he called earlier to push back the time. I'm not a big fan of surprises, but I've been unable to pry the secret out of him. All he'll say is that I should dress comfortably. That means I'm keeping on my black stretch capris from my usual Saturday morning cleaning. I did change my baggy "cleaning" shirt for a cuter top and I combed my hair and put on some makeup.

I look around with a feeling of satisfaction at my freshly vacuumed and dusted studio; even the bathroom and kitchen are spotless. The kitchen window is open, the lace curtains on either side lift in a slight breeze. The studio smells fresh and lemony. I bet I worked about an hour on the entire project, way less than I would spend on changing sheets, cleaning bathrooms and hosing down the dive deck on the Calypso.

Still, sometimes I miss the rolling sensation of the boat, and knowing that the ocean is pulsing like a heartbeat beneath my feet. I miss knowing that when my chores are done I can rest my back against the bow of the boat, smell the salt spray, and consider the horizon.

Nate will be here shortly. I'm ready to go, so I grab my purse and head outside to wait for him under my landlord's birch tree. I'm locking the door when I hear a sound near my feet like the ticking spray of an automatic, rotating sprinkler. The landing by my door is drenched in sunlight; I shade my eyes and look around puzzled. The sound seems to be coming from the small ficus tree beside me. It's louder than the buzzing whir of a grasshopper.

The ficus stands in the center of a blue ceramic pot that's deeper than I can see into from where I'm standing. I step closer and peer into the pot.

It's empty, save for the tree and some dead leaves. The dirt around it looks dry. I haven't watered it in a while. The buzzing sounds again.

Then, I see the coiled rattlesnake backed into the corner just behind the pot. Its forked tongue flickers at me; it's rattles shake a warning.

Startled, I scream. I drop my purse and keys and sprint down the stairs, my heart pounding. At the bottom, I pace back and forth, holding my right palm flat against my chest, taking deep breaths until my heartbeat slows.

Nate pulls up and parks at the curb while I'm still pacing. I don't move towards his Mazda, so he gets out and heads towards me.

"You ready?" he says. I shake my head.

"What's going on?" he says.

"A rattlesnake," I say, my voice rising. "By my front door!"

I realize my hands are empty, that I've left my purse and keys by the ceramic pot. I explain that the snake's in the corner, behind the ficus.

"I've never heard of one climbing stairs," Nate says with a puzzled look.

I stop pacing at his words. I hadn't thought of how a rattlesnake might get up the stairs and behind my pot.

"How did it get there!" I say. My voice sounds somewhat screechy.

I could swim with sharks any day and not be scared, but snakes are in a different category. I remember shrinking back when my landlord showed me the rattler he had decapitated with his shovel. I start towards my landlord's house.

"Where are you going?" Nate says

"To get my landlord," I say. "He can kill the rattler with his shovel."

"That's going to be difficult," Nate says, "given the snake's location."

My hands are trembling. I fold my arms across my chest and hide them in the crooks of my elbows.

"Maybe it will slither away while we're gone," he suggests.

"My purse, my keys, my phone…" I gesture towards the stairs. "I dropped them when I ran."

"I'll get them for you," he says heading towards the stairs.

I put my hand out to stop him. "What if it's left the corner? What if it's on my purse?" I know I'm being ridiculous, but still, I shudder at the thought of a rattler on my personal items. I frantically try to remember if my purse is zipped close. I picture the rattler sneaking into my bag.

"Let's call 911," I implore.

Soon, an animal control truck pulls up behind Nate's sedan. Neighbors walking their dogs, stop and stare at the sight of the truck. My landlord's house is quiet. I had forgotten that he and his wife are on an extended visit to one of their daughters on the east coast. I explain the situation to the animal control officer while the neighbors listen. I assure everyone I wasn't bit. The officer pulls a steel pole with a grabber at the end from the back of his truck along with a deep, metal bucket. Then, he heads up the stairs.

More neighbors and their kids wander over. What seems like a small crowd gathers at the bottom of the steps. Some neighbors crane their necks to try and see the extraction. Others tell stories of rattlers found in the neighborhood.

Very quickly, the officer returns down the stairs. The group parts to let him through.

"Want a look?" the officer asks me, holding up the bucket. The metal amplifies an angry buzzing. I decline, but Nate steps forward to peer into the bucket as do some of the neighbors and their kids.

"It's a good- sized rattler," the officer says. "Unusual to see one at the top of the stairs."

"That's a new one for me," one of the neighbors agrees, others nod. "Lucky you weren't bit."

The officer tells us he'll set the snake free in a canyon. He loads the bucket with the snake and the grabber in the back of his truck, and then he's on his way. I watch the truck disappear down the street hoping the officer will take it easy on the corners so the bucket won't tip over. The neighbors disperse sharing more stories about rattlers they've encountered. You'd think from their stories that the poisonous snakes were lurking everywhere. I shudder and turn away.

Nate goes upstairs to collect my things. I'm still shaky, wondering how that snake ended up by my door. I was wearing headphones all morning while I cleaned, my favorite playlist blasting in my ears. But I think a snake moves quietly so I wouldn't have heard it anyway.

Chapter 26

The latte Nate brought me is tepid by now. He offers to warm it up in my microwave, but I'm not ready to climb back up my stairs just yet. Instead, I thank him for his thoughtfulness, sip the latte and remind him how much I don't like surprises. I use the rattlesnake as evidence

"Trust me," he insists with a grin. "It's no snake. You'll love this surprise."

The sedan's windows are open and the air that blows through the car is aromatic with the scents of early spring: fresh mown grass, citrus blossoms and jasmine. I finally relax, considering Nate. Now that the snake's gone, I'm just now noticing how handsome he looks in a plaid collared shirt. He's freshly shaved, and I imagine kissing him, starting with his smooth cheeks and moving to his lips. The thought warms my cheeks; I lean my head towards the open window and let the breeze play with my hair.

We drive in a comfortable silence without even the radio playing. I like this about Nate. He enjoys the quiet as much as I do. Before I met Nate, scuba diving was as close as I ever got to being with other people in silence. I shut my eyes and picture the Calypso, the wind lifting my hair as it's doing now, the sun warming my skin, the ocean full of possibilities and no snakes. At least not in the Sea of Cortez.

I open my eyes when Nate slows his car and turns a corner. The noise of barking dogs grows louder as we get closer to the shelter, and then pull into the parking lot. I've been in this familiar lot so many times, even some with Nate. I first visited about a month after I'd moved back. I was still living with my parents at the time. They weren't interested in having another dog, but they never said I couldn't adopt one. Still, I wasn't ready to commit. That didn't stop me from dropping by on occasion. Nate and I drove by one day when we were headed elsewhere, and I convinced him to turn into the lot, to peruse the dogs with me just for a little bit. If you want to learn about someone (and you're not on a dive boat), one of the best places to do so is at an animal shelter.

I discovered that Nate likes all kinds of dogs. He doesn't care if they're large, medium or small. He doesn't care if a dog is all black, black with a white chest, spotted, all white or tan. I've always liked bigger dogs. But there was this one medium-sized dog we saw together once that I came close to adopting.

"This is it?" I say when we exit the car. "This is the big surprise?"

Nate grins and refuses to take the bait.

We walk to the shelter, a low concrete building shaded by a ring of eucalyptus. Nate holds the heavy glass door open for me.

"Hi Brenda," I greet the receptionist, tossing my empty latte cup into a trash can. Yes, I know her name. Yes, I've been here that many times without making a commitment and leaving with a dog.

Brenda greets me and Nate. I'm still wondering about the surprise, so I nearly miss the look the two exchange. Before I can wrap my head around what's really going on, Nate opens a familiar door and ushers me inside. It's the door that leads to the kennels. Maybe I was imagining something passing between the two. The barking is loud; the building smells clean and sharp like disinfecting soap. Someone must have recently hosed the kennels down.

We pass a few kennels, stopping to say hello to the excited occupants, and then I see him. The perfect puppy. He's black and tan with one droopy ear and a smile that seems made just for me. His brown eyes light up when I approach, and his tail wags his whole body. He's scruffy, his fur not long, but not short either. Although he's just a puppy, I can tell he'll be smaller than the dogs I usually like. But there's something about him that tugs at my heart. I know without a doubt that I'll adopt today.

"I'm guessing he'll grow to about thirty or forty pounds," Nate says.

And then I notice the sign. He's taken.

My heart drops.

"What's the matter babe?" Nate says. I was moving forward, and now my body's gone still and my shoulders are drooping.

"That dog," I say. "He's so perfect, but he's already taken."

"Maybe he has a sibling," Nate says.

"Maybe," I agree. But I know in my heart, that even a litter mate won't be as perfect for me as this dog. "Maybe the person will change their mind." My voice is hopeful.

"Maybe," Nate says. "But I wouldn't count on it. Look at him. He's smiling." Nate kneels and reaching through the bars, scratches the dog behind his ears. The dog groans with pleasure. A kennel attendant materializes next to us, jangling a set of keys.

"Want to go inside and pet him?" he says.

Nate and I speak at the same time. "Sure," Nate says. "Why bother?" I mumble, knowing my heart will simply be more broken when I can't take this dog home.

The attendant opens the kennel, and Nate steps inside. I hesitate. Nate's already got the dog on his lap, scratching the pup's belly before I enter. The attendant closes the gate but doesn't leave. "Sure is a cute dog," he says.

His words rub salt into my breaking heart. Not only do I want this puppy, but Nate looks so good with it. The dog wriggles out of Nate's lap and comes over to me. I can't help myself, I kneel and give him a good scratching under his chin.

"So, what do you think?" Nate says.

"About what?" I say. I'm still loving on the dog even though I know he's not mine.

"Should we take him?"

I look up. Nate's grinning from ear to ear.

"He's the surprise?" I say, my heart leaping.

Nate nods. I want to smack him good for teasing me, but I can't because the dog is licking my face and I'm laughing and crying at the same time.

"I'll think about it," I say when I finally get my breath.

Nate laughs.

"What are you going to name him?" he asks.

I cradle the puppy's head gently between my hands and stare into his eyes.

"He's Argo, of course," I say, thinking of Odysseus' loyal pup. The one who recognized the disguised wanderer when he returned after long years at sea.

I know I'm supposed to crate train a puppy, but as soon as possible, Argo will be sleeping on my bed. I know he'll chase away any nightmares that come my way. And in return, I'll be sure to keep him away from any snakes.

Chapter 27

If she got a puppy, Bertie would name it something cute like Coco. Too bad a puppy won't help her get a job in San Diego. Although maybe if she did get a puppy and took a picture with it she could use that on her job search profile. People love dogs, and they love people who love dogs.

She broaches the possibility of adopting a puppy with Matt. But he reminds her that if they are serious about moving, a puppy will only complicate things. Bertie rolls her eyes, says "fine" and stomps out of the room. Sometimes Matt is simply too practical.

She gets over her snit fairly quickly though because she knows he's right. There will be plenty of time to adopt a puppy once they move. Then, their puppy can play with Catalina's puppy. It'll be like a play date except without the need for knitted bonnets or diapers.

Throughout the rest of March, Bertie and Matt mull over the possibility of moving. After Easter, they finally decide to go for it. They briefly consider the southeast and Texas before settling on San Diego. The year-round mild temperatures convince them. It doesn't hurt that Catalina lives there.

Both spend some time sprucing up their resumes before plunging into the job market.

Bertie gets a couple of nibbles on her job applications but nothing serious. She feels antsy about it, although Matt points out very logically that most school districts don't hire in the middle of a school year. She notes that it's closer to the end of a school year than the middle, but she agrees Matt's point is well taken. She simply needs to stay calm and remember her yoga breathing. She's eminently qualified. The perfect job will come along at just the right moment.

In the meantime, Matt's getting all sorts of feedback from interested companies. Who knew software engineers were in such high demand in San Diego? Bertie tries to be happy for Matt, but she can't help feeling the teeniest bit competitive about the job search.

When she gets in one of those moods, Matt will challenge her to a board game that she always wins. She suspects he lets her win, but she doesn't mind. She's not *that* competitive! After, her head will be clearer. She'll realize that if Matt gets a job, they can move.

She can always find a job later. Or maybe she can consult. She likes that idea. She pictures flying into a snowy Michigan airport, solving a problem, and then flying back to sunny San Diego where Matt and their adorable puppy Coco are waiting for her.

The two agree they won't let their families know about the job search until a job is securely in hand. And Bertie doesn't remember letting the cat out of the bag about their possible move, but Matt assures her she did at the last family dinner. Her mom isn't too happy with the idea.

"When will I ever see my grandchildren?" she said, cornering Bertie in the kitchen later when she was straightening the damp towel she'd used to wipe the dishes. Her mother had made Bertie's favorite that night, lasagna. The kitchen still smelled of garlic and melted cheese. And although it wasn't Bertie's turn to clean up, she volunteered so she could scrape up and eat the last crispy tidbits in the pan.

"We can visit," Bertie said. "This house is so big. There'll be plenty of room for all of us."

Bertie's mother seemed mollified, no doubt picturing Christmases with the grandchildren in her house. Until Bertie added, "besides, we're not having kids for a long time." At least Bertie knows better than to add "if ever" out loud, even if she was thinking it.

"Don't wait too long," her mother sniffed. "I'm only getting older."

Bertie felt sad to hear her mother talk about getting older.

And she still feels moments of sadness when she thinks about leaving her home state. She knows all too well that life is short. Still, that's the very reason Bertie and Matt are moving and trying something new.

Now, her mother won't stop the grandchildren drumbeat, mentioning it every time they talk. Not even Bertie's suggestion that she and dad will have a free place to stay in San Diego stops her comments. Bertie's dad doesn't say a word about the potential move. Her brother on the other hand doesn't stop talking about the tremendous fishing off the coast of Southern California.

"You don't know anyone in San Diego," her mother will say as if that settles the decision.

"We both know Catalina," Bertie says.

"The dive master?" her mother's voice is incredulous. "You knew her for a week. You've known us your entire life."

A couple of times, Bertie tries to turn her mother's comment into a philosophical discussion about how well the family really knows each other. But the finer points of Bertie's arguments are lost on her mother.

She simply stands with her arms folded until Bertie's done speaking, and then repeats her complaint about never seeing her grandchildren.

Bertie finally learns to be quiet whenever her mother brings up the subject of moving until her mother drops it. Bertie knows her mother believes her silence means they've changed their minds about moving. After all, Bertie continues to drive to the school district each work day; Matt does the same commute he's always done to the office. They still show up for Sunday dinner and sit in the same places they've always sat. Bertie doesn't mention the wedding china or crystal again. She doesn't suggest her family call her Bertie. She doesn't talk about the San Diego weather or beaches.

Her family doesn't need to know that she and Matt have already approached realtors. They've gotten estimates on how much they could ask for their house. They're quietly fixing problems like the leaky kitchen faucet and the scuffed baseboards. Yes, Bertie loves their cottage, but she knows she can love another home as long as she's with Matt.

Bertie nods and listens to her mother talk about her friend's grandchildren without saying a word. She even goes occasionally to the basement with her dad and tries her best to laugh at her brother's dumb jokes about their childhood.

There will be plenty of time for tears and recriminations when the move actually happens.

Chapter 28

I bring Argo with me to the cafe when I go to get my latte. I've seen others on the café's patio with their dogs, and I've dreamed of having one of my own to lay at my feet while I work. Of course, it'll be a while before Argo can do that. He's still an active puppy after all. I carry him wrapped in a blanket in my arms. The vet warned me not to let him socialize with other dogs or to walk on dirt before he gets all his shots. Argo's only had his first set of vaccinations, and I want to make sure he's safe.

I didn't know I could love an animal as much as I love Argo. He kind of reminds me of Yoda, all wrapped up in that blanket with just his face peeking out. Of course, he's much cuter and furry.

He's still fairly small. I'm positive I can juggle both him and my latte at the same time. I've left my laptop at home. I figure this first visit will be simply to familiarize Argo with one of my favorite places. I imagine spreading Argo's blanket out on the patio, so he can safely play while I enjoy my latte.

Judy's working the latte machine when we arrive. The steam rises in her face. She dabs at her upper lip with a napkin, and then catches sight of me with the blanket. Her mouth drops slightly open and her eyes widen. I chuckle, knowing she thinks I'm holding a baby. I turn so she can see Argo's face. She smiles and wipes her forehead with the napkin like she's relieved.

When she slides my latte across the counter, I smile at the heart she's created on the foam.

Later, she comes to the patio where I'm on the blanket playing with Argo. He wasn't about to stay on the small square by himself, so in the interest of his health, I left my chair to join him.

"Hello down there," Judy pokes her head under the table. Argo yips with surprise, and then wags his tail. I scoop him into my arms, so I can sit down in the chair again. Argo wiggles until I flip him on his belly and scratch under his chin. Then, he settles into my lap with a contented sigh.

"Who's this?" Judy says.

"This is Argo," I say, sounding like a proud parent. Then, I coo and babble at the pup like any mom with an infant.

Judy raises her eyebrows. I can't help but laugh at her expression. "I admit it," I say. "I'm smitten."

She shakes her head. She's sipping on one of those sweet drinks with whipped cream people like to think of as coffee.

"I didn't know you like those," I say, making a face.

"I don't," she says, "but my manager wants us to sell more. She says it's good advertising if customers see us with them." She slurps her straw and smacks her lips. "So good," she says smiling around the patio.

"You figure out how the snake got by your door?" Judy asks.

I shake my head.

"Hope it hasn't given you any new nightmares." She peers at me with her brows raised.

I smile. "No, just scared the day of," I say.

"So what's with Argo?" Judy says. "He supposed to frighten away future snakes and intruders?"

My fingers continue to tickle Argo in his sweet spot. "What do you mean?"

"The name," she says. She takes another annoyingly loud slurp of her drink. The whipped cream sinks below the domed top. "I knew you were still having nightmares."

"That's quite a leap," I say wondering how she knows that I'm counting on loyal Argo to sleep by my side and be my protector.

"Is it?" Her smile is enigmatic. She loves playing at being the psychologist. "How's your drink?"

I pause at the abrupt change in conversation. "It's fine, why?" I say. "I don't want one of those if that's what you're suggesting."

Judy laughs and pushes her drink aside. "I think I've had enough of that for now. Tell me about Argo."

So, I tell her all about Nate's surprise and how he's helping me care for Argo.

"Sounds like you *are* in love," she says.

"It's too soon for that," I protest. Nate and I have only been dating for a few months.

"I'm talking about the dog," she says. She winks, swoops up her drink and tosses it in the trash on her way back to work.

Chapter 29

The spring weather is blustery, but Bertie and Matt decide they need to spend a day at the lakeshore, so they bring heavy coats and drive east to Lake Michigan. They've enjoyed many summers together on the lake. Before that, each spent a good portion of their childhood summers cruising around the lake on motor boats or sailboats, fishing and swimming. Bertie can't remember the first time her parents took her out on a boat. But she's seen the pictures of her as a toddler wearing a life jacket. She's not surprised she's smiling in all the pictures.

She's always felt an affinity for large bodies of water.

When there's no time to drive to the lake, Bertie and Matt walk the trails by the tree-lined river that's closer to home.

People sometimes compare the vast lake to an ocean. It has waves big enough to surf. The lake is gorgeous, of course. Bertie wouldn't trade it for anything. Except maybe the warm tropical waters of the Caribbean with its sugar white sand.

Catalina says the Pacific Ocean off the coast of San Diego isn't like the Caribbean or the Atlantic, that some of the beaches can be rocky in the winter but that the sand usually returns in the summer.

"The ocean's not warm in San Diego," she says.

"But people swim in it," Bertie says. "And they surf and scuba dive."

Catalina laughs and agrees. "It's not warm though," she repeats.

Bertie doesn't care. She huddles in her coat next to a deserted picnic table on the small beach by Lake Michigan. The wind whips the waves. She looks out over the restless waters and feels excited about a possible move to San Diego. She can always come back to visit…in the summer. Matt skips some rocks. The stones fly far out beyond the shore bouncing on the lake's surface, three, four, five times. When he's done, the two turn and stroll as far as they can along the familiar lake, the wind whistling about their heads. Bertie's cheeks sting with cold.

Another storm is brewing. Bertie can see it in the clouds gathering and boiling up over the water. The lake reflects the darkening skies, its waters shimmering in tones of silver, dark violet and gun metal gray. She feels exhilarated. She truly is a water person.

She holds her arms out wide and spins until she's dizzy. Then, Matt catches her. He draws her close and they exchange a passionate kiss. She can only imagine what it will be like when they live near the ocean. She hopes they can afford someplace close to the water. She won't care if it's smaller than their Michigan cottage.

Catalina says she's not sure if she'll ever return to the ocean. And Bertie can't believe it. She could no more stay away from a body of water than a moth could from a bright light.

****

Argo is young and can't be in his crate for too long, so Nate invites the two of us for a Saturday morning drive to get coffee. I carry the puppy with his blanket to Nate's car. I'm also juggling a leash, doggie poop bags, dog toys and wipes. Nate offers to help, but I can't figure out what item I could hand over without the rest tumbling to the ground.

Instead, he opens the car door wide for us. "Are you sure you didn't forget anything?" he says, after I dump everything but Argo on the carpet.

He might be laughing at my collection of dog necessities, but his question triggers a memory. "Yes," I say, "his water dish!"

I thrust Argo into Nate's arms and hurry back to my studio, Nate's chuckles following me up the stairs. When I return, water dish in hand, Nate's stroking the top of the puppy's head. Once we're all settled into the car, Nate pulls carefully away from the curb. I'm too busy making sure Argo is comfortable and safe to look out the window. Finally, I notice Nate's driving west and has passed my usual coffee shop.

"We're not staying local?" I say.

"No, there's a new place just opened by the beach I thought we could try," Nate says. When I say nothing, he adds, "You can't avoid the ocean for the rest of your life."

"I've been doing a good job at it so far," I say. "Just think how crowded the beaches would be if everyone in the San Diego area visited them all the time."

"You've got Argo and you've got me," Nate says. "Can we give it a try?"

I shrug and watch out the window as the houses, trees and cars flash by. Argo shifts in the blanket on my lap and I look down at him; he tilts his head so his brown eyes can study my face. For a moment, I think of the sea lion pup that played with Gordon, and the way the ocean helped Gordon to betray me. My arms tighten around Argo. I'm not confident I'm ready to forgive the surging waters.

But surely the cafe isn't on the beach. Argo can't be exposed to the possibility of other dogs running loose on the sand. The pup wriggles and sits up. He sticks out his tongue and wets my chin in a frenzy of licking until I'm laughing.

Nate's right, I can't spend my life avoiding something that's so huge. I don't live in the Midwest like Bertie. I'm not like those San Diegans who never go to the beach. I never have been.

A love of water – in particular the ocean- is embedded deep in my soul. And if I'm honest, part of the reason I've not been myself since my return is the fact that I've cut off something essential to my well-being. I've thought I could get along just fine without the ocean. But maybe my nightmares these past months would have vanished a long time ago if I had only spent some time with my feet in the water.

I snuggle with Argo, my cheek pressed against his. "I'm game," I say.

Nate turns on the radio and we sing along to the U-2 song "I Still Haven't Found What I'm Looking For." I smile when Nate launches into the next song "Halo" by Beyonce. We sing until the Mazda exits the freeway and Nate looks for parking near the hip new coffee locale. I've brought a pad for Argo to do his business on. When he's done, I wad it up in a bag and throw it in a nearby trash.

The new shop has a distant view of the bluffs and the ocean across the lagoon, the train tracks and the coast highway. The lagoon wanders among lush yellow and green grasses that grow wild and bright under the spring sun; a snowy egret stands lazily in the sparkling water. I imagine it's snoozing between meals.

I can smell the salt water and feel the moisture on my face, whether both are from the lagoon or the ocean, I don't know. There's a whoosh as a train speeds by headed south; we're too far from the beach to hear the waves.

When Nate selects a stool at the bar overlooking the view, I don't protest. I perch on the stool next to his with Argo on the blanket at my feet. My soul feels like its expanding, drawn to the water, much as I imagine Odysseus was when he left Ithaca (little knowing he would be gone for twenty years.) The vow I made after Gordon's disappearance to never return to the ocean seems a little bit silly all these months later. A single cloud that looks like a heart drifts towards the bluffs.

"This isn't so bad," Nate says. He's wearing long shorts and a t-shirt, a Chicago Cubs cap shades his eyes, but when he turns to me, I get lost in wondering which is bluer, the lagoon, the ocean or his eyes?

"What?" he says. The hint of a smile teases his lips as he leans in to kiss me. I'm breathless when Argo yips. He's managed to tangle his leash around the legs of my stool. I unwind the pup thinking life is pretty amazing. Why should I deny myself the first love of my life because of Gordon's choice?

"You ever thought about scuba diving in San Diego?" I say

Chapter 30

I drop Argo off with Nate. He's on spring break and volunteers to watch the pup. He sets up Argo's crate, according to my instructions, and listens carefully while I explain about feeding and walking him. I hand him a typed list. Nate raises an eyebrow at the list, but says nothing. He sets the paper on the kitchen table.

Then, he shoos me out the door. "Have fun and don't worry about Argo," he says. Argo is on his back, paws waving in the air while Nate scratches his belly when I leave.

Judy and I are planning a hike up Iron Mountain, just east of Poway. Argo is still on restriction, not having finished all his vaccinations yet. Also, the hike would be too difficult for a pup. Judy suggested the hike as a way for us to clear our heads before finals.

"You can only drink so much coffee," she said over the whirr of the coffee grinder at the shop.

"Isn't that sacrilegious?" I said, opening my eyes wide and pretending to look around for Judy's manager. Judy shrugged her shoulders and handed me my drink.

I swing by Judy's apartment building in my ten-year-old Toyota Corolla to pick her up. Judy shares a two bedroom with another woman who I've briefly met. She seems like a nice person, but Judy doesn't spend much time with her. Judy says she's too busy working and studying to hang out with her roommate. She can't wait for the day when she can live by herself like I do.

"I thought I wouldn't have to worry about money," she says, "but, as you know, the unexpected happens and there you are."

She talks airily about family conflicts and not seeing eye-to-eye on things, but she insists she's happy to be making it on her own and "learning what I'm made of."

This morning, Judy's wearing running shoes and shorts and a t-shirt from a Chicago 5K.

"I didn't know you were from Illinois," I say.

"Oh this?" Judy looks down at her shirt. "I got it at a local thrift store." She twists to look in the back seat. "Where's Argo?"

"He's too young for a seven-mile hike," I say.

"Is it that long?" Judy settles back in her seat, laughing. "Hope I can make it."

It's a weekday, so I'm surprised the parking lot's nearly half full. There must be a lot of people on spring break who got an earlier start than we did. We set off at a good pace up the tree-lined path. Soon, we're climbing up a dirt trail, winding through scrub-brush. I watch carefully for rattlesnakes. They could be nestled in any number of rocks or even slinking across the trail.

Judy forges ahead, treading lightly up the stone stairs we traverse. It doesn't seem as if she's checking underneath each step like I am. So far, I've seen lots of lizards sunning on boulders but no snakes. Hikers pass us headed back down the hill, and no one warns of a rattlesnake sighting, so I begin to relax a little.

At the top of a knoll, we pause and drink some water from the bottles we're carrying. The view to the east expands before us now that we're higher. Rolling hills and distant mountains are hazy outlines in the mid-morning light.

"Have you thought more about your plans after you finish this semester?" I say.

"Not really," Judy says. "I like to give my all to whatever I'm currently working on. I've always been like that."

"Makes it tough to plan ahead."

"Now you sound like my mom," Judy says. "Besides, you drifted for a while."

"That I did."

We continue up the trail that winds through scrub brush and tumbles of rocks and boulders. Judy sets a blistering pace.

"Are you sure you didn't run that 5K?" I ask. "I didn't know you were in such great shape." The sun is hot on my neck. My armpits are damp, my t-shirt sticks to my lower back. I can feel a line of sweat trickling down my sports bra between my breasts. I'm happy we started up the trail in the morning. I can't imagine tackling it in the afternoon heat.

Judy slows down and laughs. "I come from hardy outdoorsy stock," she says. "We were always going on some adventure."

"We never did much hiking," I say.

I'm puffing and feeling out of breath on the final switchbacks to the top of the mountain. We pass a boulder that's taller than us; there's a brief puddle of coolness as we walk through its shadow. As we climb higher, the trail is rockier, the vegetation sparser. "We spent just about every weekend at the beach," I say on an exhale.

"Don't tell me you laid around on a beach towel all day," Judy says.

"Hardly," I say. "I was usually in the water."

We're silent for a while passing by hikers who are descending. We stand aside for hikers and their dogs that are moving at a faster pace uphill. I listen to the inhale and exhale of my breath and feel the pounding of my heart in my chest.

At the top, I take a single deep breath and exhale on a cough when a breeze stirs up some dust. The peak offers a 180 -degree view of the surrounding area; not only can we see the hills and mountains to the east, we can also see the dusty outline of downtown San Diego in the southwest, some other groupings of office buildings further northwest and the blurred outline of the western coast of the Pacific where I spent so many summers. The ocean is a thick bluish outline that's difficult to distinguish below the lighter blue sky almost as if an artist used the same paint color but applied a thicker coat to the water.

"Do you ever miss it?" Judy asks. We're both looking at the coast, and I know instinctively she's asking about the ocean.

"I thought I wouldn't, but lately I've thought about getting in the water again." I touch the sea-star shape of the pendant nestled under my t-shirt. I retrieved the necklace this morning from its small pouch where I stashed it after I left the Calypso. Just feeling the shape, I can picture strapping on my gear and breathing underwater.

"Would you scuba dive?"

"I might." My voice sounds wistful. I drop my hand from my necklace.

We settle on a boulder and stare at the western horizon in silence, taking sips of water and eating the energy bars we've brought. The wind cools my sweat, and I shiver.

"Guess you have recovered from those nightmares after all," Judy says.

I look at her puzzled as to why she's brought up the subject of my dreams.

"I know this is supposed to be a break, but I can't stop thinking about my paper," she says. "I'm going to have to redo it. Ugh." She pushes up from the rock.

"Let's go," she says. "I have some work to do."

Chapter 31

Catalina is worried when Bertie talks to her that night. Argo is sick. He's been vomiting and has had diarrhea for a couple of days. She turns her phone's camera so Bertie can see the dog. The puppy's shivering and his eyes look like one of those waifs on a water-color card you see at the gift shop.

"Why is he shivering?" Bertie says. "It's not cold there is it?"

Catalina says it's not. "I tried giving him some cooked rice," she says. "But he won't even eat that."

"Take him to the vet," Bertie says. "Right now."

She's decisive like that. Besides the puppy looks terrible. In the last video chat she had with Catalina, the puppy was playful, chewing on his rubber bone, participating in a tug-of-war with a rope. His eyes were bright. He even put his wet nose right up to the camera. The difference is obvious to Bertie, but maybe the change has been subtler to Catalina who sees the pup every day.

"Really?" Catalina says.

"Go," Bertie urges her.

Catalina thinks she can make it to the vet's office before it closes. The two disconnect with a promise from Catalina to keep Bertie informed about Argo's condition.

When her phone rings on her bedside table after midnight, Bertie picks up. It's Catalina. Bertie leaves Matt sleeping and tip-toes to the bathroom where she sits on the closed toilet seat lid for a whispered conversation.

Argo is staying overnight at the vet clinic. He's being treated for Parvovirus. Catalina explains it's a disease that can kill in days if left untreated. But the vet thinks she can save the puppy. Still, there's a ten- to-fifteen percent chance he won't make it. Catalina's voice breaks when she shares the statistic, Bertie can barely understand her friend when she thanks her for urging an immediate trip to the vet.

Bertie brushes aside the thanks and focuses on the statistics. "That means there's an 85 to 90 percent chance he'll live," she says in a fierce whisper. "Sounds like pretty good odds to me."

"I was so careful," Catalina says.

Neither one mentions Gordon, but given their shared history, Bertie knows Catalina is wondering if she was as careful as she imagines.

"I know you did everything the vet told you," Bertie says. "You're a good owner."

"Argo could have gotten the virus from one of his litter mates," Catalina says. "He could have already had it when I adopted him." Her voice is hesitant. "Or maybe Nate wasn't as careful. He watched him for me the other day."

"There's no sense in worrying about it," Bertie advises. "Try to get some sleep, and when you wake up in the morning, I bet Argo will be fine. Do you have any sleeping pills?"

Catalina says she never takes them.

Matt opens the bathroom door, yawning. "What's going on?"

Bertie shushes him. She turns towards the gray- tiled shower, pressing her phone closer to her ear. She speaks quietly to Catalina, and then, when Catalina disconnects, Bertie prays Argo will live to see another day. She doesn't know if Catalina can handle another death within the space of nine months.

When Bertie swivels back, Matt still hovers in the doorway looking like a confused zombie with sleep-heavy eyes and wild hair. He scratches his face, his fingertips sounding like sandpaper on his unshaven cheek.

"What's the emergency?" he says, yawning again.

"Catalina's puppy might die."

"Seriously?" Matt studies her, and then does a U-turn. Bertie hears him shuffling back to bed.

Since she's already up, Bertie takes the opportunity to use the toilet. After she washes up, she applies a thick layer of lavender scented cream to her hands and neck. Maybe she should have suggested Catalina put some lavender under her pillow to help her sleep. She considers calling her friend back, but the pull of bed is strong.

Bertie switches off the bathroom light and feels her way across the darkened bedroom, thinking about what Catalina said about Nate. Bertie can't imagine that Nate would do anything on purpose to hurt Argo. She's never met him, but from what Catalina has told her, she thinks he sounds like a great guy.

"Why would someone help you get a puppy only to kill it?" Bertie says climbing into bed.

"They wouldn't," Matt mumbles.

Bertie snuggles next to her husband under the covers, pressing her head into his shoulder. The night is cool, and she's chilled from talking to Catalina in the bathroom. The skin on Matt's arm is still cold from his venture to the bathroom, but his body is warm.

"You're right you know," Bertie says into his chest. Matt wears an old college t-shirt to bed with his boxers; the material is soft after years of washing.

"About what?" Matt's voice is sleepy.

"Getting a puppy," she says. "Catalina says it could cost more than a thousand dollars to save Argo."

"When we get a puppy, we'll spend the money to keep it alive," he says. "But money requires working and working requires a clear head so I'm going to sleep now." He pulls the covers further up his shoulders, turning so that his back is to her.

Bertie sighs. Despite the lavender on her hands and neck, she doesn't think she'll be able to sleep well until she knows Argo is ok.

Chapter 32

I pull open my door at the knock expecting to see Nate. Last night, I called him from the vet clinic while I was waiting alone for the test results. I couldn't stop my mind from going to terrible places while I sat on the molded plastic chair in the waiting area that smelled of antiseptic despite the lavender scent dispenser plugged into the nearby wall. I couldn't bring myself to look at the cute photos of happy puppies and kittens on the walls.

Nate didn't answer his phone. So, I kept staring at the floor until the vet called my name. Her words were a blur. I told her to save Argo no matter what. I'd figure out how to pay the bill later.

I was already home when Nate called back. I'd already stepped inside my too quiet studio. I'd already looked at the scattered dog toys with tears in my eyes. I told him not to come over. I told him I was exhausted.

But the truth was, I couldn't stop thinking about whether he'd been careful enough with Argo. It was easier to blame Nate than to think once again my own careless actions might lead to death.

This morning when he called and asked if he could come over, I said he could. I was thinking more rationally by then because the vet contacted me earlier and said Argo would survive. It took a while for her words to sink in. But when they did, I danced around the kitchen, holding my phone to my chest.

I'm going to have to sanitize or discard all of Argo's toys and blankets. The carpet will need a steam cleaning as well as all the furniture. Nate can help me. The cleansing can be an act of atonement we can share.

Now, I step lightly to the door already making a mental list of cleaning supplies and new dog toys and blankets. When I open it, Judy is standing on my landing.

"What are you doing here?" I say. Judy's holding paper coffee cups. Steam rises from the tiny hole in the plastic lids.

"Home delivery!" Judy sings out as she hands me one of the cups. I can smell the Latte through the hole.

"Do we have plans?" I say. If we did, I've forgotten them in the rush to the vet and the worry about Argo. I didn't sleep much last night. I'm sure Judy will understand that I'm just not up to any physical activity today.

"Can't a friend stop by with a latte?" Judy says.

"Aren't you supposed to be at work?" I'm still standing in the doorway, confused. I haven't taken a drink yet from the cup that's warming my hand.

"I took the morning off," she says. "Can't you see these are from another shop?"

I hadn't noticed the difference, but now that I look more closely, I can see the logo on the side of the cup is different.

"Can I come in?" she says.

I step aside with an apology. Judy comes into the kitchen and settles at the table. "Try it," she says. "I bet it's not as good as mine."

I leave the door ajar for Nate and take a sip. "Is this some sort of psychological experiment?"

She laughs. "Where's the rug rat? I brought him a treat." She shakes a white paper bag.

"Argo's in the hospital," I say sinking onto a chair at the table. "He almost died."

"But you brought him to the coffee shop just the other day," Judy says. "He looked fine."

"This came on fast." I fill Judy in on what's been happening with the puppy over the last few days. I remember that he had a slight case of diarrhea the morning I left him with Nate. Nate said it wasn't that uncommon in puppies. But the fact that he might have already been sick makes me feel better. Maybe he did have the virus when I adopted him at the shelter.

"Nate's been helping you with Argo?" Judy says. She looks pensive. "Maybe he took the puppy somewhere he shouldn't."

I shake my head, setting aside my cup. I've already drunk the full pot of coffee I made this morning, and I feel somewhat jittery. I cross my legs and bounce my bare right foot.

"Why would he do that?" I say.

Judy purses her lips. "Why do you think he wouldn't?" She pauses then adds, "I'm just glad you didn't have Argo when that rattler turned up at your door.

"I can only imagine Argo sticking his nose into that corner and the rattler sinking its fangs in. He'd be dead for sure." She shivers and pushes the latte towards me. "It's getting cold."

Before I can tell her that I can't drink any more coffee or my head will explode, Nate knocks and comes into the kitchen through the unlocked door.

Judy's words are still rolling around in my thoughts. Her comments about the rattler remind me how I nearly got bit. I still step carefully when I leave my studio. I've never figured out a good explanation for how the poisonous snake got upstairs.

Out of the blue, I remember how Nate postponed our date from morning to afternoon on the day the rattlesnake showed up. Allowing plenty of time for the snake to mysteriously appear on my door step. I think about his offer to watch Argo, and I can't help but look at him suspiciously.

"Hi Nate," Judy says. Her voice is welcoming as if she's greeting a good friend rather than someone she was just casting doubt on.

I lean back in my chair and finger my latte. My thoughts are racing, and my welcome is muted.

Chapter 33

"Great news!" Bertie says when I tell her how well Argo is doing. I've decided to juggle my schedule, so he will be solely under my care until he gets his last shots which will be next week. Bertie applauds my decision. I'll be making payments on my credit card for a long while but I can't imagine paying for anything more important than keeping Argo alive.

"Did you get a haircut?" I say squinting at the video screen on my phone. I'm sitting on my bed while we talk. Argo is tussling with one of his new toys next to me. "You look different."

Bertie laughs. "I got some highlights. Now that we're moving to California I thought I'd get a jump start on the sun."

"You're moving? You got a job?"

"Matt did." Bertie is all smiles. "We're moving at the end of May."

"Woohoo!" I'm excited my friend will be close by. Argo yips and jumps on me, caught up in my exclamation of joy. I tell him no and ask him to lay down. Instead, he darts around the bed in circles. What can I say? I have a lot of work left to do with the dog training.

When Argo finally calms down, his little pink tongue hanging out of his mouth, Bertie fills me in on the details of Matt's new job, She hopes to land a job once they get to San Diego.

"So dust off your scuba gear," Bertie says, "we can spend some time underwater together before I get a job."

"I might." I say.

I actually feel excited about the idea of showing Bertie the sights off the San Diego coast. Maybe we should start with the kelp beds near La Jolla Cove. Kelp forests are rare, and we have one of the few in the world just off our coast. I know Bertie will love swimming amongst the swaying, green kelp stalks. I smile thinking about her reaction when I tell her the water is a "warm" 64 degrees.

"Maybe Nate can come too," Bertie says. I can tell she's probing for information. I haven't talked about Nate much lately. In the past, I told her he's a diver. I might have mentioned that we talked once about diving off the coast.

"We'll see." I change the subject to possible locations where Bertie and Matt can live in the San Diego area. I'm not ready yet to dissect my feelings for Nate with Bertie.

All I know right now is that my feelings for Nate have cooled in the wake of my doubts surrounding the rattlesnake and Argo incidents. Maybe I was moving just a little too fast with him. There's no reason we need to continue full speed ahead.

I can't easily forget how the Bakers' abused my trust. I'm still a little gun shy when it comes to relationships.

Nate did apologize profusely for anything he might have done to trigger Argo's brush with death. He even offered to help pay for the vet bill. I thanked him and declined. I accepted his apology, but I couldn't stop from wondering if he was being sincere.

I hate my skepticism and doubt, but for now, I think I'll just let it be.

I did ask him to help me sanitize my living space. He agreed and cleaned with a diligence that reminded me of my days on the Calypso working with the boat crew to get the ship ready for the next set of divers. Who knew Nate could mop a floor so well or steam a couch? I vacillated between admiring his form and blaming him that we had to do this work in the first place.

My parents want to know when I'm bringing Nate to dinner. I tell them we're not to that stage yet. I bring Judy instead, and we all have a good time talking about movies and laughing while she psychoanalyzes my family. When it's time to leave, she hugs my mom and then my dad. Her eyes are all wet and glittery when we leave.

"What's with the tears?" I say on the way to my car. Argo trots beside me on his leash. He's gotten all his vaccinations so he's good to go anywhere with me. I open the door to the backseat where I've set up his crate with his blanket, and he jumps in.

Judy brushes the moisture away with her fingertips. "You're lucky to have both your parents," she says.

I look back at the house where I grew up; light spills from the kitchen window. I imagine my parents cleaning up together after dinner. Maybe dancing to some music on the little speaker they have in the kitchen for their phones. And I know she's right. I am lucky. I'd forgotten how lucky all those years I was gone chasing water and air and the sight of another unusual underwater creature

I pat her shoulder because she's told me of the rift in her family, and then, I drive her home. Judy compliments my parents talking about the delicious meal, the homey atmosphere, and the obvious love they have for each other. Then, she shifts her comments to Bertie.

"You must be excited your friend is moving here," she says, staring out the window. "She was in the dive group with you and Gordon?"

"You'll like her," I say, smiling at the thought of Bertie, ignoring her reference to Gordon. "She can be a little off-putting at first, but you'll discover you can't resist her."

"Hmmmm," Judy mumbles.

I can tell from her tone and her averted face, she's still down about her family. Sometimes, she gets in these glum moods that I've learned are impossible for me to break. There's nothing I can do but trust she'll emerge eventually. And I'm in too good a mood for her to get me down tonight.

Still, I'm sad for her when I watch her walk into her apartment building alone, knowing her roommate is gone on a business trip. I hope she won't spend the night brooding and that she'll watch that romantic comedy she mentioned she might.

I spend the next few hours at home studying for an upcoming exam and working on another draft of a paper that's due soon. Argo sleeps on his blanket near me. I'd still be sitting at my computer except Argo's ears perk up, and he runs to the door with a yip. It's the first time I've heard him bark. And I don't know who's more surprised, me or him.

"What is it boy?" I say.

He yips again, so I stand from the chair where I've been perched all this time. The kitchen window is open. I signal for the puppy to quiet down while I listen at the window, leaning over the sink.

I think I hear the soft tread of footsteps descending the stairs leading to my apartment. But then, the breeze picks up and the leaves in the tree just outside make a clicking rustle. I can't be sure if the footsteps were real or simply my imagination.

Argo is quiet. He trots to his water dish where he noisily laps some water.

"You probably need a walk," I say. The puppy looks at me and wags his tail.

Still, I wait a while longer before leaving my studio, slowly putting on my shoes and gathering Argo's leash. All the time I'm listening, waiting to see if Argo will bark at the door again. I've never seen a rattlesnake at night, but still, I worry about another one on my doorstep.

Argo doesn't bark, so I pull on a light sweatshirt, sliding my cell into a pocket along with the dive light I use as a flashlight. When we step outside, I immediately shine the light into the corner behind the ficus. The area's empty except for some dust and a spider web.

It's chillier out than earlier, and I'm glad for the warmth of my sweatshirt. We start around the block; it's a short twenty- minute route that I've seen other neighbors walk with their dogs. It's late. I checked the time on my cell before we left. But my neighborhood is safe. I've walked around this block at later hours when Argo wasn't fully vaccinated and needed to avoid other dogs.

Most of the houses are dark; there's the glow of a T.V. screen in a few windows; porch lights are on here and there. Shadowed sedans and small pickups are parked in many driveways and along the street. The neighborhood is quiet except for the occasional breeze in the trees, and the owl that often hoots as we turn the corner. Argo is busy sniffing light posts, bushes and trees. I'm thinking about my exam when we turn the last corner before my studio.

Somewhere in the recesses of my brain, I recognize the soft creak of a gate's hinges. I notice the movements of a dark figure out of the corner of my eye, and then a large shape comes barreling towards us with its teeth bared.

Chapter 34

Bertie's family has lived in Michigan since her great-great grandmother was a baby. According to family lore, the Mayers were among the first to farm in the area. Her mother has done all the genealogical research and has documents proving the migration of both sides of the family to this specific area. Family ties are very important to the Mayers. Very few have left for other states. In fact, Bertie can't really name those who have left. But maybe that's because no one talks about them once they do.

Bertie remembers an awkward family reunion one summer when a smaller (or as her mother would say wayward) branch of the family showed up from Oregon. They had migrated just a little bit too far west. Bertie doesn't remember ever seeing that family again. Although she might have seen pictures on Christmas letters. She wonders if her mother is friends with them on Facebook now. She's afraid to ask. The relatives might have just posted pictures of grandchildren.

In any case, Bertie's not looking forward to telling her parents about the impending move. She supposes she should at least tell them before the *For Sale* sign is staked on their front lawn. One of her mother's friends might happen to drive by and tell her about it. Her mother and father haven't been to Bertie and Matt's for a while. The two have been too busy looking for jobs and getting rid of stuff to host a get together. And after the initial leak that they were thinking about moving, both have stayed quiet. It's easier that way.

Matt's parents won't be too happy with the move either. Bertie thinks the Clarks can also trace their family roots back a few generations to Michigan. At least Matt will have the pleasure of telling them. She wishes she could talk him into telling her family as well. Maybe she could convince him of his expertise in sharing the news if he tells his parents first. He'll have practice at it after all.

Bertie wishes they could simply leave as if they're going on vacation. But that wouldn't be fair. Her parents are the ones who raised her, and she knows they love her. She tries to put herself in her mother's shoes, imagining her daughter telling her she's moving to another city more than two thousand miles away. Bertie tears up at the scenario, and she doesn't even have a daughter.

"How can I possibly do this to my parents?" she says to Matt as they drive another carload of stuff to the Goodwill trailer that's parked behind the local supermarket.

"Babe," Matt says. "This is a decision we both made. We're excited, remember?"

Bertie stares out the window at the newly green lawns, the bright leaves popping out on the trees and the blue sky. "That was in the winter," she says.

"Close your eyes," Matt says. Bertie closes her eyes. "Think of the gray skies, the snow, the ice and the bare branches."

Bertie shivers, but opens her eyes just in time to see a particularly breathtaking display of tulips in someone's front garden. She sighs.

"We can go diving in our own backyard," Matt says. "We can wear sandals and shorts year- round. Goodbye snow boots, wool hats and scarves."

There's a bag full of the aforementioned objects in the trunk.

Matt picks up Bertie's hand. "We're going to love it," he says.

Bertie leans her head back against the seat rest. She knows he's right. She's been wanting to move for months. They had an extra special celebration when Matt got his new job. She blushes and gets all hot just thinking about it. She squeezes his hand.

"I'm just nervous about telling my parents," she says.

"Let's go by right now," Matt says.

"Looking like this?" Bertie's hair is piled on top of her head in a messy bun. She's wearing yoga pants and her finger nails are chipped. Matt hasn't shaved yet, his jeans are ripped and his feet are thrust into scuffed loafers.

"Sure, why not?" Matt turns the car around. "We'll go to my parent's house first. Get some practice in before we face yours."

"Since you'll be so good at it, with the practice and all," Bertie says. "You can tell my parents as well."

Matt laughs. "Not on your life."

Matt's parents look like they've just gotten out of bed. Both are in robes; his dad's unshaven; his mom's face is free of makeup. They invite Bertie and Matt into the kitchen for coffee. They take the news well. They wish Bertie and Matt good luck on the next chapter in their lives, clinking their University of Michigan coffee mugs together. Bertie is certain their good cheer is due to the fact that Matt is one of four siblings, and his brother and sisters are all still in town, not to mention at least three grandchildren. Plus, Matt's the second boy so he's never gotten much attention, especially once his younger sister arrived.

Bertie freshens up as best she can in the powder room at her in-laws. She dabs at her armpits with a piece of tissue. She straightens her bun, smooths her yoga pants and applies her favorite lip balm that she's dug out of her sweatshirt pocket.

She drums her fingers on the car door on the way to her parents' house. Matt suggests she text them before they drive over, and make sure they're home. Bertie rolls her eyes. Her parents are always at home. At least her dad always is; Bertie can't remember a weekend when he wasn't puttering around the yard or in his workshop, especially this early in the morning.

Bertie imagines her mother working peacefully in her garden as usual, tending to her roses, talking to the flowers like they're her babies. She tells Bertie its good practice for being a grandmother. But she's been doing it for as long as Bertie can remember. Surely, she hasn't been hoping for grandchildren Bertie's whole life?

"What's that babe?" Matt says.

Bertie doesn't realize she spoke out loud. "Just practicing my speech," she says. She pictures her mother rising from her flower bed, her garden hat shading her eyes, her trowel tipped with fresh soil in her hand, her lips open in shock. Bertie groans.

Matt pats her leg. "Almost there," he says.

When they pull into the drive, the living room curtains are still drawn. "I hope they're ok," Bertie says. True, they haven't been to her parents' house early on a Saturday for quite some time, but Bertie is thrown off for a moment. The sight doesn't line up with her memories of early Saturdays, her parents always getting a jump on the day and the weekend chores.

Her mother opens the curtains as they walk up the brick path to the door. She looks surprised and then pleased. Bertie knows her mother thinks they're showing up unannounced because they have other big news. Her stomach clenches. The front door swings open before they reach it.

Chapter 35

My neighbor's dog, a huge mixed-breed, lunges towards us. I step in front of Argo, reach into my pocket for the dive light and whack Rocket on the nose. While he's shaking his head, I switch the light on and shine it directly in his eyes.

"Rocket!" I say in a firm voice. "Go home!"

Rocket stops growling, but doesn't head for home. Instead, he stands with his lips drawn back over his teeth. In the bright light, I can see the saliva glistening on his fangs. The skin on his snout is wrinkled; the hair on the back of his neck is ruffled.

I can't remember his owner's name. But I do remember that his owner is always careful to move to the other side of the street while on walks; that his owner is meticulous about keeping Rocket safely in his yard. I don't know how he escaped. I can't see his owner, but I don't dare take my eyes or my light off Rocket's face.

"Come get your dog!" I yell.

I hear running footsteps cross the street, a car door slamming and the noise of an engine starting up. I want to know who let this dog out, but still, I'm afraid to swing the light away from Rocket.

"Come get your dog!" I shout again. I hear Argo growl behind me. I fear a dog fight that my pup, who weighs little more than twenty pounds, will surely lose.

I start walking backwards towards my studio, keeping Argo behind me. The detached garage I live above was so close when Rocket approached. I risk a glance behind me. The light in my studio shines a welcoming glow of safety. I don't know how I'll make it up the stairs, but for now, I'm concentrating on keeping my footing on the sidewalk. If I trip, both Argo and I could be bitten as I plan to throw my body over the pup as a shield.

Rocket surges forward, attempting to sneak behind my legs and get to Argo. My puppy yips and growls. I hit Rocket on the nose again with the heavy light. This time, I shove him away with the ball of my foot.

I swing the light back around so that it's shining in his eyes. Rocket stays his distance, but starts barking; deep, sharp barks that thrum in my ears and remind me of the male sea lion we encountered underwater that time on the Calypso.

I can barely hear running footsteps over the noise Rocket is making. This time, the footsteps are coming towards me, slapping hurriedly on the pavement. I hear someone shouting Rocket's name. The dog's head swivels, and he peers into the darkness. Another shout and Rocket bounds out of the circle of my light.

I'm frozen in my defensive stance, my light still shining on the now vacant spot where Rocket stood mere seconds ago. My ears still ring with the sound of his barks. Finally, I move the light towards the street.

Rocket's owner is snapping a leash on the dog. I can hear him scolding Rocket for scaring me. The dog wags his tail, his tongue lolls out of his mouth.

The owner shields his eyes with his hand. Only then, do I lower my light.

"Are you okay?" he calls from the middle of the road. "I'm sorry Rocket scared you. I don't know how he got out."

I say nothing. I'm still shaken from the encounter. I train the light on Argo, running my hands over his fur and his snout to make sure he's ok. Nothing seems amiss, so I tell the neighbor we're fine.

We head home climbing the stairs to my studio where I firmly shut and lock the door behind us. When he's free of the leash, Argo trots to his water dish. He then jumps up on my bed and promptly falls asleep.

My heart is still racing. I set the dive light and my cell on the kitchen counter then strip off my sweatshirt. I run a washcloth under warm water and hold it to my face until I feel calmer. Only then do put on my pajamas and crawl into bed.

My dreams morph into nightmares where I'm the one being blinded by a dive light and I can do nothing to protect my puppy from certain death. The nearby howls of coyotes celebrating a kill weave in and out of my consciousness. It's difficult for me to separate reality from illusion.

I wake up sweating, my sheets tangled around my legs, Argo pressed to my side. My hair is damp on my neck. I stumble into the kitchen for a glass of water. It's a long while before I can fall asleep again.

In the morning, my neighbor climbs the stairs to my apartment and knocks on my door. When I answer, he introduces himself.

"I wanted to make sure your puppy is all right," he says. I step aside so he can see Argo is perfectly fine. The pup is in the kitchen where he's busy chowing down his breakfast. When he's done, he dashes to the door with his tail wagging. My neighbor bends to scratch behind Argo's ears.

"Someone messed with my gate last night," he says, standing again. "I found a large rock holding it open. It was only a matter of time before Rocket got loose."

I remember the footsteps and the sound of the creaking hinges before Rocket appeared. Was someone watching for me? Someone who opened the gate knowing Rocket would get out?

"Will you call the police?" I say, holding Argo back with my foot. I don't want him sprinting down the stairs.

"No, the gate's not damaged and no one seems to be hurt," he says.

"I hit Rocket on the nose pretty hard," I say. I'm not planning on apologizing, and it doesn't appear that my neighbor expects one.

"Don't worry about it," he says.

After he leaves, I'm still thinking about the footsteps I thought I heard on the stairs, the shadowy figure I saw and the car pulling away. I power up my computer and put in an order for pepper spray that I can carry in addition to my dive light.

Chapter 36

Bertie hesitates on the doorstep. She's perspiring again. She can feel the moisture in her armpits. She unzips her sweatshirt, and fingers the lip balm in its pocket.

"We were in the neighborhood and just thought we'd pop by," she says. "But if it's too early, we can come another time." She starts to turn away.

"Of course it's not too early for my daughter to visit," her mother says, sweeping her hand to welcome them inside. "Come in, come in."

Matt clears his throat. Placing his hand on the small of Bertie's back, he propels her forward. She steps into the shadowed hall, feeling like she's marching toward the principal's office, and she stiffens her back for a scolding. In the kitchen, her mother offers them fresh squeezed orange juice.

"I just got it at the farmer's market," she says. "Good thing you didn't come earlier or I wouldn't have been here." She calls down the basement stairs for Bertie's dad. Bertie notices for the first time that her mother is fully dressed. She even has a dash of color on her lips.

"I picked up these fresh scones," her mother says. Bertie gets a whiff of the scones; they smell like her mother just pulled them from her own oven. Her mother opens a drawer and brings out a knife. She's bought two scones for their breakfast, but she prepares to cut them in half.

"Mom, no, thank you," Bertie says, holding out her hand to stop her mother's actions.

Her dad arrives from the basement, and there's a flurry of greetings and juice pouring. Bertie's mom goes into detail about the farmer's market; she's thinking of maybe bringing some of her roses to sell. Her friend Susan is having fun at a booth set up by the local knitting club; she's apparently having great success selling her darling knitted baby booties and caps.

A pregnant silence falls over the group; they're all still standing around the generous kitchen island. Matt wiggles his eyebrows at Bertie so much she wonders they don't wander off his face. He clears his throat again. He and Bertie speak at the same time.

"Bertie has something to tell you," he says.

"Guess we'll be going," Bertie says.

Bertie's mother sets her juice glass on the granite counter and grabs Bertie's hand. "What is it dear?" she says, all smiles.

Bertie looks between her parents. Her father has started to pick at his scone and has spilled a few of the scone's crumbs on his Detroit Lion's shirt.

"We're moving," Bertie blurts.

"To a bigger house?" her mother says. Bertie can tell she's still hoping for an announcement of another kind.

"To San Diego," Bertie says. Matt winks at her and gives her a thumbs up.

Bertie's mother releases Bertie's hand and picks up her juice for another sip. Her dad stops brushing the crumbs from his shirt.

"Why?" he says. Bertie and Matt explain about his new job, about their excitement to try a new location while they're still young.

Bertie's dad nods, "I hope it makes you happy Alberta."

"It will," Bertie says. "And you both can come visit anytime, get away from the snow for a while."

Bertie dares to sneak a look at her mother. She's patting her mouth with her napkin, but Bertie could swear she was just using the napkin to dab at the corner of her eyes.

"I knew this would happen someday," her mother says. "With all that gallivanting around the world scuba diving and such." She sighs, but then she surprises Bertie by wishing the two well.

There's no reason to stay longer. It's not as if they're moving today and will never see her parents again. Bertie carries her juice glass to the sink, where she rinses it carefully just like her mother has taught her.

"We're not moving until the end of May, but we wanted to let you know," she says.

"We're grateful," Bertie's mom says. She surprises Bertie further by giving her a hug. Bertie's the one with tears when they break apart. Her father hugs her as well. Bertie wipes the tears from her cheeks with the hem of her sweatshirt when she and Matt return to their car.

"That wasn't so bad," he says. He pulls away from the curb, turning the car back towards the Goodwill.

Bertie watches her family home diminish in the side mirror until it's out of sight, hidden by the familiar trees lining the street. She feels sad, relieved and excited.

Chapter 37

Bertie will be surprised when she sees me. I was so tan when she knew me on the Calypso. My skin had a healthy glow from being outside near the ocean every day. My dark hair was lighter. Now, I look in the mirror and even I think I look whiter than usual. And, the other day, I noticed a couple of warts on the backs of my hands.

I haven't had warts since I was a kid. My mother jokes that its because I'm growing old. My father tells me I'd better hurry up and get married before I start growing hair out of a wart on my chin. His jokes don't bother me anymore. Now, I laugh and joke that it looks like he's been painting a white ceiling with all the speckles in his dark hair.

I figure my pale complexion and warts are all because I'm inside too much. My body's probably in shock, and possibly dried out, because it's used to more water and air.

I'm determined to finish my coursework before Bertie arrives though. I want to have at least two weeks off when she gets here. So, getting outside into the sun is just going to have to wait.

I haven't been to the coffee shop in weeks. Instead, I'm drinking pots of my own terrible brew. I text occasionally with Judy. We haven't spoken since dinner that night at my parents. I know she understands as she's busy with her own school deadlines.

Nate calls. He's not satisfied with texts. He's not satisfied with my attempts to keep him at arm's length. He brought over take-out one night, insisting that I need a short break to eat. He's right, of course. I do enjoy his company, but still I make him leave after an hour.

Bills must be paid, however, so when my mom schedules a huge balloon event at a local hotel, I pause my studies to help her out. It's a good thing Argo loves going places with me. At my parent's house, I load Argo into the front seat of the truck she's rented. Just this once, his crate goes in the back. The two vans are not big enough to handle an event of this size. My mom spent most of yesterday inflating balloons that are bagged in the back of the truck. I smile watching my short mom climb up into the cab, then maneuver the truck down the street. She glances over at me and laughs.

"Bet you never thought you'd see this," she says as we pull onto the freeway.

"No. I didn't," I say.

My spirits lift as we drive to the hotel where An Elegant AffAir has been hired to decorate one of the ballrooms for an on-site convention. I've discovered I enjoy spending these times with my mom. I'm eager to see what new balloon creations she's designed.

The heavy, morning traffic is gone. I feel like I'm sitting on a ladder as we speed towards our destination, higher up than I normally sit in my Corolla.

The hotel is a twelve- story, white building near the San Diego harbor. As my mom drives into the parking lot, I can see rows of sail boats and motor boats moored in the water nearby. A few boats move slowly about the harbor, passing the USS Midway Museum and the Star of India. Sunshine reflects off the mirrored buildings downtown; the blue sky is an upside-down bowl of unblemished glass. Airplanes take off and land from the airport less than a mile away, but the hotel and the harbor seem untouched by the roar of jet engines.

We pull into a parking spot around the side, and then the three of us veer past the lobby and enter the hotel through a side door. Argo wears a blue and yellow vest I bought on-line. It's not an official service dog vest, but no one says anything when I bring him along on jobs. He can still fit in a smallish, soft-sided crate that looks almost like a suitcase. He usually keeps quiet when he's inside. I carry a pocket full of treats to make sure he stays that way. Treats go hand-in-hand with successful dog training as far as I'm concerned. I'll get Argo set up in his crate in the ballroom, and he can stay there safely while we unload the truck.

My mom has already scoped out the ballroom, so she knows where to go. She did a walk through before she submitted her proposal to the event coordinator. The open doors to the ballroom are just down the hall from the lobby. I can smell the coffee set up for the guests. I'll grab a cup later to help me power through the job. The dinner won't start until this evening, but we have a lot of work to do.

The same thick blue carpet with some sort of entwined design of gold that softens our footsteps in the hall continues into the ballroom. Round tables with white tablecloths are already set up. There's a moveable podium near one wall. My mom explains that we will be creating a tropical scene complete with palm trees, pineapples and coconuts. We'll build a cresting wave near the podium, and a surfer if there's time.

I set up Argo's crate in a corner while my mom makes a trip to the truck. Once the truck is unloaded of all the bags of balloons, the tanks and the metal structures we'll use to create the trees, the wave and the surfer, we set to work.

We build the trees on heavy square steel bases and bent poles with balloons my mom inflated at home. The lower sections of the palm fronds are created with green, air-filled balloons that will hang down; we fill other green balloons with helium so that part of the frond will stand up. Every couple of hours, I take Argo out of his crate and walk him along the harbor. It's nice to get out in the fresh air and away from the smell of latex for a short while.

We've finished the palm trees when the event coordinator bustles into the room. She looks at her watch, and then surveys our work. Three palm trees with coconuts are artfully placed around the room as well as several bunches of balloon bananas. The table décor will be completed last; my mom envisions centerpieces of balloon pina coladas. The coordinator chats for a few minutes and then says, "I'll let you get back to work."

I see her again a few minutes later while I'm walking Argo outside. She's carrying a clipboard and talking to a man dressed in black. She raises her eyebrows at me. I smile and wave. Then, I stop to snap a photo for Bertie. She responds to my photo share with a line of heart emojis.

Our next project is the wave. My mom directs our work; I'm simply there to tie balloons and pop as few as possible. When she tells me to attach a balloon of a certain blue at a particular spot, I follow orders. Of course, I listened when she first sketched out her idea of a wave done in the organic style, but I'm not artistic so I couldn't visualize the completed project. But once it's done, I'm amazed at how perfect it is. We're admiring the wave, when the event coordinator pops into the room again. I can tell she's looking for Argo, but I've hidden his crate behind a table at the back of the room.

"Ladies," she says, "you've come highly recommended. I hope there's not going to be an issue with finishing as promised."

I've helped my mom often enough to know the coordinator's words are code for what kind of discount will you give me when you don't live up to my expectations. My mother always seems to grow taller at this point. I imagine her as Odysseus' wife Penelope staring down the unwelcome attentions of her suitors.

"We're the best in the business for a reason," she says. Her frosty tone usually shuts down the challenge, and this event coordinator is no different from the rest.

"I'll leave you to it then," she says, turning on her heel and dashing out of the room.

We laugh and shake our heads. Then, we get to work on the pina coladas. I'm having a hard time getting the balloons to cooperate, and my mom finishes most of the tables. Hotel wait staff have been in and out of the room by now, setting the tables with silverware, glassware and napkins.

"This looks amazing," I tell my mom when we're done.

She nods with a pleased smile, then takes pictures for her portfolio. And it's true, the room is transformed into the illusion of a tropical paradise.

Sometimes, I shake my head at the audacity of my mother's art; her creativity and cheerfulness in the face of its temporary nature. No doubt all of this will be popped at night's end by the cleaning crew, the air that turned the balloons into palm trees and bananas, released back into the atmosphere through the tiniest of pinholes. The shriveled latex tossed into the trash.

But really, is this use of air that different from the tanks of oxygen we use to descend underwater for relatively brief moments in time? I think of Penelope weaving, promising her unwelcome suitors that she'll choose a husband when she's finished with her project. Then, secretly pulling apart the threads at night, starting all over again each day.

We're loading the last of our equipment on a cart, along with Argo's crate when the event coordinator comes rushing in all out of breath.

"You did it!" she exclaims with wide eyes.

We smile and leave, knowing that our work speaks for us.

We load up the truck and head for my parent's house. My phone buzzes while we're on the road. Judy wants to know if I can get dinner with her. I let her know I'll be eating at my parents', and then heading home for more studying. She asks about coffee after, but I decline. My mom's pulling into her driveway when my phone buzzes with an incoming call. It's Nate. I tell him the same thing I just told Judy. I promise to get in touch when I have some free time.

My dad's home from work, so he helps us unload the truck. Dinner is leftovers. I've brought Argo's dinner in a plastic bag. Argo and I linger longer than I intend. It's easy to relax at the table with my parents. It's late when we climb into my Toyota.

"Get some rest," my mom blows kisses to me through the window and coos to Argo where he's ensconced in his crate in the back seat. My dad loops his arm over her shoulders and the two wave as I back out of the driveway, my headlights raking across their darkened figures.

My mom's advice sounds good to me. I decide I will get some rest after I take Argo on a short walk. First, I'll need to grab the pepper spray and my dive light.

I'm yawning when I turn onto my street, more than ready to take a break from studying with a good night's sleep. I can set my alarm to wake up early.

I'm already thinking of how nice it will be to crawl into bed when my headlights illumine a dark figure with white hair sprinting towards me down the middle of the street. Its shadowy arms wave like a crazed sports fan.

I glimpse Gordon's face; his piercing blue eyes behind a dive mask; his mouth open in a terrible scream. And I jerk the wheel of my car, slamming into a parked pickup.

Chapter 38

In the sudden silence after the bang of the crash, all I can hear is my heart thumping. I'm afraid to get out of my car. What if Gordon's ghost attacks me? I press shaking fingers to my sea star necklace and whisper, "I'm not superstitious."

Argo's whimper snaps me out of my thoughts.

"It's ok boy," I say. I feel a jolt of pain in my ribs when I shift to look behind me at the pup, and I suck in a breath causing another stab of discomfort. My seatbelt must have bruised my ribs. I'm grateful Argo's in his crate, buckled to the back seat. For the moment, I'm forced to assume he's all right.

My old Corolla doesn't have an airbag. But I don't believe I was driving fast enough anyway to deploy one when I smashed into the truck. Still, my head jerked forward. I must have hit my face on the steering wheel, my lower lip feels swollen and when I touch it my trembling fingers come away wet. My smashed headlights still glow, and I can see the wetness on my fingers is black. I can only assume its blood.

Argo whimpers again. I release my seatbelt and try to open my door, so I can get around to the back. But no matter how hard I jiggle the handle the door is stuck.

We're not going anywhere. I just have to hope Gordon's ghost is gone.

A loud rap on my window startles me, sending my heart into the stratosphere and my ribs into another spasm of pain. I'm afraid to look. What if I see Gordon's face at my window?

I shudder. Argo yips. I force myself to think logically. Gordon is dead. It's impossible for him to be on my street. I don't believe in ghosts.

I remember yawning. Maybe I fell asleep. Maybe the figure running towards me was nothing more than one of my nightmares. They've become less frequent but are not gone all together.

Another loud rap jangles my already anxious thoughts. Someone shouts through the closed window, asking if I'm ok. The door handle rattles urgently as the person tries to get in.

I can't sit here forever.

I'm careful when I turn to look. I don't know what I'll do if the face at my window is Gordon's.

I breathe a sigh of relief to see a woman I don't know, pressing her face to my window. Her hair is scraped back from her brown face. Her cheeks are round. Her nose is squished flat. She's squinting. I imagine she's trying to see into the interior.

I push a button, but my window won't budge either.

"Try the back door," I yell. I push another button, praying my automatic locks will open. They don't.

The woman disappears. I'm alone in the car with Argo. He's quiet. I hope that's a good sign. Now, I'm thankful to see people milling about my car most likely attracted by the loud bang like a cannon shot when my car hit the truck. It seems like forever before I hear the sound of metal crunching, and a man pries open my car door with a crow bar.

A cheer goes up among the assembled neighbors. The man assists me out of my car, and then guides me by my elbow to the side of the street where he helps me lower myself to the curb.

"Argo," I say, gesturing towards my wrecked Corolla. "My dog."

Someone brings Argo still in his crate and my purse, setting both near me. A woman who says she's a nurse leans in to examine me. I can see the hints of gold in her dark eyes. I assume she's my neighbor, but I don't recognize her.

"You been drinking," she asks, "doing drugs?" Her voice is matter-of-fact. She shines a pen-light into my eyes. I blink. She leans forward, and I know she's sniffing my breath for the smell of alcohol, smelling my hair and clothes for the tell-tale scent of marijuana.

I'm thankful I declined my dad's offer of a glass of wine at dinner. I wonder if she would call the police if I was drunk or high.

"You're eyes aren't dilated," she says. "You probably didn't hit your head."

I ask if she'll take a moment to look at Argo. The minute the pup emerges from the crate, I know he's ok. He squirms against me, his tongue licking my hand. I smooth my fingers over his body and find no injuries. A wave of relief washes over me. Someone finds his leash in the car. I snap it on his collar, so he won't run off.

"What about the other person?" I say to the woman. I've thought more about what happened. And I'm not convinced I fell asleep at the wheel. That I dreamed the figure with Gordon's face running towards me. "Are they all right?"

"Was there someone else in the car?" the woman says

"Not in the car," I say, "in the road. I swerved to miss them."

"No one else appears injured," she says. "The truck is empty and so is the road."

None in the cluster of people step forward to say they were hit.

She offers to call me an ambulance, but I decline. She helps me to my feet, noticing when I wince and hold the palm of my hand to my side.

"You have someone who can stay with you?" she says.

"I'll be fine," I say.

"At least call a doctor," she says. "You might have injured your ribs."

Now that the excitement is over, the neighbors start to trickle away, heading home. I'm grateful for their attention and care. I don't recognize a soul. My landlord is still out of town. I don't see the neighbor who owns Rocket. I stand by the curb, gripping Argo's leash in my hand, wondering what I should do about my car. Whether I must stay here and wait for a tow truck. I'm not eager to be left by myself in the dark.

An older man and woman approach. I recognize her as the one who leaned her face against my car window. She tells me they live down the street, and that they were out for an evening stroll when they saw the crash. Both wear light jackets and loose slacks. The man wears a cap on his brown, grizzled head; the woman wears a nylon pouch that's strapped around her middle. I ask them if they saw someone running in the middle of the street. Neither one did.

They apologize for not being much help. The man shifts his thick glasses up his nose and mentions something about needing a new prescription. They say they don't know the owner of the pickup, but they offer to help me move my car to an open spot near where I'm sitting.

Working with another neighbor who hasn't yet left for home, they put my car in neutral and push it against the curb. I dictate a note that the woman prints on the back of a discarded flyer she found in my car. She leaves it under one of the pickup's windshield wipers. By now, everyone else is gone, back inside their houses I assume.

I'm still shaking from the adrenaline of the accident. My legs wobble, and the woman reaches out her hand to steady me.

She asks where I live. When I point out my nearby studio, the man carries Argo's crate up my stairs, while the woman helps me, allowing me to lean on her. At my insistence that I'm going to be all right, they leave me on my doorstep. As they disappear from sight, I realize I didn't even ask their names.

Argo follows me into the studio where I flip the deadbolt and depress the door handle button. I wrap some ice from my freezer in a kitchen towel and lower myself gingerly to the couch, grimacing when the pup jumps up beside me. Argo circles a few times before curling in a ball next to me. I hold the ice to my lip, and think about what just happened.

But the more I think, the more nervous I get. I jump when the owl hoots in the birch. I sit still, hardly breathing, and listen for any noises that are out of the ordinary. Finally, exhaustion overtakes me and my eyes close.

But I can't allow the nightmares that will form. I force my heavy eyelids open and fumble in my purse for my cell. Bertie will know what to do. She'll have a sensible answer for what I saw tonight.

Chapter 39

Bertie's sitting cross-legged on her living room area rug, holding a mauve ceramic chip and dip set. Her leggings are covered with lint and bits of neon circle stickers. She's wearing one of Matt's old shirts that she plucked from the donation pile.

She's up late executing the final tagging push for the huge moving sale she and Matt are having tomorrow. Every night this week, the two sorted, packed and tagged. But there's still more to be done. The two are determined to clean out as much as possible before the move. She fixes a tag to the bottom of the ceramic, and then adds it to a pile of kitchenware. She's surrounded by piles of varying sizes, items sorted into categories of bedroom, kitchen, bathroom, décor and clothing. When she's done, the two will carry the piles out to the garage where tables are already set up. Tomorrow morning, they'll just need to open the garage door, and spread out blankets on the driveway to display larger items.

While she finishes up tagging, Matt is driving around the neighborhood posting bright orange flyers he printed about the sale. Moving sales are big deals; Bertie knows people will be waiting in their trucks and vans when Matt opens the garage door just after sun-up, signaling the start of the sale. She used to be one of those waiting; in fact, tomorrow they'll be selling some of the furniture she bought at other sales and re-finished.

She continues tagging items even though she knows some people will surreptitiously remove the tags and ask for a different price. She's promised Matt she won't get upset if someone offers an insultingly low price for an item she spent way too much money on or a piece of furniture she spent way too much time refinishing. She's going to wear the tie-dye shirt she made the summer she was into tie-dye, the shirt with the peace symbol she learned to stencil in the middle. She's going to channel those beachy vibes she just knows are prevalent in Southern California. She's going to smile and bargain and make lots of money.

The two are also up late tonight, because both are racing to meet work deadlines before they leave. Bertie's been put in charge of several projects that have led to longer hours at the office and at home. She feels like the school district is squeezing every last drop out of her brain before she moves. She's expected to not only wrap up the projects, but also to train whoever is hired to take her place.

Also, her mother has started inviting her and Matt over for dinner more often. Family dinners used to only happen on Sunday. Now her mother wants Bertie to come over twice a week. At these dinners, she offers Bertie some sort of memento to take so she "won't forget those she's leaving behind." The first is a mint-green music box from Bertie's old room. Bertie decorated the box with glittery pink heart and white daisy stickers. She remembers sitting at her childhood desk, stressing over which stickers to pick and how to place them.

"Remember how you begged for this?" her mother says. She winds the box and the music tinkles "Somewhere Out There." Matt chokes back a laugh. Bertie shoots him a dirty look.

Bertie takes the music box because she doesn't have the heart to tell her mother she left it in her old room all those years because she didn't want it anymore.

The next time, her mother hands her a small, plain wooden box which Bertie has never seen before. The wood is oiled and smooth. The brass hinges are shiny.

"Open it," she says looking like a kid giving a birthday present.

Bertie opens the lid to find a stack of neatly printed recipe cards. Before she can speak, her mother reaches in and selects a random card.

"Oh look," she says. "Here's Grandma Mabel's recipe for tuna noodle casserole. Remember how much you loved this?" She taps the card with her fingernail; it looks as if she's gotten a fresh manicure. Her salmon colored nail polish is immaculate. Bertie hasn't had time to care for her nails, and she curls her fingers around the box in an effort to hide them.

"You always wanted a heaping serving with the corn flakes and melted cheese on top," her mother says.

Bertie doesn't remember. She doesn't dare look at Matt, because she knows he'll be grinning from ear to ear because Bertie doesn't cook. At least not like her mother does. She mostly fixes up pre-packaged meals, making them look nice on their plates. When it's Matt's turn to make dinner, he'll cook a few favorites his mother taught him. Bertie's never told her mother. She represses a shudder at the horror her mother would express at this failing. Still, she appreciates the effort her mother made to write down all the recipes. Maybe she'll keep them to look at, sort of like a photo album.

"Your father made the box," her mother says.

Now, Bertie's eyes dampen. She rubs the box with her thumb thinking of her dad down in his workshop creating something for her. She hugs her parents and thanks them.

Her dad shuffles his feet. "It was just sitting on a shelf gathering dust," he says. "Looks nice all cleaned up with those recipes inside."

On the way home, Bertie holds the box in her lap and sighs. "What am I going to do with this?" she says.

"Cook me up a casserole?" Matt says.

Bertie laughs and pretends to throw the box at him. "You wish."

"You can always sell the items at our garage sale," Matt says.

"That's not going to happen," Bertie says. "What if my parents come by? There's no way I can get rid of this. We'll just have to bring them with us to San Diego. Knowing my mom, she'll ask about them when she visits."

"Maybe they can get lost in the move," Matt says.

The next time her mother invites them to dinner, Bertie says she's busy with work and moving. She promises they'll come over another time.

"I've found something I know you'll love," her mother says. "I'll just add it to the box I've put by the door."

Bertie doesn't even want to imagine the stuff her mother is setting aside. She doesn't tell Matt who she knows would have a good laugh. She doesn't have time to expend the energy thinking about her mother's box.

Bertie sighs and adjusts the bun on top of her head. The piles around her are bigger than when she started. She's almost finished. She pushes up from the rug and pads on bare feet into the kitchen for a glass of water. She's sitting amongst the piles again when her cell rings.

Catalina tells her about the accident. She describes swerving to avoid the figure running towards her. She recounts the nightmarish sight of Gordon's face, her voice trembles.

"Are you sure you didn't fall asleep at the wheel?" Bertie says. "I know you've been cramming for exams."

"I'm positive," Catalina says. "I was on my street. I could see my studio."

"Stress could cause hallucinations," Bertie says. "Maybe you're feeling out of control about all that's going on, and it triggered thoughts of another situation where you felt out of control?"

"Maybe," Catalina says. "Have you heard of that happening?

Bertie admits she hasn't. Still, Catalina's experience defies logic. She's silent for a moment, thinking. She picks up a pair of candlesticks, another wedding present, and snagging a rubber band from a supply heap, she fastens them together.

"This might sound paranoid," Catalina says, "but I think someone let out a dog that nearly attacked Argo a couple of weeks ago."

"You didn't tell me that," Bertie says. She sets the candlesticks with the kitchenware, but then shifts them to the décor pile.

Catalina explains about the dog appearing out of nowhere, the figure she saw and the car driving away. Her voice gets higher. She definitely sounds stressed. Bertie will do some research on whether stress can lead to hallucinations.

"Then, there was the rattlesnake by my door," Catalina says. "I'd forgotten about that."

Bertie asks about the snake. She's not familiar with rattlesnakes. She supposes she'll need to learn about them before they move. From what

Catalina's telling her, it sounds like rattlers are common in the San Diego area and something to be avoided.

"But it's not usual for them to be upstairs?" Bertie asks.

Catalina's no is emphatic. The two talk for a few more minutes. Catalina assures Bertie her door is locked; she promises to see a doctor tomorrow.

After Catalina hangs up, Bertie feels badly she's not already in San Diego where she can help her friend figure out what's going on. She thinks Catalina's probably not handling the pressure she's under very well. After all, Catalina spent all those years focused solely on diving. Now, she's juggling master level classes, a job, a studio and a dog.

But what if Catalina's right? What if all those incidents are somehow tied together?

Bertie considers the piles that encircle her. Between work and moving, Bertie feels as if she doesn't even have a moment to breathe. She closes her eyes and mentally rids her brain of useless clutter like the box her mother is keeping for her. Then, Bertie envisions saving the information Catalina shared tonight in a file; a file that's not at the front of her brain, but a file that's nonetheless being investigated and scrutinized. This is where her most dynamic ideas emerge. When she's not focusing on something, somehow her brain is working away on the solution.

Chapter 40

My ribs are still sore in the morning. I'm a little dizzy when I stand up. I need to hold onto a piece of furniture or the wall until my studio stops spinning. My lip is tender. I'm careful when I sip my coffee and eat my breakfast. I choose a blouse from my closet that I think will be easy to get on and off. I call the doctor and get an afternoon appointment. Argo is fine. I take him on a very short walk, just so he can do his business.

My car looks bad in the daylight, the front is all smooshed in like an accordion. The headlights are splintered. Just down by the truck, I can see shards of glass glinting in the sunlight. I suppose I need to sweep them up. I circle my car with Argo. The driver's side door hangs crooked on its hinge. I don't know how the couple got it closed last night. I'll have to call a tow truck. Still, I hope it's not completely totaled. I don't have the funds for another car.

I wander slowly to the truck where I examine it for damage. Its back wheel well is dented where my Corolla struck it. Apparently, my car bounced off the truck's oversized back wheel. There's a wide smudge on the tire. I'm no expert, but it appears to me as if the dent can be pounded out.

I'm exhausted from the short excursion, and I slowly climb back up the stairs to my studio holding Argo tight on his leash so he doesn't bound ahead and strain my injured ribs. I'll go back down later with a broom.

I spend the rest of the morning talking to the man whose truck I hit, my insurance, and attempting to study. I try to sweep up the glass in the street, but when I bend to hold the dust pan, my ribs hurt. For now, I push the glass against the curb and out of the way of traffic.

Now that the sun's out and my studio is filled with light and I'm sitting at the table with my books, I feel embarrassed about my late- night phone call to Bertie. She's probably right about my stress level. Knowing her, she'll do some research on stress and hallucinations.

Eventually, my eyes grow heavy from all of my morning activity. I set my books aside, climb onto my bed and fall asleep, meaning to take only a short nap. I wake up when Argo shifts against me. I need to leave right away for my doctor's appointment. I call a ride sharing service, crate Argo and make my way down the stairs, holding onto the railing.

X-rays show tiny cracks in one rib. The others are most likely bruised. The doctor says my swollen lip will eventually return to normal. He suggests I take it easy for a few days, maybe take a break from driving. I don't know if I'm ready yet to drive, especially at night.

I leave the doctor's office, ready to request another ride share when my phone buzzes with a text from Judy. She's done with work. She's wondering if we can meet. I text and ask her for a ride. I give her the doctor's address and say I'll explain when she picks me up.

I wait on the curb until she arrives, pulling her silver Honda up with a quick tap of her horn. She grabs a stack of papers off the passenger seat and thrusts them into the back.

"I opened the store this morning and literally just got off work," she says. She apologizes for not thinking to bring me a latte.

"It's ok," I say, climbing into the car and gingerly buckle my seat belt. Her car is fragrant with the smell of coffee. I can only assume it's emanating from her work clothes, a white blouse and black slacks, and possibly her hair. "Thanks for the ride."

She stares at me for a moment, leaving her car idling at the curb. "What happened to your lip?" she says.

I gently touch my lip. I know it looks like I got into a fight. My other injuries are more painful, but I suppose they're not visible I give her a brief description of my accident, and my injuries. I mention the figure but not the glimpse I had of Gordon's screaming face. I don't have the energy for her psychoanalysis right now. She starts to ask a question, but a car pulls up behind her and beeps, before she can finish. The curb is painted white for passenger drop-offs.

"Can you drive me home?" I say. "I don't feel up to going out."

She swings the car away from the curb, and heads towards the general direction of my studio. "Would it be ok if I picked up something to eat first?" she says. "Work was crazy. I had zero time for lunch."

I tell her I don't mind.

"Somehow I need to take it easy these next few days," I say. "Not sure how I'll do that with exams and papers and work."

"I doubt your mom would expect you to show up for work," Judy says.

I know she's right, even though I haven't called my parents yet and told them about the accident.

We're silent for a while. Judy flips on the radio to a 80s station that's mostly ads.

She pulls into a burrito place we both love. "I'll just dash in, and be back in a jiffy," she says. "You want anything?" Suddenly, I'm famished, and I ask her to get me a California burrito. I close my eyes while she's gone, enjoying the quiet. When she's back, I hold the warm bag on my lap. The smell of beans, cheese, meat, and fries wafts from the bag.

The tow truck is pulling up when we arrive at my studio. I was given a four-hour window of when the truck would show up, and here it is on the early end of the four hours. Maybe it's a sign my luck will be changing.

"Your car," Judy says, rubber necking as she slowly drives by and then parks. "It's worse than I thought it would be." She makes a show of opening the door for me. "I'm worried about those burritos you're carrying," she jokes. I hand her the bag. Then, she stands aside so I can work my way out of the car with the least jiggling of my ribs as possible. She hovers nearby while I speak to the tow truck driver.

We head up the stairs after my car is gone.

"You still seeing Nate?" she says from where she's standing behind me.

I'm fumbling for my key in my purse. I push aside my cell and wallet. "Sometimes," I say, extracting the key and inserting it in my front door. "Why?"

"I don't know," she says. "Just thinking about Argo, and then this. It makes you wonder."

"Wonder what?" I say, pushing open the door. I let Argo out of his crate. He jumps around Judy, but comes when I call him and sits beside me where I've settled at the kitchen table. I slip him a treat.

Judy sets the bag on the table, fills water glasses for each of us, then sits down. "You know," she says continuing her train of thought, "your dog almost dies, and then you get in a wreck because a mysterious figure runs across the road."

Even though I had the same thoughts last night about whether the strange events I'd experienced lately are connected, I don't comment. My brain is still where it settled this morning with the idea that I overreacted and imagined seeing Gordon's face. I bite into my burrito; the sauce and salt sting my lip. I ignore the discomfort because it tastes so good.

Judy chews on her burrito. Some of the sauce drips onto her blouse. "Dammit," she says, wiping at it with a napkin. "These are so messy." She dabs some more, going to the sink where she turns on the faucet. When she comes back, the red spot is gone but a larger, wet spot is in its place. "Was the figure a man?" she says.

I close my eyes and picture the previous night. I remember driving down my dimly lit street and seeing my studio just ahead. I recall a dark shadow with Gordon's face dashing straight at me. I remember being so focused on the face that the figure refuses to settle into a definite shape.

"I don't know," I finally say. I reach for the water and take a sip. "What reason would anyone have to hurt me or Argo?"

I'm curious to hear her theory. I'm surprised she's not going down the same psychological path Bertie did, theorizing I'm stressed out and hallucinating, considering her pursuit of a degree in psychology.

"It can't be that big of a mystery," Judy says. "Even you questioned whether Nate took good care of your dog."

"Nate?" I say, surprised she's mentioned him again. "What does he have to do with my accident?"

When Judy mentioned Argo almost dying, I wasn't thinking of Nate or the Parvovirus that Argo suffered through. I thought of the night my neighbor's dog got out and tried to attack my puppy. I realize I've never told Judy about that night. And why would I? I didn't think anything of it until after my car accident. And I don't mention it now. I don't want to sound hysterical like I did last night on the phone with Bertie.

By now, I've eaten half of my burrito. I rewrap the rest in the paper and push it aside. It's delicious, but I feel full. I'll eat it later for dinner. Argo is laying quietly at my feet. I'm slipping him another treat when Judy says, "Maybe Nate was one who ran at your car last night."

Chapter 41

I think of Nate and I think of the figure running towards me. I try to merge the two in my mind. I don't see a connection, but maybe I'm refusing to see it because I like him.

"Why would he want me to crash?" I say.

"Maybe he's a woman hater," Judy says, leaning forward in her chair. "Have you searched for information about him on the internet?"

I laugh at the idea. "That's not something I typically do." Judy narrows her eyes at me. "Do you?" I say.

"Of course!" she says.

"Did you search for information about me?" I ask half in jest.

"Why wouldn't I?" she says. "I'm using you for my research. I can't have some weirdo as my subject."

I raise my eyebrows at her admission.

"Don't judge," she says. "Everyone does it. I can't believe you've never searched for an old boyfriend." She finishes her burrito, then wads her own discarded wrap into a ball and stuffs it in the bag. "Let me help you to the couch," she says.

I thank her for the offer and tell her I can toddle to the couch on my own when I'm ready. Judy cleans up the table, throwing out the burrito bag and saving my wrapped burrito in the refrigerator. She washes and rinses her water glass. Then, even though I didn't ask for it, she retrieves my laptop and sets it on the table before me. Argo leaves my side to follow her to the door where she turns the door handle button to lock before leaving with a wave and pulling the door shut behind her.

I listen to her light footsteps on the stairs. It almost sounds as if she's skipping. There's the sound of her car engine roaring to life, a short beep of her horn, and then she's gone.

I think about her suggestion that Nate could be the cause of my accident. Much as I don't want to believe that Nate would want to harm me, it doesn't take long before I'm remembering my misplaced trust in Gordon and the Baker family. How many others have I blindly trusted, thinking my gut instincts were all I needed to judge someone's character and motives? Just because I operate from a basic sense of integrity and loyalty, it doesn't mean others do the same.

Maybe I've been blinded by Nate's charm. I have thought at times that he's too good to be true. And he does have blond hair like Gordon and the same sea blue eyes.

My cell rings. I'm surprised to see the caller is my dad. I can't recall a time he's phoned in the middle of the day.

"Everything all right?" I say when I answer.

"Yes, yes, of course," he says. "Can't I call my daughter to say hello?"

"Are you on break?" I say. My dad is a program manager at a local electronics company.

We chat for a few minutes about nothing important. And then, I don't know if it's the aftermath of my accident or my growing realization that my dad is someone I can count on, I tell my him about my car accident. I tell him I'm ok, that I've been to the doctor. I've called my insurance. I've gotten my car towed. All the things that make me a responsible adult.

I don't tell him about the figure. Then, I'd have to tell him about what happened on the Calypso. And my gut clenches just thinking about sharing that story with my parents and letting them know how someone died on my watch.

My dad says he loves me, and then we disconnect.

I decide I'm too tired to do any studying. I push back my chair and stand. My legs wobble like they used to when I'd leave the Calypso for a shore excursion. I skip the couch, heading straight towards my bed. Argo leaps onto the bed before I reach it. I adjust the pillows around me to protect my sore ribs, settling one behind my head and yawn. Argo executes a few circles, and then collapses next to me, his head snuggled into my hip. I close my eyes.

Gordon frolics with the sea lion pup, his blue eyes brilliant behind his dive mask. His long white hair floats about his head like sea foam. I watch amazed as he swims in circles with the animal. He's clearly human, but he moves with the grace of a sea lion underwater.

Lucky and Lauren join the play, but unlike their father, their faces have snouts and whiskers instead of noses; their eyes are pools of liquid brown. Even Ava joins in the fun.

But the dive can't last forever. I check my dive computer and signal to the Bakers that it's time to leave. Although they're slow to depart, eventually the women encircle Gordon and prepare to ascend to the surface. One moment I can see them clearly in their ceremonial ascent, the next their shapes are hidden from me. I strain to see through the murky water that swirls with sand.

I'm not certain, but Gordon appears to be holding something in his arms. I move closer.

It's the sea lion pup. The pup gazes up at Gordon and licks his chin.

My heart races at the danger of removing the pup from his home. I'm ready to push my way into the circle, to warn Gordon he must leave the pup behind. But before I can, Gordon's face flashes inches from mine. His unearthly blue eyes pierce to my soul.

My cell rings, and I struggle to resurface from my dream. It's silent by the time I groggily come to in the darkened studio. I push myself into a sitting position, forgetting about my sore ribs, and I cry out in pain. I reach for my cell, and then remember I left it on the kitchen table. Argo licks my cheek. It's probably way past his dinner time.

My phone rings again. I'm still on the bed, in the dark, when it stops. When I feel ready, I swing my legs over the side. I'm careful to stand slowly, careful of my ribs. When I'm fully upright, I flex my toes on the small braided rug at my bedside. Argo jumps to the floor with a thump. The kitchen curtains are open, and there's enough ambient light I can see him wagging his tail beside me.

"Let's get your dinner," I say. My voice sounds scratchy. I stop at the table and finish the glass of water Judy set before me earlier this afternoon, before snapping on the light and filling Argo's dog dish. He's busy eating when my cell rings a third time.

"Catalina," Bertie says, her voice sounds breathless. "Are you all right?"

I yawn and rub my eyes. "I just woke up from a nap," I say. My nightmare is still fresh in my mind. My thoughts are divided between Bertie's voice and my underwater visions. I grip the cell phone, pressing it to my ear, leaning my hip against the solid table. My gaze falls on my laptop. I'll have lots of studying to catch up on tonight.

I ask Bertie about her move, but she brushes aside my questions.

"I've been thinking about who would want to harm you," she says.

"What time is it there?" I ask.

"It's late," she says, "but I couldn't wait to tell you. You see, that's how my brain works. I get it set on solving a problem, and it does without me really thinking about it."

I don't see, but I'm still waking up, still disentangling myself from my nightmare, so I wait for her to keep talking.

"You still there?" she says.

I nod forgetting that she can't see me. "Yes, I say. "Go on."

"Anyway, I remembered that the Bakers have another family member," she says. "One time we were talking, and a sibling named Jordan was mentioned."

"So?" I say. I carry my glass to the sink and fill it with water from the faucet. Argo is lapping at his own water.

"I'm thinking this sibling didn't come on the trip because he didn't agree with Gordon's plan," Bertie finishes in a triumphant rush of words.

"That seems farfetched," I say. I'm feeling better, fully awake now. "Maybe this Jordan simply isn't a diver and wouldn't have enjoyed a week on a dive boat." I drain the glass of water, setting the empty container on the counter. Argo sniffs along the bottom edge of the cabinets where they meet the floor, no doubt looking for any crumbs that might have dropped from previous meal preparations. I haven't swept the floor lately, and don't plan on doing so after the pain of sweeping the street this morning.

"I don't think you should dismiss the possibility that somehow Jordan is behind what's going on with you," Bertie insists. "Maybe he blames you for his father's death."

"Bertie," I say, "I appreciate you taking my phone call last night seriously. But I realize today that I was overwrought. I think you were right when you suggested I might be hallucinating from stress." Bertie is silent on her end. I add, "Honestly, I thought you would do some research on stress and strange sightings."

"At least think about the possibility of Jordan," Bertie says.

"What should I do?" I say. "Look up the Bakers on the internet?" I remember Judy's suggestion this afternoon that I search for information on Nate.

"I already did that," she says with a disappointed sigh, "but there are too many Bakers. Of course, I found Gordon's obit, but it's very brief. Still, there's definitely a Jordan listed among the surviving family. And get this, donations are requested for a foundation that works with injured seals and sea lions."

The back of my neck prickles at this information, my recent nightmare flashes in my mind, and I don't know what to say. Argo starts licking the top of my foot. He must have found all the crumbs. Before I can comment on the foundation, there's a loud knock at the door. I jump and inadvertently kick the pup.

"Someone's here," I say. "Sorry boy," I whisper to Argo.

"Don't answer," Bertie says.

"They know I'm here. The light is on, the window's open and they can hear me talking to you."

"You want me to stay on the phone?" she whispers.

The knocking continues. Argo dashes to the door and adds his barks to the noise. Holding my phone to my chest, I pull open the door. Nate's on my doorstep, holding flowers and a restaurant take-out bag

Chapter 42

Catalina tells Bertie the person at the door is Nate. Then, she hangs up. Bertie listens to the brief dial tone before her phone goes silent. She knows Catalina won't answer if she calls back. She shivers. The bathroom is cold; she's sitting on the closed toilet seat lid again. Maybe she should get a cushioned lid at their new house. This one is definitely uncomfortable and not meant for long phone conversations.

Holding her cell, Bertie moves to the sink and looks in the bathroom mirror. The lighting is not flattering at all. She really needs to get some sleep. Her skin looks pasty. Her eyes are red and the skin below them is puffy. She fluffs her hair, and then shrugs at her reflection. She flips off the light and pads to the bed, returning her cell to her nightstand. Then, she crawls back into bed, pulling up the blankets in such a way as to wake Matt – if he was close to being awake that is. She's nowhere near sleep. In fact, her brain is on full throttle now. Matt groans and rolls over.

"What's wrong babe," he mumbles.

"I figured out whose out to get Catalina, but she doesn't believe me," Bertie says.

"How do you know?"

"I could tell she was blowing me off. She said I was right about her stress level."

"I meant how do you know someone's out to get Catalina?"

Bertie reminds Matt about the workings of her brain, and how she remembers the conversation on the Calypso with the Bakers. She tells him about the obit confirming the existence of Jordan.

"That's a hell of a speculation," he says. "Everything could simply be coincidences."

"What about the figure that jumped out in front of Catalina's car?" Bertie's not ready to give up the argument or go to sleep just yet.

"She could have imagined the figure," Matt says. "You said yourself she was tired and stressed." He swings his legs off the side of the bed and stands. "Might as well take care of business now that I'm awake." He heads into the bathroom and closes the door. When he returns, Bertie is still sitting up in bed.

"It's late," he says. "Can we talk about this in the morning? You've called Catalina. There's nothing else you can do for her from Michigan." He pats the bed beside him. "Now that we're awake," he winks.

"How can you think of that now?" Bertie says.

"How can I not?"

Bertie laughs and lays down. Soon, thoughts of Catalina have retreated once more to the back of her brain.

Argo jumps around Nate's feet. I'm glad for the distraction. I didn't expect Nate to turn up at my studio while my head is swirling with Bertie's theories and Judy's innuendos. My neck feels hot. I tell Argo to stop, and when he doesn't, I reach for his collar. The movement jiggles my bruised ribs. I gasp and lean against the door jamb holding my side. Argo must realize he's done something wrong, because he drops his tail and slinks behind me.

"You get in a fight?" Nate asks. He's still standing outside, holding the flowers and the brown bag.

Now the heat warms my cheeks. I touch my bruised lip, and then move my hand up to my hair.

"Do I look that bad?" I say.

I haven't looked in the mirror since I got out of bed. It feels like I have a rat's nest at the back of my head. My eyes are probably smeared with mascara. My blouse is wrinkled. I step aside and invite Nate in, then excuse myself for a visit to the bathroom, snagging a clean blouse on the way.

I can hear him moving about the kitchen, opening cupboards, setting out plates and silverware. I slip off the crumpled blouse and toss it in the hamper. I wet a washcloth with cold water and dab my warm cheeks and neck. Cold cream and a tissue solve the mascara smudges. I apply more water to my hair and give it as vigorous a brushing as I can before gently pulling the new top on. I finish by brushing my teeth, then dabbing a little perfume on my neck where I can see my pulse is working overtime. I tell myself it's because changing tops was an uncomfortable process.

The flowers Nate brought are in a vase in the center of the kitchen table when I emerge. He's moved the candle I keep by my bedside to the table as well. A small flame flickers and dances in the draft coming through the open window. The kitchen light shines on his blond ponytail, highlighting the wisps of hair that have escaped and wave at his temples. I think again about Bertie's theory of a vengeful Baker sibling.

"I'm not really hungry," I say. But, then my stomach growls, betraying me. Whatever food he's brought smells delicious. I imagine steam rising from the bag and wafting cartoon-like to my nose.

"That must be Argo's stomach I hear then," Nate smiles, showing a flash of his teeth. My heart flutters. Argo watches me from his blanket. He holds a new rubber toy between his paws.

Nate opens the bag. "It's from that restaurant we've talked about trying together," he says.

I consider the flowers, the candle, the food and the new dog toy. It would be rude to simply send Nate on his way. He's done nothing wrong. In fact, he's doing everything right.

I sit at the table.

The food is as good as the online ratings promise. Nate waits until we're nearly done to ask me again about my lip and why I held my side earlier. In the interest of fairness, I tell him about my accident, mentioning the figure that ran at my car. I leave out the minor detail that the figure looked like Gordon. I decide to tell him about the neighbor's dog.

I look into his eyes when I tell him about Bertie's idea. He doesn't flinch when I mention the missing Baker sibling.

"The Bakers were all very blond," I say, my voice trailing off. I drop my eyes to my plate, using my fork to push around the tiny amount of food that's left. I don't want him to see me staring at his hair. But he's not fooled.

"Making me a prime suspect I suppose," he says. "I'm blond and I'm a scuba diver."

I look up to see his eyes are blazing. He's frowning. I'm flustered. Uncertain of his reaction, and what it means if anything, I stand to clear the table of the dirty dishes and silverware, but I've moved too quickly and the room whirls. I swallow hard. The dizziness passes. Argo chews his toy roughly making it squeak.

"I never said that," I say. "I never even said I agreed with Bertie's theory." I carry the plates and silverware to the sink.

Now, my defenses are up, and my anger is rising. I'm frustrated with my injuries and with the unsettling thoughts I'm having. I drop the silverware into the sink with a clatter.

"What about Argo?" Nate says. His chair scrapes, and I know he's left the table as well.

"What about him?" I turn on the faucet, my back still towards him, and scrub the plates with soap until there's no sign we even used them. I feel the bulk of his presence directly behind me.

"You haven't let me take care of him since he was sick," Nate's voice sounds accusing. "Do you think I deliberately put him in harm's way?"

I swivel to face him, my hands dripping with soapy water. He's less than two feet from me. I can feel the heat of his body. I want to kick him or kiss him or run away in fright. I can't decide.

I wish Argo would run over and nip Nate's calf so I wouldn't have to make a choice. But instead, the pup's busy on his blanket giving his new toy a thorough chewing. I can hear more vigorous squeaking from the dominated toy.

I want to deny Nate's accusation, but I can't. Tears well in my eyes. I hate it that I cry when I'm angry.

I'm saved from speaking when someone knocks. I wipe my hands on my yoga pants and slide past Nate to pull open the door. I catch my dad in mid-knock, his fist raised to pound. The night air cools my cheeks.

I'm simultaneously grateful for my dad's well-timed visit, yet embarrassed that he might have heard us arguing. He's never met Nate. And this isn't how I pictured introducing him to my dad. Still, there's nothing to do now, but welcome my dad inside.

"This is a surprise," I say, standing aside and gesturing for him to come in.

"I wanted to check on you," he says, "see in person how you're recovering from your accident." He pauses at the sight of Nate, but then moves forward with his hand outstretched.

"Dad" I say, watching the interaction. "This is Nate."

"Nice to meet you Mr. Rodrigues," Nate says, gripping my dad's hand briefly. There's an awkward moment of silence, then Nate moves towards the door.

"I'm going to take off," he says.

"Don't leave on my account," my dad says.

"No worries," Nate says. He reaches for the door knob. "I believe we're done here." He looks at me for a moment, and I can tell he's disappointed. But before I can stop him, he's out the door, his retreating footsteps hammering down the stairs. I'm stunned at this unexpected turn of events.

My dad closes the door. "Don't want Argo getting out," he says.

I lean against the table with the heels of my palms pressed to my eyes. Argo works his toy. My dad gathers me into his arms and rubs my back. I lean into his shoulder. My injuries, Nate's sudden departure, Judy and Bertie's speculations overwhelm me, and I don't even try to stop the sobs that shake me.

"Want to tell me about it?" my dad says when I've quieted. And I do, starting with Gordon's death on the Calypso.

Chapter 43

Today's a busy day with escrow closing. They'll have ten days to finish packing and cleaning up. Matt's new company is sending movers. He tells Bertie not to spend a lot of time boxing things up; the movers will take care of everything. But she's heard horror stories about breakage and movers packing full cans of trash.

"If you pack it and it breaks, the moving company won't pay for it," Matt warns.

Bertie doesn't care. She knows she can do a better job than the movers packing fragile items. She's taken the day off from work to sign the papers, and now that they're all signed, she's at home, and changed into stretch capris and a sports bra. It's unexpectedly warm outside; her hair is tied up in a high ponytail. When she moves quickly, she can feel the soft ends of her hair brush against her neck. Matt couldn't get the time off and rushed back to work.

She's in the middle of sorting when her mother calls and invites them to dinner. Bertie begs off saying she's too busy packing.

"You have to eat," her mother insists.

"We'll just get some take-out," Bertie says.

"I'm bringing dinner to you," her mother says ignoring Bertie's protests.

When her mother arrives, she arranges the food in Bertie's nearly empty refrigerator. Bertie stands by waiting for her mother's comments about the absence of fresh food, but she has none.

"Just remember those are my dishes," her mother says, "and don't pack them." She smiles and heads into the living room. "Now, how can I help?"

Bertie indicates the boxes, the tape, newspaper and the piles of items to be packed. She doesn't mention the labels she's mentally assigned to each pile. Like the one she's made of the "important" mementos her mother has gathered. The mental label she's chosen for this pile is "Castaways." It makes her think of people lost on a deserted island; they're not forgotten; they're not useless; they're just not contributing to society at this moment in time – through no fault of their own of course. The dilemma for Bertie is: does she want to rescue these particular castaways? And if so, does she want to save some, all or none? And wouldn't it be better to make that decision now in Michigan before they start anew in San Diego?

She mentions none of these thoughts to her mother. She wouldn't dream of hurting her mother's feelings.

Bertie bites her lip when her mother starts to work right away on the pile of mementos. Her mother carefully wraps the old music box in several layers of tissue before taping more layers of newspaper around it. She gives the wooden recipe box the same treatment as well as the myriad of other items she's found for Bertie to keep as mementos.

Bertie tries not to think about storing these items in San Diego. She's researched the housing market, and she knows their house will most likely be smaller since houses cost more there. She's told her mother there's a good possibility they'll be downsizing, but her mother simply lists all the things Bertie can do without. None of the mementos are on the list. Bertie pictures having to remember to set out all the "special" items before her mother visits. She can't help but sigh.

"I'm worried this will break," her mother says, cradling the huge newspaper wad she's created around a ceramic figure Bertie shaped and painted as a child. "Maybe you should bring it in your suitcase on the airplane." She holds the wad out to Bertie.

"You've done a fabulous job wrapping it," Bertie says. "I'm sure it will survive the move unscathed. Besides, airport security probably won't let me bring a wrapped object through the gate."

"You're right," her mother says, finding the perfect spot for the figure in a box she's lined with kitchen and bath towels. "Susan had to unwrap the present she brought back for the baby from her recent trip."

Bertie peels a strip of tape from the roll and seals the box.

"I wish I could be there to help you unpack," her mother says.

"Me too," Bertie says. She doesn't doubt her mother's sincerity. But she also knows her mother won't take any action to be present when Bertie unpacks. She's sad, but understands that what her mother is really saying is "I'll miss you." And Bertie will miss her mother as well.

"We'll be renting an apartment while we look for a house," Bertie says. "I know you're busy and who knows how long our things will be in storage?"

"What about the mice and rats?" Her mother starts on another box.

"What rats?"

"In storage," her mother says. "They're all over the place in California. I've heard they dig into your boxes and use your newspaper and tissue for nests. Sometimes you don't even know they've been there until you find a pile of poop in your towels."

Bertie grimaces at the thought, although she's fairly certain her mother is simply pointing out yet another downside of their move.

"I'm sure everything will be safe," she says. "Besides, the movers are putting all of our stuff in a sealed pod."

It's close to dinner when her mother dusts off her hands and gathers her purse to leave. "Don't forget about my dishes," she says, kissing Bertie on her cheek.

Bertie pulls her mother close for a hug. "I won't," she says. She waves goodbye from her front porch. "Thanks for the food!" she yells. Her mother drives off with a wave.

Back in the living room, Bertie considers the box she just taped. It would be easiest if the movers could "forget" the box her mother filled with mementos. Bertie wants those towels though, and she debates whether it's worth repacking the box. Maybe the items will break, and since she packed it, the movers won't replace it. Bertie smiles, writes "towels" in black marker on the box and gets back to work.

"I'm going to miss you mom's cooking," Matt says later while they're sitting at the kitchen table eating the dinner her mother brought. They're eating on paper plates, using plastic utensils Matt scrounged from the back of a drawer.

"What's that supposed to mean?" Bertie says.

She's in a bad mood. She feels dirty, dusty and sweaty from her afternoon of packing. And there's still the bedroom and bathroom to finish up. Not to mention the work deadlines that are looming. Maybe she should let the movers do their job like Matt suggested.

"Nothing," Matt says. "Just that I like your mom's cooking."

Bertie watches Matt enjoying the fried chicken her mother cooked. She feels badly that she snapped. "Maybe I'll learn how to cook while I'm looking for a job in San Diego," she says.

"You do have that recipe box," Matt says, grinning at her between bites. Bertie pretends to throw her plastic fork at his head. "I thought you were planning on spending your spare time diving with Catalina."

Bertie smiles at the thought. "You can come too," she says.

"It's too bad about Nate," Matt says gathering up his plate and utensils. "You done?" he asks Bertie before collecting hers and carrying the pile to the trash. "He sounded like a good guy."

Bertie feels irritated again. "I suppose you want to knock back some beers with him," she says.

Matt drops the plates into the trash. He looks puzzled. "What are you talking about?"

"Were you listening when I told you about Argo - Catalina's puppy?" Bertie says with frustration. "Or when I told you about the snake, the attacking dog and her car accident?"

"I know who Argo is," Matt says.

"You were there on the Calypso. You heard the Bakers talking about a sibling who didn't come on the trip."

"Honestly," Matt says, "I don't remember that conversation. It's been almost a year since we were on that boat."

Bertie folds her arms across her chest and narrows her eyes at her husband.

Matt holds up his hands in surrender. "So the guy is blond with blue eyes. I didn't know that was a crime. Like I said, he sounded like a good guy."

"Catalina's heart is broken," Bertie says. "I know that for a fact."

Matt steps towards Bertie and wraps his arms around her; her arms are a folded barrier between them. He kisses her forehead. "Sounds like you'll be arriving just in time," he says into her hair.

Bertie melts against him, her arms sliding around his waist. He's right, of course. Bertie can be a better friend when she lives nearby.

Chapter 44

I type the last sentence of my term paper about the meaning behind Athena's many disguises in the Odyssey. Some have argued her deceptions are unbecoming in a goddess, but I take the counterpoint that her disguises are required for her to operate effectively as a woman. Particularly in that period of history. Just look at what happened to Calypso. She was forced to give up her love because it didn't fit with Zeus's plan. Then there was poor Penelope who was required to host her unwanted suitors. She had to resort to trickery to keep them at bay. Don't even get me started on Circe.

Argo lays beside me, his head resting on my bare foot. My sandals are safe on the chair next to me. Argo can't be trusted not to chew them. I stretch my arms above my head and wiggle my fingers and toes. For the first time, the movement doesn't bother me. Physically, I feel good. In fact, this morning was my first venture out driving on my own. It seemed appropriate to come here to my favorite coffee shop.

Unfortunately, my car will not recover. It was totaled. I'm waiting for my insurance to send me a check. In the meantime, I've used ride-shares or asked Judy to take me places. Today, I'm driving my dad's Ford.

I don't know how the old pickup is holding together; it's got more than 150,000 miles on it, and a few dings and dents. My dad says it's safe, and I do feel safe, sitting up high where I can get a good view of what's ahead. I'm grateful it's not a stick shift.

Argo sticks out his legs and arches his back, making that peculiar noise dogs do when they stretch. I lean to scratch behind the loyal pup's ears. Then, I hold a treat close to his nose. When he opens his mouth just wide enough to stick out his tongue and suck in the treat, I let him have it. I tell him he's a good boy.

Now that I'm no longer focused on my paper, I realize how busy the coffee shop is. The air is filled with the buzz of chatter even on the patio. I notice people eating sandwiches and salads instead of muffins and avocado toast. My coffee cup is long empty, my napkin crumpled beside it.

It's getting warmer, the shadows shifting since I claimed a table in the shade earlier this morning. The sun spills onto my shoulders. I shed the long-sleeved blouse I no longer need to cover my tank top. I refill Argo's dish with water from my bottle.

While he's drinking, I pack up my laptop and the scattered dog toys I brought to keep him occupied while I worked. I dump my napkin in the trash, unwind Argo's leash and head for the exit with a sense of accomplishment.

Judy comes out from behind the counter intercepting me before I can leave. Her co-worker is frowning behind her, scrambling to line up drinks and work the steamer. Judy seems oblivious to his displeasure.

"I saw you on the patio but couldn't get away," she says.

"It's just as well," I say with a smile. "I finished my paper!"

"That's great! Wish I could say the same," Judy grimaces.

Something metal crashes to the floor behind the counter.

"Sounds like you're needed," I say.

She shrugs her shoulders, walking to the door with me and holding it open so I can get safely through with Argo.

"How about tonight?" she says. "Are you free?"

"Bertie's coming," I say, at Judy's raised eyebrows, I add, "you know, my friend from Michigan. She and her husband might be here tonight."

"You're not sure?"

"They're driving, so it depends on how far they get today. Plus, I've got to help my mom with a couple of jobs. I feel badly not being able to work for a while."

"Sounds busy," Judy says, "I'll be in touch then." She retreats behind the counter without saying goodbye. I watch her back, wondering if I've hurt her feelings. Besides giving me rides, she's come over to my studio a couple of times since my accident to keep me company. Maybe she's wondering if Bertie's arrival signals the cooling of our friendship.

There's a long line of orders, and soon, Judy's swamped creating various concoctions. Now's not the time for a heart-to-heart. I leave the café with Argo, resolving to bring Bertie and Judy together. I'm positive we can all be friends.

Fortunately, Argo is a good jumper, and he easily leaps into the pickup. He's getting bigger. I haven't had to pick him up since my accident. I'm not sure if my ribs have recovered enough that I can carry his weight. I buckle him into his doggie seatbelt. He's too big now for his travel crate. My dad bought and installed the special seatbelt so I'd accept his loan. I climb into the driver's seat and roll down all the windows.

My cell dings. I don't know why, but every ding makes my heart leap with the thought that this might be the time Nate is texting. Of course, my cell is lost somewhere at the bottom of my purse. It dings again while I dig for it. The text is from my mom. She's sent a link to the address where we will be working this afternoon.

I hold my phone, debating whether I should text Nate.

I miss him.

I hate how he left that night. I don't like the misunderstanding that's between us. Still, I'm hesitant. I don't know whether to believe I fell asleep at the wheel, hallucinated from stress and imagined Gordon running at my car, or actually saw a person. And I can't completely exorcise the niggling doubts I have, doubts sown by my friends. It's too easy to hear Bertie's and Judy's voices in my head questioning Nate's care of Argo, speculating about a Baker sibling.

I can't forget how the Baker's tricked me. I think of Nate, his handsome face, his dazzling blue eyes, his sun-bleached blond hair, and although it's been nearly a year since I spent a week with the Bakers, it's easy for me to imagine Nate's a dead-ringer for them.

I drop my cell back into my purse and start up the truck. My nightmares returned in vivid detail for a few nights after my accident, but are nearly gone. After my talk with my dad and his reassurance that I did all I could as a dive master, I felt as if the burden of Gordon's death had truly and finally slipped from my shoulders.

I'll talk more with Bertie when she gets to San Diego. Maybe I'll arrange a double date with Nate, so she and Matt can meet him. I remember how observant she was on the Calypso. How she saw things others missed. She'll know if Nate resembles the Bakers.

Until then, I'll wait.

Chapter 45

Bertie's both eager and sad as they drive her Volvo southwest from Michigan. She's hopeful for what she anticipates is ahead, yet sorry to be leaving her family and all that's familiar. They've motored through hours of farmland, small towns and cities, past mountains and into long stretches of desert with nothing but dirt, weird looking cactus and the occasional unpaved road winding into rock-strewn hills. They've passed through rain storms that pounded the roof, unexpected hail that iced the road, whirling dust that skipped across the highway like miniature tornados and scorching temperatures that rose in waves from the asphalt. The trash bag in the back is filled with used coffee cups, crumpled chip bags, wadded up fast-food containers and apple cores.

When they cross the border into California, Bertie's stomach feels just like the times she takes that first giant stride off a dive boat on a scuba trip. She knows she can breathe underwater. She's done it before; she's confident her equipment will work; she's checked her tank has enough air. Still, her stomach flutters, and she feels the stirrings of a mild panic. That's why she always waits to be the last to jump. She can't stand to be on the surface too long; to truly consider what she's about to do by willingly descending below the water.

Now, as Matt maneuvers the Volvo through low hills piled with giant boulders, she feels like she's standing on another precipice. But this time, she's not familiar with the outcome. She imagines rattlesnakes hiding in the cracks between the boulders, slithering out to sun themselves on the hot surfaces. A hawk circles in the cloudless sky.

Sure, scuba diving has its risks, the possibilities of unexpected outcomes. Bertie knows all about the possibility of equipment failure and other potential underwater emergencies. Yet, once she gets past that first time, she feels confident she can handle anything and get to the surface with enough air to keep living.

Now, her breathing becomes shallow. She wonders *what were they thinking when they decided to leave Michigan?*

"You okay babe?" Matt says. His ball-cap is on backwards. Sunlight illuminates the bristle on his chin and the parts of his cheek that aren't in shadow. He's wearing his dark sunglasses. The ones he always wears on dive trips because he says they're best for the glare. He put on shorts in Michigan. He's pulled on a sweatshirt when it was cold, but now the sweatshirt is in the back with the trash and the other last- minute items they found after the movers took everything.

"We're in sunny California!" he says with a grin.

Bertie cracks the window. Warm air streams in, and she lifts her face to breathe, slowly inhaling and exhaling until the moments of panic pass.

She rolls her shoulders.

"My legs are so pale," she says rubbing her bare thighs. She's wearing denim cut offs, a dive t-shirt she bought in Fiji and sandals. "And my arms," she says. "I look like a ghost."

Matt squeezes her hand. "We're going to love it," he says. "Just remember to breathe."

After dropping Argo at my studio, I drive the pickup to my parents. The pup's old enough to be left alone in his crate for several hours. My mom's waiting in her van. We'll only need one today, so I climb in beside her. Our first event is an anniversary party at a restaurant. The address isn't easy to find, and we circle the block twice before realizing our destination is the unassuming brick building on the corner. My mom maneuvers the van into an open spot near the front door. She knocks on the restaurant's locked doors; a manager opens up for us and shows us where to set up.

The space is divided into two good-sized rooms filled with the afternoon light that spills through leaded glass windows. A highly polished mahogany bar is in the back corner of one room. The other room features a beautifully restored fireplace with a carved wooden mantelpiece. About fifteen round tables are arranged around this room.

I imagine the building was once someone's residence. I can hear the clank of pots and pans in the kitchen. The manager leaves us to our work, vanishing into the kitchen through a swinging door. I smell a hint of garlic and basil before the door closes.

We unload bags of pre-inflated balloons from the back of the van and carry them into the restaurant. Then, we bring in the stands we'll need for the table décor and the mini-arch that will highlight the anniversary cake. The color scheme mirrors the original wedding colors of blue, white and teal.

The setup is quick, and we move on to the next job: a retirement party at a country club. This one involves a spiraling pillar of gold, silver and black balloons topped with a balloon shaped like a gold watch. The table décor is assembled around a gold fountain of shimmering ribbon that spills out of the top of the smaller balloon swirl and reminds me of confetti. Waiters are setting up the buffet line with metal warming plates when we finish.

After we load her van with our paraphernalia, my mom suggests we sit for a while in the lobby where there's a nice view of the golf course through the picture windows. We settle into cushioned arm chairs angled for the view. The sun has set but the sky is still tinged with a rosy gold. The verdant green and oak tree studded golf course glow like an oil painting by one of the Dutch masters.

"It's nice to have you back," my mom says, reaching for my hand and giving it a squeeze. "I've missed you."

"I missed you too," I say. I know she's talking about my recent hiatus from the job due to my car accident. But I think about all those years I was away. How I didn't return home for six years, not even for a short trip; how I didn't realize what I was missing; how I forgot that it was my parents after all who first introduced me to the ocean.

"I hope this wasn't too much for you," she says.

"No, I'm good."

We sit in companionable silence. People dressed in golf attire come in and out of the lobby, speaking in hushed tones. The golf course slowly darkens, the shadows deepen. Now, people dressed for dinner in suits and ties and cocktail dresses and heels cross the thick carpet. I watch a couple who look to be in their thirties. They're leaning into each other, heads nearly touching as they pass in front of us. "Whatever happened with Nate?" my mom says.

"Nothing," I say.

"Hmmm."

As a daughter, I can hear a wealth of curiosity and comment in that sound. But she doesn't say any more. My phone dings in my pocket. I resist the urge to pull it out and check to see if it's Nate.

"It's getting late," my mom says, standing. "Want to have dinner?"

"Another time," I say. My phone dings again. "Bertie and Matt are arriving tonight."

"Your friends from the boat?"

Although we've never talked about what happened on the Calypso, I'm positive my dad has filled her in on the details. I've learned these past months that she won't press me for information I'm not ready to share.

"Yes,' I say, "the ones who were with me on that day."

Her smile is loving and sad, and I know I don't need to say more. She links her arm through mine as we walk out to the van in the gathering darkness for the drive back to her house. The text is from Bertie.

Before I leave my parents', I go in their garage and grab my wetsuit, fins, mask and snorkel. We can rent the rest of our scuba gear if we decide to go diving.

My heart hammers with excitement and nervousness as I load the gear in my dad's pickup and head home to Argo.

Chapter 46

I open the door, and Bertie springs into my studio. It's exciting but also weird to see her here. She's wearing normal clothes, shorts and a tank top, and not the bikini or wetsuit I was used to seeing that week on the Calypso. Hoops dangle in her ears; the diamond on her ring finger sparkles in the kitchen light. She laughs and holds up her right hand for a high five just like she did all those months ago when she first leaped on board the dive boat. Argo barks and jumps around her. I step forward and slap her palm. Now we're both smiling and laughing. Argo whirls around us in a paroxysm of joy. I love the happy energy Bertie brings to my small living space.

We hug, and then Bertie kneels to greet Argo. He rolls onto his back, his legs waving in the air, so Bertie can rub his tummy.

"He doesn't do that for everyone," I say. I can't help but think of Argo assuming the same position for Nate on that day I left him so I could go on a hike with Judy.

Bertie gives Argo a good scratching so that one of his rear legs kicks the air. Before she can stand, he rights himself and licks her lips.

I laugh. "He's in love," I say.

Bertie stands and wipes her lips with the corner of her tank top. "I'm not sure I wanted a kiss there," she says. She turns to Argo, and shakes her finger at him pretending to scold him. "Watch it buddy or Matt will come after you." Argo sits at her feet, staring up at her adoringly, the tip of his tail swishes back and forth.

"Where's Matt?" I say.

"He's at the hotel," Bertie says, "exhausted from the drive. All he wants to do is sleep. But I couldn't wait to see you, so I snagged the keys and drove right over."

"I'm glad," I say. The flame on the candle I've lit on the kitchen table flickers, and I realize the door's still open. I close it so Argo won't run out.

"Cute place." Bertie surveys the studio. "And I see you've got your diving gear." She smiles and points at the couch where I've spread my wetsuit across the back so Argo won't get to it. My mask and snorkel are hanging on a hook in the kitchen.

"I just got it from my parents' today," I say grinning. The thought of getting into the water enthralls rather than terrifies me. I drove home from my parents with a smile on my face imagining the dives Bertie and I could do together. I don't know if it's because I know and trust Bertie or if I've fully put my experience with Gordon behind me. I decide that tonight I don't care. What matters are my positive feelings.

"My fins are in the closet," I say. "Argo was eyeing them like they were dog toys for him."

I offer her some wine from the bottle I have chilling in the refrigerator. I pop the cork and pour us generous drinks.

"Let's toast," Bertie says, "to friends and future underwater adventures."

We clink our glasses together.

"Did you eat?" I say. "Can I get you something?"

Bertie says they grabbed a burger and fries on the road. She pats her stomach and says she's still full, and then she sinks onto the couch, crossing her legs beneath her. Argo's not far behind her. He jumps up and lays down with his head in her lap. I smile and sit at the other end of the couch.

"I've told Matt we need a puppy," Bertie says running Argo's silky ears through her fingers.

"I'm not sure Argo would allow that," I say.

We sip our wine and talk like old friends, our conversation skipping around from Bertie's drive, to her feelings about leaving home, to my happy completion of my paper and the most recent event I helped my mom decorate with balloons. We're nearly done with our second glass of wine before Bertie mentions the Bakers and more specifically Jordan.

Bertie almost hates to bring up the subject of Jordan. Catalina looks so relaxed and happy, drinking her wine with her feet tucked up under her. And Argo. What a sweet pup! He's fallen asleep on her lap. Every once in a while, he'll snore or whimper a little. Catalina says he's dreaming when he whimpers.

Catalina's studio is adorable. The scented, flickering candle, the brick red couch, the art posters and the lace curtains fluttering at the kitchen window all give Bertie a deeper insight into her friend. There was no room for homey touches on the Calypso. The one time Bertie saw Catalina's bunk, it struck her as very utilitarian and neat. Now, she can see that Catalina's bed covers are rumpled. A messy stack of books towers on her small, carved dresser. Catalina's glorious hair tumbles about her face in beautiful disarray. Catalina's hair was always in a ponytail on the Calypso. Bertie puts a hand to her own straight hair knowing that strands are sticking out like straw from the bun on top of her head.

Maybe she shouldn't have mentioned Jordan yet. A shadow darkens Catalina's face at the name. Her lips turn down, and there's a palpable silence in the room. Not even Argo utters a sound. But there's no turning back now. Bertie sips her wine and waits for Catalina to speak. She did a lot of waiting this past year in her dad's basement workshop; although it was hard for her and didn't produce the results she hoped for, Bertie learned that sometimes it's better to wait than forge ahead. Something she never could get the hang of while diving.

Now, while she's waiting for Catalina, she thinks of all the sea creatures Catalina turned up underwater in the Sea of Cortez. And it occurs to her, that she wouldn't have seen half as many on her own or even known what to look for or where to look despite her sharp attention to detail. It will take the two of them to figure out what's happening to Catalina.

Bertie strokes Argo's nose with the tip of her finger, marveling at the softness of his fur in that particular spot.

"Jordan," Catalina says. "I don't know…." She gazes into her wine glass as if she expects to find an answer in the liquid. She swirls the glass like there's tea leaves at the bottom that will reveal her future.

"What other answer could there be to the string of events that have happened?" Bertie says. She shifts her position on the couch, disturbing Argo. The pup jumps down and heads to his water bowl for a drink.

"Maybe they're not a string," Catalina says. "Maybe they're simply coincidences."

"We need to be smart this time," Bertie says leaning forward. "We missed so many clues on the Calypso."

Bertie's voice is impassioned. I know she feels just as badly as I do about Gordon's death. Although she wasn't the group leader, she is certified as a rescue diver. She's agonized with me over what she could have done differently.

I think of the group ascent the Bakers always did at the end of each dive: the ceremonial nature of it. I think of Gordon's ear troubles on the drift dive; the smile on his face when he didn't know I was there, and our conversation on the dive deck when he expressed no regrets. And I know Bertie is right.

I can't vacillate anymore about what's been happening to me, brushing the incidents off as mere coincidence. I need to trust my gut, my spidey sense, like I did after my car accident when I called Bertie. I need to seriously consider that someone is behind the seemingly unrelated events. I need to seriously think about that someone being related to Gordon. Because I simply can't think of another reason why someone would want to harm me.

On the surface, Odysseus' many travails could be viewed as the bad luck of a seafaring wanderer. But his story makes clear that a vengeful Poseidon, god of the sea, is at the root of his troubles, wanting to make Odysseus pay for the blinding of his son.

Chapter 47

I tell Bertie I don't know how we'll figure out who Jordan is. I tell her my gut says Nate isn't responsible but I can't bring myself to apologize to him. I was so very wrong about the Bakers. What if I'm wrong again?

"Maybe you've never seen Jordan or met him," Bertie says. "He could be hiding in the shadows for all we know."

Her words should frighten me, but instead, I feel a sense of relief. A stranger could be behind the string of incidents. It probably isn't someone I know. It's likely not Nate. Argo jumps up onto the couch again. But this time, he settles near me, curling up next to my thigh. I run my fingers over his warm, fuzzy body, thinking about the day Nate surprised me with Argo at the shelter. The loyal pup has become more important to me than I imagined he could. I picture the last time Nate was here and I'm ashamed I suspected him of intentionally harming Argo. I look at Bertie, tears pooling in my eyes.

"What is it?" she says, reaching out her hand towards me.

"I feel so badly about Nate," I say. "Maybe I should call him." I look around the studio for my cell.

Bertie holds up her hand. "Wait," she says. "There's no rush. You can call him later."

I sink back against the couch, dabbing the corner of my eyes with the tips of my fingers. "You're right," I say.

It's obvious to Bertie that her friend is relieved to remove Nate as a suspect. Bertie isn't so sure about him though. What about all those things Catalina said to her about Nate on the phone? What about Nate's physical appearance? Still, Bertie's willing to talk about Jordan as a stranger if it helps Catalina be more careful.

"I wish we could call up the Bakers and ask them about Jordan," Bertie says, finishing off her wine. She stands and carries their two empty glasses to the table, where she tops them off with the rest of the wine. She hands Catalina her wine glass, then she settles back on the couch.

"Why can't we?" Catalina says.

"We could if we wanted to spend a ton of time or money on finding them," Bertie says. "The obit didn't mention where they currently live. It was published in a newspaper from Gordon's home town of Chicago. I can't even tell you how many Bakers are listed in that city." Bertie shakes her head, and then sips her wine.

"I don't even remember where they said they were from," Catalina admits.

"I got the impression they moved around a lot," Bertie says. "At least Gordon and Ava did."

We're silent. I'm thinking about what steps we can take to identify Jordan. I imagine Bertie's doing the same while she sips her wine.

"Call Nate and organize a double date with us," Bertie says.

I look at her suspiciously. "Are you planning to grill him?" I say.

Bertie widens her eyes. "Of course not!" she says. "We don't know what to do next so I figured you might as well call Nate. You wanted to earlier remember?"

I'm not completely certain of Bertie's motives, but I do want to call Nate. I search my studio, Argo following at my heels, and find my cell on my bed. I don't mind that Bertie's listening in while I make the call. I figure her presence will help me keep the conversation light.

Nate doesn't answer, so I leave a long message apologizing for our last conversation and asking him to come on a double date with Bertie and Matt. I end by saying I'm looking forward to him meeting my friends. When I hang up, I look at the cell I'm holding and I hope I've done enough to get a positive response.

A bone-deep weariness settles over Bertie. The excitement of seeing Catalina is gone, and the long days on the road are finally taking a toll. She feels stuck to the couch, her limbs heavy. Her eyelids are weighted. Between the glasses of wine and the trip, Bertie doesn't think she can make it safely back to the hotel. Catalina tells her she can stay at the studio tonight. Matt doesn't answer his cell when Bertie calls. She leaves him a message so he won't worry.

There's no sense talking about Jordan anymore tonight. The two can discuss Catalina's options in the morning when Bertie's feeling more alert. Catalina loans Bertie a washcloth and towel. When she's done in the bathroom, Bertie settles on the couch with a pillow and a blanket. The studio is dim. Catalina's switched on her bedside lamp. The candle on the table provides the only other light.

Now that it's her turn in the bathroom, Catalina's decided to take a shower. Bertie closes her eyes and listens to the sound of running water. Argo is a warm ball at her feet. She can feel him lift his head when an owl hoots in the tree just outside the kitchen window.

Bertie's drifting off to sleep when someone knocks on the front door.

Chapter 48

Bertie ignores the knocking. But whoever it is persists. Argo leaps from the couch and bounds to the door with a sharp bark. Now, the person, a woman, calls Catalina's name. Bertie groans. She swings her legs from the couch, pushes her fallen hair out of her eyes. Yawning hugely, she pads on bare feet to the door and swings it open just enough to see the young woman standing on the other side. She blocks Argo with her legs so he won't dash outside. She can feel his damp nose pushing against her bare calves.

The woman has black hair and a nose ring. She's holding a blouse and a bottle of tequila. Something about her seems familiar, but Bertie can't see her clearly without the kitchen light on. Obviously, the woman knows Catalina. She's on her doorstep calling her name.

"Can I help you?" Bertie says.

"I'm Judy," the woman says, "and you must be Bertie." She shifts the blouse so it's draped on her arm and holds out her hand.

Catalina has told Bertie about Judy. She knows the young woman is a friend, so she puts out her hand in greeting. "Catalina's in the shower,"

Bertie says. "We're just about to turn in." She smothers another yawn behind her hand.

Judy's smile disappears. "I found her blouse at the coffee shop," she says. "She left it there this morning. I thought I'd bring it by, and a bottle of tequila to celebrate that she finished her paper. Margarita time!" Judy shuffles her feet in a dance move.

Bertie feels badly about turning Judy away. She's Catalina's friend after all. Let Catalina decide whether she should stay or go. Bertie opens the door wider and invites Judy inside, flipping on the kitchen light. Judy passes close enough that Bertie can smell the lingering scent of coffee mixed with shampoo on Judy's hair. Argo sniffs Judy's sandals. Judy sets the blouse and the tequila on the table, and then pats the dog on his head. When she doesn't offer a treat, he wanders back to the couch and settles on a cushion.

"Looks like you've already been drinking," Judy says indicating the empty bottle on the table and the wine glasses in the sink.

Bertie can't tell for sure, but it almost sounds like the young woman is jealous of the time she spent with Catalina tonight.

"We just arrived in town," she says. "My husband stayed at the hotel, but I was eager to see Catalina."

Judy smiles and nods. "I wish I could have joined you," she says. "I know how much Catalina's been looking forward to your reunion."

"Catalina should be done soon," Bertie says. Judy is leaning quite comfortably against the counter. She's plainly been in the studio many times before. Bertie hopes Judy won't stay long. She really is very tired. She looks with longing at the couch where Argo is sound asleep and snoring. "Can I get you a glass of water?"

Judy declines the offer, but Bertie fills a glass for herself. Now that the kitchen light is on, Bertie is struck again with a sense that she's met Judy before. While she's thinking about how she knows the young woman, Judy looks around the studio.

"I see Catalina's got her diving gear from her parents' garage," Judy says. "She must be eager to get out in the water with you again. I've heard all the stories about your time together on the Calypso."

"Yes," Bertie says. This time she doesn't bother to cover her yawn. "Sorry," she says, blinking, "long drive." She swallows some water. "Catalina tells me the ocean's cold here."

"I've heard it is," Judy says. She lifts the dive mask from the hook.

"Are you a diver?" Bertie says.

"I was at one time," Judy says. "My family spent nearly every vacation at some dive resort or on a dive boat."

"But you don't dive anymore?" Bertie leans against the table. She's struggling to make polite conversation; working to keep her yawns at a minimum. "I'm sorry," she murmurs again after one particularly wide yawn.

"No need to apologize," Judy says. "You've come a long way." Her voice is soothing. Bertie can only describe it as sounding like the school counselor she was forced to meet with that time she disputed her teacher's statements in front of the whole class. Catalina has told her Judy is a psychology major.

"I'm glad you're here tonight." Judy fingers the rubber seal on the dive mask. "I haven't dived in a while. About the same amount of time since Catalina gave up the sport."

Bertie's brain is sluggish. She and Matt got up early this morning so they could make the final push to San Diego. She's been in a cramped car for a few days. She hasn't slept well on the road. And she hasn't gotten off Michigan time just yet. Then there's the wine to consider. Still, all this time Judy's been talking Bertie's brain has been working away like the hard drive on a computer. Thoughts are coming together and pushing to the forefront of her mind.

Bertie stands taller, and stares at Judy. She's positive she's seen the young woman somewhere before but she can't quite make the connection.

Judy holds the dive mask up to her face. "Bet you remember the last time you saw this."

And Bertie does.

Chapter 49

Bertie's sleepiness disappears in a flash, although her mind is still befuddled with the wine. Gordon's blue eyes are staring at her through the dive mask. Judy laughs, and then takes the mask away from her face. She sets it on the table where Bertie is holding on for support.

"Everyone always said I was the one who looked the most like my dad," Judy says. "I knew you recognized me. I could tell you were wondering about it from the moment I walked in the door."

"You're Jordan," Bertie says in a whisper. She's still trying to wrap her thoughts around the fact that Jordan is a woman, and not a man like she assumed.

"I am," Judy says with a smirk. "Catalina told me how observant you are. She agonized for months over the fact that you didn't realize my dad's plans before he died." Her lips tighten, and her blue eyes narrow. "You could have stopped him."

"You're lying," Bertie says. "Catalina never blamed me for what happened with Gordon." She wishes her denial sounded stronger. But she's slurring her words. Her thoughts are fuzzy. She wishes she hadn't drunk so much wine. She wishes she'd followed Catalina's example and not drunk that last glass.

"Maybe she should have," Judy says. "Aren't you a certified rescue diver? Along with your husband?"

Bertie feels nauseous at how much Judy knows about her. The woman's clearly disturbed. She ignores Judy's question, pressing her with one of her own.

"Are you the one behind all that's been happening to Catalina?" she demands. Her tongue feels thick in her mouth.

Judy moves closer to Bertie, her lips twisted into a sneer. "What if I am? She deserves to pay a price for letting my dad die."

Anger wells inside Bertie, quelling the nausea. She's furious that Judy pretended to be Catalina's friend and that she dared to harm Catalina. She pushes away from the table towards Judy, hardly knowing what she will do with the young woman. Maybe she'll give her a good thrashing. Maybe she'll simply force her out of the studio. Maybe she'll call the police. She grips Judy's arm.

"You're a sick person," Bertie says, yanking Judy towards the door.

But before she can make any progress, the young woman jerks her arm from Bertie's grasp. Bertie stumbles at the abrupt movement. Her arms flail as she grabs again for Judy. The younger woman steps away, and Bertie's too far off-balance to right herself. Her fingertips graze Judy's t-shirt, before she falls to the floor. Her head smacks the table on the way down. There's a sharp pain in her temple, then everything goes black.

I hear Bertie's and Judy's voices in the kitchen. I'm surprised Judy's come over so late, but I'm glad the two have met. Hopefully, Judy won't mind leaving soon. Bertie's tired. We can all get together for coffee another time.

I finish pulling on my pajamas, an old soft pair of loose cotton pants I've had forever and an even older t-shirt. I brush my teeth and wind my hair on top of my head. I turn out the bathroom light. I'm reaching for the door when I hear a crash in the studio.

I yank on the knob and see Bertie sprawled on the kitchen floor, her hair spread like a halo around her head. Her arms are flung sideways out from her body like she's flying, and her legs are splayed. The empty wine bottle rolls on the table top, and comes to a rest against my blouse and a full bottle of Tequila

I rush over to Bertie, kneeling beside her, feeling her throat for her pulse. I'm relieved when I feel Bertie's steadily beating heart, and I see her chest rising and falling.

"Bertie," I say, "can you hear me?" I get no response. Argo licks her cheek. I push him away before he can lick her lips, remembering her response when he did that before.

"What happened?" I say, looking up at Judy.

She shakes her head and shrugs her shoulders. She's holding her hand to her mouth as if she can't quite believe Bertie fell over.

"Did she faint?" I say. I stand and move to the kitchen sink, where I wet a towel to dab on Bertie's face. A nasty lump is swelling on her temple. "Get some ice," I tell Judy.

But she doesn't move. I push past her for the ice, which I wrap in the towel and hold to the lump. Maybe I should call Matt. Maybe I should call an ambulance. Bertie moans, shifting her position, but she doesn't open her eyes.

I stand and grab Judy by the shoulders. She appears to be in shock, her eyes are closed. Her lashes flutter on her cheeks. I shake her gently. Her eyes open. And I'm stunned by how blue they are like the ocean on a day you can see forever.

"Are you wearing contacts?" I say. I know it's a strange question to ask while my friend is lying unconscious on the floor but the words fly unbidden out of my mouth. Judy has brown eyes. Almost as dark as her black hair.

"We were talking and she just keeled over," Judy says. "She was telling me how tired she is."

Something about Judy's words doesn't ring true, but I'm too worried about Bertie to pursue the matter further so I drop my hands from Judy's shoulders and turn back to Bertie.

"Argo, leave it," I say, noticing that the pup's crept close to Bertie's face again. I kneel and do a better job of sweeping Bertie's loose hair away from her face. She must have taken out her bun and brushed her hair before laying down on the couch. I hold the ice in the towel to her head. Her eyelashes flutter. She murmurs something I can't make out.

I hear Judy moving about the studio by my bed, then walking back to the kitchen and opening a cabinet. There's the sound of a bottle top being twisted, the soft pop as the seal is broken. Then, I hear liquid being poured into a glass. Maybe Judy needs a drink to calm down.

I lean closer to Bertie. "Bertie," I say. "Wake up Bertie." I rub the ice across her forehead and around her cheeks. Her lips move again. I bend my head so that my ear is pressed to her mouth.

"jdan" She whispers.

"I don't understand," I say. I put my ear to her mouth again, but now she's silent. I check her pulse and breathing, then stand. Judy's hovering by the table with a shot of tequila. I can't tell if she's drunk any. She appears to be staring off into the distance. I can't help but turn to see what she's looking at. But all I can see is the lace curtain hanging limply at the kitchen window. I shake my head.

At least I can make Bertie comfortable. I hurry to the couch, grab the pillow I loaned her and bring it to the kitchen. Kneeling, I lift her head, and slide the pillow underneath it. The ice is melting in the towel and Bertie is still unconscious.

"I'm going to call Matt," I say. "He needs to take her to the hospital."

"I don't think that's a good idea," Judy says. Her voice is muffled. I look up at her and freeze. She's wearing my dive mask. My snorkel is held fast in her mouth.

And all I can see is Gordon.

Chapter 50

My mind flies back to all those times I saw Gordon's face underwater in the Sea of Cortez. For a few unnerving moments, I struggle to separate those memories from my more recent nightmares.

Bertie moans beside me. My friend is hurt and helpless on my kitchen floor.

I swallow down my terror. I suck in a deep breath. I remind myself that Gordon is dead, that I'm not having a nightmare or a hallucination, that this is real, and that Judy stands above me.

Not Gordon.

"What are you doing?" I say. I push to my feet, and stand before my friend wondering how I could have been so gullible all these months? How could I look at Judy and be fooled by her dark eyes and black hair? How could I be blind to her clear resemblance to Gordon?

Judy snickers.

With a swift movement, I lean towards her. Before she can get away, I pull the mask up and over her head with one hand. I don't care that it catches strands of her black hair or that she yelps in protest, the snorkel mouthpiece dangling from her lips that reek of tequila. I yank the snorkel away from her with my other hand.

"How could you lie to me?" I demand. "How could you listen to my nightmares and not tell me who you were?" Now, I'm angry at myself and at her. Bertie groans. Judy looks at her as if she's a bug to be squished.

"What did you do to Bertie?" I say in a loud voice.

Judy shrugs. "Your friend fell and hit her head," she says, drawing out the word friend with a sneer. "She got what she deserves."

"Why?" I say, trembling, my hands gripping my mask and snorkel. "I thought *you* were my friend." I hate that I sound like a grade schooler upset that her friend wasn't true. Tears pool in my eyes.

"How could I be friends with the person who let my father die?" Judy says. She blinks her eyes and smooths her hair. "I'm glad to be rid of those contacts. I look so much better with blue eyes. Don't you think?" Her smile is chilling.

"I'm calling Matt," I say. I drop the mask and snorkel on the kitchen table and move towards my bed where I left my cell phone. Argo shadows my movements. I toss aside my blankets and pillows but can't find my phone. I head to the bathroom, thinking I might have left it there.

"You're wasting your time," Judy says. She pats the purse that dangles on her shoulder. "I've got both of your phones," she says. I hear one of the phones ding inside her purse. "Guess one of us is missing a text," she says in a sing song voice.

I stare at Judy wondering what happened to the person with whom I felt safe sharing my secrets? Her mood swings and tears at the rift in her family make sense to me now. It's clear she's Jordan: the sibling who didn't come on the dive trip.

"Your parents wouldn't want you to do this," I say, holding out my hands in front of me to show her I mean her no harm.

"You only knew them a week," she says, her voice trembling. "My father shouldn't have died on that trip."

"Is that why you didn't come along?" I say. I look between Bertie and the door. I debate whether I should leave Bertie here while I go to my landlord's and use his phone. Then I remember, he and his wife are out of town. The key to their house is in a kitchen drawer behind Judy. I decide I shouldn't leave Bertie alone with her. But maybe I can convince Judy to help me with Bertie. Maybe I can get my phone from her.

"My family knew I was against what he was planning," she says. "They deliberately didn't tell me when or where they were going." Now her voice sounds sulky, like a teenager denied something she wants. Her lips form a pout.

"You admit your father planned his death?" I say, inching closer towards her. Maybe if she sees I'm not afraid of her, she'll remember our friendship. Argo trails behind me.

"Don't try that psycho-babble on me," she says her voice suddenly furious. "You were his dive master. You were in charge of his safety. You should have never let it happen."

"What do you want?" I say, stopping my forward movement. It suddenly occurs to me that Judy's behind all that's been happening to me from the rattlesnake by my door to Rocket getting loose and the figure that jumped in front of my car. It was her face I saw wearing a dive mask. Bertie is right about the missing Baker sibling looking for vengeance.

"I want you to pay for what happened to my father," she says in a calm voice that sends shivers up my spine.

One of the phones in her purse dings again. And I wonder. What else does she have in there? I've given up on any thoughts of swaying Judy. All my focus now is on figuring out how to get Bertie and me out of my studio and away from Judy.

I look around the studio for a weapon I can use to defend myself if I have to. My gaze settles on the kitchen table. Maybe I can grab one of the bottles and hit Judy with it. I shuffle forward.

"I know you don't mean that," I say, doing my best to keep my own voice steady.

She ignores me and steps in front of the table, blocking my view of the bottles. Bertie shifts on the floor and moans.

"I'm glad Bertie's here for this," Judy says. "She was a part of your dive group. She's as much to blame for my father's death as you are."

I say nothing. I've given up on any thoughts of swaying Judy. All my focus now is on figuring out how to get Bertie and me out of my studio and away from Judy.

"I so enjoyed listening to your nightmares." Judy says. Her voice is familiar now, the caring friend who studies psychology. She smiles as if my frightening dreams provide her with fond memories. "I wasn't really writing a paper," she says, chuckling. She sighs. "But the nightmares didn't last," she says, "and now you're planning to pick up where you left off. Moving on with your life as if my father's life and death were meaningless."

"I don't think that at all," I say, holding my palms together as if I'm praying. "Your father was a wonderful person." My voice trembles. Judy appears to be listening, so I continue. "His life-long passion for the ocean was admirable. I remember one dive we did with a sea lion pup…" My voice catches and trails off.

My memory of Gordon playing with the sea lion is as clear as the day it happened, and I extend my hand towards Judy thinking perhaps she will understand I that I grieved Gordon's loss.

But she scuttles away, screaming at me to stop talking about her father.

She swoops up my dive mask and drops it to the wood floor. Then, she stomps on it. The plastic doesn't crack, but I imagine it will be scratched and unusable. Judy curses at the mask. She grabs the snorkel, pulling and twisting the plastic tube that connects the mouthpiece to the open spout that sticks above the water. It too isn't easy to destroy.

I'm shocked by her actions. I don't know how she's planning to make Bertie and me pay. But given how she's behaving now, I don't care to wait to find out if she has a gun or a knife or some other weapon in her purse. While Judy's face reddens with the effort of destroying my snorkel, I rush towards her.

My head lands in her gut. We both fall to the floor, knocking the table over with a clatter. Argo barks and skitters around us. I can hear his nails on the wood floor. The two bottles bounce against each other and fall to the floor. I hear glass shatter.

Judy squirms under me. I try to pin her down. We wrestle on the floor in the spilled puddle of tequila, the smell of alcohol imbuing both of our clothes. The flicker of a flame distracts me, and as I turn to look for the source of the fire, Judy slips from my grasp.

I grab at her, but it's as if she's a ghost. I can't get a hold of her clothes, legs or purse. She pulls open the door. The whoosh of air fans the mysterious flames higher. I can only describe Judy's laugh as maniacal.

"Let's see if you can do a better job of saving your friend than you did with my father," she says before stepping into the night. Her footsteps pound down the stairs. Argo dashes after her, barking, and ignoring my commands for him to stop.

Chapter 51

I slump on the floor.

Judy's clomping footsteps and Argo's barks fade into the distance. Bertie groans.

"What happened?" she mutters. She raises her head from the pillow, and then falls back against it with her hand pressed to her forehead. I crawl towards her. The flickering light in the kitchen grows stronger. I can see now that the source of the flame is the fallen candle. It tumbled to the floor with the table and the bottles. As luck would have it, the flame wasn't doused. Instead, it's now catching hold of the tequila, heading towards my blouse which was also swept to the floor.

"Bertie," I say, "Can you get up?" I grab hold of her hands and try to pull her into a sitting position. Her head lolls back, her hair dangling behind her.

The flames are advancing towards us, licking up the tequila. The thin material of my blouse is not flame retardant and the edge of one sleeve blackens. My pajama pants are soaked with the alcohol. They stick to my bare legs. I shudder, thinking about the fire reaching me and Bertie. I gently lower Bertie back onto the pillow.

I grab the towel, damp now from the melted ice, and beat at the fire. But the tequila is everywhere. Air from the open door and window creates a brisk breeze. Papers I'd left on the table flutter and blow about. The fire spreads, greedily licking at the papers.

Smoke curls towards the ceiling, and the smoke alarm emits a shrill beep that's painful to hear. I dash to the bathroom, grabbing the damp towels I used to dry off from my shower. Rushing back to the kitchen, I throw the towels on the flames. Some are snuffed out, but not all. I don't have a fire extinguisher, and I curse my disordered priorities for not taking the time to purchase one. But this isn't the time for self- flagellation. I need to think clearly; I need to remember all I learned in my dive certification classes about how to save a life.

Bertie coughs. Smoke swirls around her. Flames inch closer to her; the stench of burning material grows stronger. Fire consumes all but the collar of my blouse. Somehow, I need to get Bertie up off the floor.

This time, I position myself behind her and push on her back. She stays upright, but only because I'm helping her. I feel pain on my leg. Flames touch the hem that flares out from my leg and quickly devour a small bite out of my pants. My skin blisters. A sob escapes my lips, as I turn to beat out the fire with the palm of my hand.

"Bertie," I say, "you've got to help me." I'm determined to save both of us. I won't fail this time.

She mumbles, at least I know she's semi-conscious. I push her forward so her head bobs above her knees, and then tip her onto her side so she's further from the fire that's now burning along the tipped table top.

We're both coughing when I grab her feet and drag her towards the open door. My burned hand screams in protest. But I grit my teeth and keep pulling my friend towards the fresh, life-giving air that's just a few feet away. I don't know how I'll get us both down the stairs. But I'll figure that out when we're both outside.

I dig deep into muscles and a resolve I'd forgotten I had. Inch by inch, I move Bertie towards the door as the fire grows more intense in the kitchen, now consuming the entire table top and racing along the legs.

Finally, we're outside.

I lean Bertie against the frame, and shut the door to my studio behind us.

The night air is cool on my hot cheeks, but stings my burned hand and leg. I pause for a moment to breathe deeply, to check that Bertie is breathing as well. I adjust her position, helping her away from the building, looping her right arm around the ceramic pot for support. I can't imagine bumping Bertie down the steps. It'll be faster if I go for help on my own.

Still, I worry that Judy might be lurking somewhere in the shadows. What if she comes leaping up the stairs while I'm gone?

I hesitate, peering into the gloom at the bottom of the stairs. I freeze as a shadow detaches itself from the small portion of lawn I can see. I brace myself, ready to fly at the shape and knock it backwards. Then, Argo appears on the bottom step. My heart swells at the sight of him. He wags his tail and bounds up the stairs towards us. We greet each other joyously. Then, I tell him to stay and watch over Bertie. He sits beside her, his ears forward, alert.

"I'll be back," I say. I don't have the key to my landlord's house, but I figure he won't mind if I break a window to get to his phone. I know the broken window will set off an alarm. All the better if the police are called while I'm phoning the fire department.

Although I want to dash down the stairs and sprint to the nearby house, I'm still unsure where Judy is. I pad silently to the bottom step. Holding my breath, I peer around the corner. The street appears quiet beneath the mature, leafy trees that arch above it. Amber circles illumine the asphalt below the widely spaced street lights.

I can hear the high- pitched tone of the smoke alarm in my studio, but no one else seems aware of it. Light spills from my kitchen window, casting a square onto the lawn below, but it doesn't look out of the ordinary just yet. I know it's only a matter of time before the fire engulfs my studio. I can't leave Bertie sitting on the doorstep too long.

I take a cautious step away from the stairs. The leaves rustle in the tree behind me. There's a whoosh as an owl spreads its wings to fly across the street. I keep moving. When nothing happens, I walk more quickly to my landlord's house. I debate whether I should break a window in the back, but the back of the house is a deep pool of dark shadows. I veer towards the front, hoping a neighbor will see me. Maybe the neighbors who helped me before will be out for another night time stroll. Maybe the neighbor who owns Rocket will be out for a walk.

My heart is racing. I'm hardly breathing by the time I reach the bushes and begin my search for a rock or stone left behind from paving the front walkway.

"You made it out." Judy's voice comes from just behind me.

My breath catches in my throat. My fingers close around the rock I've found.

I whirl to face her, the rock in my hand.

Chapter 52

Judy's face is shadowed. Her hair is loose and swirls around her shoulders. I imagine her hidden features look something like Medusa with her hair of snakes, and for a moment I expect to see wings unfurling from Judy's shoulders.

"You're alone," she says. "Why am I not surprised you left your friend? I suppose she's gasping for air now. Just like my father when you left him."

I grip the rock tightly, refusing to be intimidated by her or her cutting words. "You don't look a thing like your father," I say. "He was a kind and gentle soul."

"You know nothing about my father!" she says, her words fierce. Her figure is silhouetted by the light, and I can see her fists are clenched at her sides.

"I know he loved your mother and your sisters," I say. "I imagine he loved you too." I hold onto thoughts of Judy as my friend. The times we spent at the coffee shop. The moments when I thought she was comforting me after a particularly bad night of nightmares. The hike we did together. I also hold onto the rock, prepared to use it as either a weapon or as a window breaker.

A guttural growl comes from Judy's direction. I can't tell if she's angry or grieving. She steps towards me only to suddenly fall to the ground with a sharp exhale of breath. Rocket plants his paws on her upper back and barks. I grip the rock tighter as the barks seem to reverberate through my body and down into my soul.

"Rocket!" My neighbor sprints towards us carrying a leash. "Stop!"

He grabs the dog by its collar, pulling it off of Judy, and snapping the leash to the collar in one motion. "I'm so sorry," he says. Rocket stands quietly beside him, panting.

Judy doesn't move.

"Miss," he says to her, "you okay?"

She lays unmoving on the lawn. Even when sirens wail down the street and a fire truck pulls to a hard stop by the garage below my studio, she keeps still. Red and white lights flash over us.

I want to help her, but I don't trust her. So, I don't kneel beside her to check for her pulse or to see if she's breathing. The man, his dog, and I simply stand beside her while firefighters rush towards us. I direct them up the stairs. One kneels beside Judy and gestures for a paramedic.

Two people join our little group. It's the older couple who helped me move my car. They tell me they heard my smoke alarm while they were passing. They discussed whether they should call the firefighters while they walked home, and finally decided they should. They explain they wanted to err on the side of safety. They apologize and hope they've done the right thing. They're sorry if they disturbed me over a false alarm. I'm too shaken to thank them.

The paramedic's still working on Judy and I'm still holding the rock when I see a firefighter come down the stairs with Bertie slung over his shoulder, her head and hair dangling in front of his chest. I drop the rock at the sight of Argo. Rocket barks at my dog. But I don't care as I'm already rushing towards Argo and Bertie. I grab up Argo, and hold him safely in my arms. I press my lips to his fur and tell him he's a good boy.

The firefighter sets Bertie gently on the lawn. I sink down beside her keeping a tight grip on my pup. I'm vaguely aware of other firefighters pulling a hose up the stairs. Bertie appears to be awake. She's able to sit up on her own. We hold hands while a paramedic checks her out, strapping an oxygen mask to her face to help her breathing. Argo sits by me, my fingers looped through his collar. The paramedic recommends a ride in the ambulance, but I offer to drive Bertie to the hospital in my dad's truck. I tell her we can pick up Matt on the way.

"I want to call Matt," she says, holding the oxygen mask aside. Tears are running down her face, making tracks in the smoke stains. "But my phone's in your studio."

The paramedic says the firefighters might be able to save it. I look over to where I last saw Judy. She's being strapped onto a stretcher. The flashing lights illumine the scene enough so that I can tell her neck is held tight in a brace.

I let go of Bertie's hand. "I just need to check on something," I say.

"Who's that?" Bertie asks, peering around me and noticing the stretcher for the first time.

"Judy," I say. "Keep hold of Argo for me."

Bertie cuddles Argo in her arms.

I walk over to where the paramedics are preparing to lift the stretcher. Judy's purse is on the lawn.

"Let me get this for her," I say. I pick up the purse and surreptitiously and carefully feel inside for our cell phones. I don't want to cut my finger on a knife, or accidentally touch a gun. But my fingers find only three phones and a set of keys. Otherwise, her purse is empty.

The paramedics are moving towards the ambulance. I don't have time to figure out which phones are ours or to think about why there's nothing else in her purse, not even an ID. I scoop the phones out, and drop all three on the lawn. I catch up with the paramedic and set the purse on the stretcher beside Judy. Her eyes are closed and she's not moving.

"Will she be all right?" I ask. And I do feel concern for her. After all, she was my friend, before she revealed herself as my enemy.

The paramedics tell me Judy hit her head on a paving stone when she fell. They inform me of the name of the hospital where they'll be transporting her ; they say I can follow in my truck if I want. I thank them for the information. My voice is flat as I tell them her name is Jordan Baker, and watch the ambulance pull away. Then, I scoop up the cell phones and hustle back to Bertie.

By the time I help Bertie and Argo into my dad's truck, the firefighters have doused the flames in my studio. I imagine it's a wet, smoky mess inside. But I'll deal with the damage later.

I pull away from the curb thankful that, this time, I've managed to save what really matters.

Chapter 53

The sun is climbing above the eastern horizon when the Serenity motors out of the Avalon Harbor towards our first dive site. Rows of sailboats and motor boats rock gently in the wake as the Serenity cuts ripples through the still, shadowed water. Flags are no more than limp pieces of cloth tied to the tops of the forest of masts. Only a few early risers sit on their boat decks sipping coffee.

Our dive boat is equipped with a small upper sun deck, a lower dive deck with utilitarian benches, two exit ladders, two hot water shower heads, camera tables and a fresh water rinse tank. The dive deck smells of neoprene with an underlying hint of bleach. I imagine the captain or possibly the dive master swabbed the deck earlier. I don't miss the chore.

The two tanks we'll each use for our dives are lined up behind us. There's eight of us divers on board not counting the boat captain and the dive master. Although there's a head, there are no cabins, dining room, lounge or bar. The 45-ft Serenity is not a live-aboard.

I watch the dive master as she moves about the deck, arranging snacks, stacking plastic cups for our use, and securing the drinking water dispenser. And, I realize, I don't envy her. I'm happy about the choices I've made. I'm excited about pursuing a career on land.

Both she and the captain greeted us when we stepped on board from the dock. There were the expected comments about my name; we are leaving out of the Catalina Island harbor after all. I smiled and shrugged good-naturedly. There's no sense in taking offense at trivial comments, something I learned in my many years as a dive master.

Bertie's high five to the crew was more subdued than I remember from our initial meeting on the Calypso.

She's been cleared by the doctor to dive again, but she told me she might just do one dive. She's sitting between me and Matt, spinning her wedding ring. Nate's on the other side of me.

We've been taking things slow. He was understandably reluctant to jump right back into a relationship with me. And I'm feeling my way, learning how to fully trust again. Sometimes, I look into his blue eyes and I see an unwavering devotion that both attracts and frightens me. Someday, my mom says, I'll just have to take that leap of faith. I'll have to believe that what's underneath the surface appearance is the truth.

"It's the same with scuba diving," she says. "Every time you take that giant stride and descend underwater, you're taking a risk to see what's below."

I know she's right.

I don't think of Judy as often as I used to, and when I do, I rarely think of her as Jordan. I found another coffee place where I don't know the names of the baristas who make my lattes. It was too painful to return to the cafe where we met, and where Judy spent so much time pretending to be my friend.

Ava came to the hospital where Judy was taken. The staff was able to call Ava when I brought Judy's phone to the emergency that night. The police told her how Judy left Bertie and me in the burning studio. I doubt they filled her in on what else I reported. I had no proof Judy was involved in the string of other incidents. Only Bertie's and my suspicions.

Ava showed up at my parent's house a couple of days after the fire. She'd been able to find my parents' address because they're still listed in the phone book. Ava didn't know I'd be there. She hoped to ask them for my contact information. But my studio suffered too much smoke, fire and water damage to be habitable. I'm still at my parents while my landlord works to restore the studio.

That day, Ava sat with me and Argo in my parents' living room. They left us alone to take care of some chores outside. Ava told me the doctors recommended Jordan be committed to a psychiatric ward for treatment. I suppose that's the best place for her while she comes to terms with her father's death.

Ava apologized for her daughter's actions, her soft brown eyes pooling with tears, and I remembered how she took my hand when she left the Calypso and thanked me for my leadership. This time, our conversation was short. I wished Ava well when she left. I no longer have hard feelings towards her, Lucky, Lauren or even Gordon. I understand now that they would have done the same to any dive master. It wasn't personal like it became with Judy. I didn't send along good wishes for Judy. It was too soon for that.

The Serenity's motor slows and stops, the dive master leans over the railing to hook the boat to a mooring ball. I feel a flutter of anticipation as I adjust my equipment for our first dive.

Nate checks my straps and extra regulator are in place. I do the same for him. We're buddies. I'm trusting him with my safety today just as he's trusting me. I figure it's as good a first step as any.

The other four divers are strangers to me, but I don't need to worry about them. I'm here to simply enjoy the dive with my friends. I smile as the four who I don't know take turns jumping into the ocean.

Nate goes next. When it's my turn, I don't hesitate on the dive platform like I used to in my nightmares. I step freely into the air, falling and immersing myself in the water. I bob to the surface, moving my fins beneath me in a familiar motion, letting the water flow easily through my gloved fingers. My soul expands.

I inhale the salt air, eager to get below and see what the ocean has to show me.

Bertie feels tremulous: a new feeling for her when she's on a dive boat. The emotion is different from the usual nerves she experiences before a first dive. She's not been dizzy for at least two weeks now. She can breathe freely. And the doctor has cleared her to dive, assuring her that her lungs are fully recovered from the minor smoke inhalation she suffered. But still, she worries about what will happen underwater. She checks Matt's equipment, and he checks hers. Because of the water temperatures, their wetsuits and hoods are thicker, their weights heavier than what they used on the Calypso.

"You okay babe?" Matt says. He's wearing his mask, ready for his giant stride, but his snorkel hangs loose outside his mouth. They'll be the last into the water.

Bertie shakes her head. "I don't know," she says. She puts her gloved hand over her stomach. "I'm feeling queasy."

"More than usual?" Matt says.

At Bertie's nod, he tells her they don't need to dive. But Bertie can see behind him to where Catalina waits on the surface. Her friend waves to her, beckoning her to jump in.

"Come on in," Catalina shouts. "The water's fine!"

Bertie knows what happened in Catalina's studio is to blame for her reluctance now. She's never had a problem rushing into anything, including diving, before. She hates how tentative and unbalanced she's felt this last month ever since she charged Judy, hit her head and nearly died. It was like a switch was flipped inside her, emphasizing her anxieties about the unknown. She's wondered whether moving to California was the right choice after all. She's questioned her dissatisfaction with her family relationships. She's moved cautiously in her job search; she's wavered about an apartment. She's even introduced herself a few times as Alberta.

Matt's been patient with her, as he is now. He's already reaching to remove his dive mask.

Bertie looks at Catalina's hooded head in the water, her brave friend taking her first dive in nearly a year. She's surrounded by other hooded divers.

The group could just as easily be the hooded divers of their group on the Calypso. She remembers Gordon's love of diving and his love for his family. She thinks of Ava, Lauren and Lucky's love for Gordon, the closeness it was obvious they shared, the respect for Gordon's decision. A closeness and respect, she remembers is missing in her own family; a closeness she realizes now Judy didn't understand.

Bertie raises her arms above her head and takes a deep breath of the clean ocean air. On the exhale, she lowers her arms to her sides with her palms up and a smile.

She won't let what happened in the studio spoil this dive. It will be a first step towards regaining her confidence. Actually, it's a giant stride; she can work on the rest later.

Bertie reaches for Matt's hand stopping him from removing his dive mask.

"Let's do this," she says.

The two shuffle their fins to the spot where they'll take turns making their giant stride, leaping off the boat and committing to the dive. She waits while Matt splashes into the ocean, then bobs to the surface and swims towards the others.

Now it's her turn. She's the last on the boat besides the captain and all eyes are on her.

"For Gordon," she shouts, just before inserting her snorkel and launching herself into the air.

Bertie and I sit on the bow of the Serenity, our shoulders touching. Our wet hair is wound on top of our heads. The wind teases the loose strands blowing them dry and whipping them around so that sometimes my hair is in Bertie's face and sometimes hers is in mine.

We've already talked about our two dives. We've discussed and exclaimed about the fish we saw in the kelp. Now, we lean back in comfortable silence. The air is warm, but we're bundled in sweatshirts, damp towels wrapped around our bare legs, chasing away the water's chill.

The boat parts the deep blue sea before us with a satisfying hiss. I watch as flying fish leap out of the water on either side of the racing boat's hull. Their silver scales flash as they thrust into the air for a brief period of flight; their wing-like fins beat furiously to keep their bodies aloft. Then, they drop back to the water for a splash landing, only to repeat the process all over again. Bertie leans forward, expressing her delight at the fish she's never seen before.

"Remember the bat rays?" she says.

And I do. I remember the moments we spent together on the bow of the Calypso, watching the bat rays fly: the strange creatures blasting out of the water only to plummet below the surface again. And I realize, it's shared moments like this that make my life rich. The temporary flight is spectacular and exciting, breathing underwater is wondrous, and the ocean is gorgeous in all its mystery, but it's the community of family and true friends that hold the fabric of my life together; a community that's worth the risk of discovery.

I relax beside my friend, leaning back against the boat, the warmth of Bertie's shoulder soaking into mine. The captain steers the Serenity in a wide turn, and now, the open ocean unfurls behind us as we head towards the harbor.

The End

Book Club Questions

What do you think of Gordon's choice? Do you think his family helped him? Would you assist a loved one in his situation to do what Gordon did?

The Water's Fine includes three different families, Catalina's family, Bertie's family and the Baker family. How would you describe each? Did Catalina and Bertie have realistic views of their families?

It can be easy to drift through life without taking the time to develop friendships. What is your experience with how difficult or easy it is to connect with others?

Would you ever scuba dive? Why or why not? Is there another risky sport you enjoy?

Acknowledgements

Writing this novel would not have been possible without the support and encouragement of my family and friends. You are my inspiration and my cheerleaders, so I thank you. Thank you for meeting me for monthly writing sessions, thank you for ideas, thank you for reading and providing feedback, thank you for showing up and carrying my stuff to library appearances. Thank you for being my buddy on our many scuba diving trips, and thank you for helping me find my lost bootie!

I also want to thank my readers. As someone once said, "An author only starts a book, a reader finishes it!"

Cover design by Pamela A. Meistrell at PM Graphics and Design